PURSUED

The Vampire Syndicate

REBECCA RIVARD

Wild Hearts Press

THE VAMPIRE SYNDICATE
SERIES

"A must-read series!" - *Paranormal Romance Guild*

They call us the Dark Angels: Gabriel, Zaquiel and Rafael.

We're brothers. Princes. Billionaires.

The richer-than-sin heirs to one of the world's most powerful vampire Syndicates.

But we're not vampires, we're dhampirs. Half-human, half-vampire, with panty-melting good looks.

The media love us.

Vampires hate us.

And Slayers, Inc. will do anything to take us down.

Pursued (Gabriel)
Craved (Rafael)
Taken (Zaquiel)

Want to be the first to hear about Rebecca Rivard's vampire romances and other steamy paranormal books?
Sign up for her newsletter:
https://rebeccarivard.com/newsletter

❧ 1 ❧
MILA

I'd been running so long that when the syndicate vampires finally caught up with me, I almost welcomed it.

Almost.

I was hungry. Painful, gnawing, can't-think-about-anything-else hungry. Somehow, I'd found myself in a Giant Eagle grocery store, doing something I'd promised myself I'd never do—shoplifting.

I slipped around a big man in striped shorts to snag a couple of avocados. A hand latched onto my wrist.

Not the big man in the shorts. Another man.

Cold lips touched my ear. "Security would be very interested in what you have in that backpack, cher."

A vampire, with a hint of New Orleans in his voice.

I froze, heart banging against my lungs so hard I could barely breathe.

No, no, no.

The big man rattled down the aisle with his loaded cart, oblivious. In the next aisle, a woman with a flat Ohio accent asked where the wine was.

I sipped in air. "I don't know what you're talking about."

"No?" The vampire started to unzip my backpack.

I closed my eyes, picturing myself busted in the produce aisle for three chocolate bars, a can of sardines, a hunk of cheddar and a bag of peaches.

"Stop it!" I twisted away, but he was right there.

Powerful fingers clamped onto my upper arms. "Then come with me."

I licked my lips and willed myself to calm down. A vampire can hear your pounding heart, turn your fear against you. "What's this about?"

Like I didn't know. Karoly Kral's men had been hunting me for three years.

"You'll see." The vampire turned me to face him. He was blond and inhumanly beautiful, with dark brows and a lean, sculpted face.

My gaze went to the black wolf tattoo on the side of his neck. A Kral Syndicate enforcer.

So I was right. My blood chunked to ice.

A woman trailed by a kid in a dance leotard turned into our aisle.

The vampire glanced at them. His mouth curved. "Say you'll come, Camila. Or that pretty lady with the little girl in the tutu"— he jerked his chin at the woman and the kid—"will be food for me and my friend."

Bile filled my throat.

No, no, no.

But in my three years on the run, I'd learned some things about vampires, like that they tend to underestimate humans.

I hunched my shoulders, made my tone sullen. "I'll come."

For now.

The enforcer's hum of satisfaction raised fine hairs all over my body. He removed my backpack and dropped it on the floor. "You won't need this."

A peach fell out and rolled across the aisle. I stifled a moan.

Insane, right? To be worried about fruit when you're being kidnapped. But I'd lusted after those peaches like a teenager craves the one boy she can't have, my shrunken stomach grinding at the sight of all that sweet, juicy fruit.

The vampire put an arm around my shoulder and walked me out

the doors. I slipped my hand into my back pocket and palmed the silver switchblade concealed there.

His scent was dark and earthy, like the deepest part of a forest. My chest constricted. I didn't want this man close to me—he made my skin crawl—but that familiar forest aroma made my insides knot with yearning.

Outside, dusk spread its wings over the parking lot like a malevolent black bat. The humid July air pressed on my skin, gluing my curly hair to my nape.

My gaze locked on the limo with tinted windows idling at the curb. Stupid, to let myself get caught out this close to nightfall, but it had been weeks since I'd seen one of the undead.

My captor hooked a finger into the waistband of my too-loose shorts. I'd lost weight, the past few months.

"You know what I am, right?"

I dipped my chin. "A vampire."

"Then you know I can outrun you without breaking a sweat."

"You *can't* sweat," I muttered.

"Exactly."

He caught my wrist in a tight grip and with his other hand, opened the limo door to usher me inside. Polite and slick as hell.

A frazzled mom, juggling a toddler and two bags of groceries, sent me an envious look, taking in the sexy vampire in the ten-thousand-dollar suit helping me into the limo like I was his pampered thrall, not his prisoner.

It's not what you think, I wanted to scream.

The vampire glanced at her—and I struck, releasing the switchblade and stabbing him in the ribs with the silver point.

He snarled and swore at me, but his grip loosened enough for me to wrench free. I sprinted across the access road—right into the path of a big, double-cab truck. I threw myself out of the way and continued across the parking lot, dodging shopping carts and gawking onlookers.

My car was unlocked—always. I'd learned even a few seconds could make a difference. I yanked the door open and scrambled inside. I hit the lock and started the car at the same time.

3

The ancient engine jerked, hesitated.

I turned the key again. "Come on, come on. You can do it."

I glanced around, lungs working in short, panicked bursts. I couldn't see the blond vampire, but I knew he was out there. A Kral enforcer wouldn't let me go this easily.

The engine stuttered.

I drew a sobbing breath. "Please, please, please..."

The engine ground to life just as fingers clamped on the rim of the door. On the other side of the window, the blond vampire appeared like something out of a horror movie. Long white fangs and dark eyes with a glowing blue rim.

All the spit left my mouth. The bright, glowing blue around his irises was a bad thing. Very, very bad. You didn't see blue rims unless a vampire was aroused—or furious.

A sharp jerk, and the rusted door gave with an earsplitting screech.

I slammed the car into gear, but he plucked me out of the seat by the nape of my neck like I was a runaway kitten. I snatched the switchblade off the seat as he reached across me to shove the gearshift back into *park*.

He set me on the pavement in front of him. I planted my feet and brandished the switchblade.

We faced off. But vampires don't play fair.

Blue-rimmed eyes captured mine. "Come with me, Camila." His voice held the force of compulsion.

I strained backward, resisting with everything I had, but I couldn't drag my gaze from his.

"*Now*," he commanded. "Drop the knife and take my hand."

"No." The word scraped out of my throat.

But he was too powerful for me. The switchblade clattered to the pavement and I took his outstretched hand like a freaking zombie.

Forgetting my car. Forgetting the switchblade at my feet. Forgetting everything but the compulsion to obey.

He speared his free hand in my hair, dragging my head back. He shoved his face into mine. "No more fighting. You will come with us."

Somewhere deep inside, I shrieked *no*, but my head bobbed up and down. "Yes."

The limo pulled up next to us. Inside were two other men: a human at the wheel with a boxer's bent nose and beefy arms, and another vampire, this one with dark hair and sleepy eyes, sprawled on the leather seat, long legs stretched out before him.

"Get in." My captor shoved me into the back seat.

The sleepy-eyed vampire shifted his body enough to allow me space on the seat beside him. "Camila."

I growled.

"I am Stefan," he said. He had an accent, too, but his was Central European—Russian, or some other Slavic country. "And that is Martin." He looked at the blond, who'd taken the seat on my other side, a hand to his ribs. "What happened?"

"Bitch stabbed me with a silver blade."

Stefan chuckled. "You will live."

Martin sent me a dark look. "No thanks to her. Lucky it didn't go deep."

The limo pulled out, leaving me sandwiched between the two lean, cover-model-gorgeous males. The forest scent filled the limo's interior. A vampire's way of enticing us poor, stupid humans to come closer.

I crossed my arms over my stomach, fighting down panic. I was weaponless, my only clothes my hoodie, T-shirt and cargo shorts.

On the other hand, I was still alive. Maybe these weren't the same vampires who'd been trying to kill me for three years?

We pulled onto the highway. "What do you want?" I asked.

"The crown prince has never forgotten you," said Stefan.

The crown prince? My heart skipped a beat.

It was Gabriel who'd sent them, not his father Karoly?

"Yeah?" Longing twisted through me. I scowled to hide it. "Then why scare the crap out of me by sending you two to snatch me? Why not just ask politely—you know, in the usual way—a phone call? A text?"

"Would you have come?" asked Stefan.

"No," I said flatly.

Silence.

You didn't say no to a vampire syndicate prince. Especially the crown prince.

"Besides," Martin said, "you're using a burner phone."

"Like you don't know the number." The fact that they even knew I had a burner phone proved my point. "So. What does he want?"

"Our orders were to pick you up," Martin said.

"And take me where?"

"New York."

I swallowed. The Kral Vampire Syndicate headquarters were in Manhattan.

"What if I don't want to go?"

Martin's smile was white. "What makes you think you have a choice?"

"Fuck you, too," I said, but fell silent as the limo took the exit for the airport.

There was no use arguing. They wouldn't let me go. I might as well save my energy for the upcoming confrontation with Gabriel Kral.

Because I couldn't stay with him, no matter how much I might want it.

I stared out the window as night fell over the flat midwestern countryside. In the past few years, I'd lived in four different states, always in small, out-of-the way towns with none of the money and glitz that attracts a vampire. Three months ago I landed in this aging suburb near Cleveland, and taken yet another dead-end, low-income job.

I'd barely saved enough to move into a basement apartment—a room, really, with a tiny kitchen at one end and a single pint-size closet—when the store manager called me into his windowless beige office and ordered me to shut and lock the door. He'd moved closer, licked his thin lips.

I'd known what was coming, and God help me, I'd almost said

yes. This job had taken me almost a month to find and I was down to my last fifty dollars.

But I'd refused and stood by the open door as I told him to go to hell, saying it loud enough that the ladies out front would hear me. Two days later, he fired me for being five minutes late to work.

The vampires were still scrutinizing me.

Another wave of longing washed over me. There was something so seductive about how a vampire watched a human.

Gabriel had watched me like that, his green eyes hungry, and I'd fallen into his lap like a ripe plum.

But I'd been young, then. Barely out of my teens and starry-eyed with love. I was older now, and harder.

My shoulders curved inward, the adrenalin surge that had carried me across the parking lot gone. Almost too exhausted and hungry to be afraid, and mourning the loss of those damn peaches nearly as much as the switchblade, my only silver weapon.

"Fine." I forced my spine to straighten. "Just tell me there's going to be food on this jet."

T hey did feed me on the flight to New York.

And I ate, even if I felt a little like beef-on-the-hoof being fattened for the butcher.

A pretty flight attendant handed me a menu and invited me to order anything I wanted. I started with three appetizers, then moved on to a salad of tender greens topped with cranberries and candied pecans. Next was crab-stuffed flounder with a side of herbed red potatoes that I washed down with what was probably an expensive white wine, given I was on a private jet.

The vampires slouched on leather couches, sipping wine and speaking in undertones to each other.

I was full now, but I stubbornly kept eating, only because I caught Martin's envious glance. A vampire can drink a glass of wine and maybe have a bite of food once every few days or so. Other than that, they have to stick to blood.

After a while, I'll bet it gets pretty damn boring.

A chocolate mud pie topped with whipped cream and shaved chocolate rounded out my meal. I held Martin's gaze as I forked up a large bite.

Eat your heart out, blood sucker.

We landed at La Guardia well after dark, and took another limo into Manhattan. My palms were sweaty now, all that rich food churning in my stomach.

Another limo conveyed us to the Upper East Side, a street right on Central Park that reeked of old money and behind-the-scenes power. Prewar apartment buildings. Carefully trimmed trees. Small rectangles of annuals surrounded by miniature black-iron fences. Even the trash cans were brand-new and of coated green steel.

The heat was still stifling as I exited the limo flanked by Stefan and Martin. They were silent now, cold-eyed. They marched me between two potted orange trees. One doorman let us in, and another pushed the elevator button.

The ride up was so quiet I could hear the frantic pounding of my heart. I pushed my back against the brass bar and stared at the shiny metal doors.

Gabriel.

Ironic, that a vampire prince had an angel's name. And not just any angel, but God's left hand man. Protector—and destroyer.

I should hate him for dragging me back like this. He'd sworn the decision was up to me.

But a small, secret part of me was excited. The part that still wanted him, no matter how wrong it was for both of us.

The elevator reached the top floor. We stepped out into an apartment with high ceilings and a parquet floor polished to a golden sheen. The tall windows were made of that special dark glass that allows vampires to see out even on a sunny day. Right now, though, the view was of Central Park at night, its winding wooded paths dotted by lights.

Stefan and Martin escorted me through a big-ass foyer into a living room. The lighting was dim—vampires have eyes like cats—and the furniture elegant but comfortable. Butter-soft black leather, a plush red-and-black carpet, black metal lamps with shades shaped like tulips and lilies. I suppose if you live as long as vampires do, you appreciate comfort as much as beauty.

Four women in skimpy black dresses lounged on the couches or on velvet pillows near an unlit fireplace. Their necks were bare, the tiny marks from a vampire feeding barely visible. They would've been beautiful if not for their empty eyes. They smiled a greeting at the two vampires with me but remained where they were like the obedient thralls they were.

We entered a long gallery hung with dark, moody paintings that together were probably worth as much as the entire apartment building. I glimpsed the name Degas scrawled in the corner of a painting of a woman drinking alone in a bar. Another depicted a hazy river at sunset that even I recognized as a Monet.

We entered a library filled with wall-to-wall bookshelves. A tall, dark-haired man stood by a window, looking out at the busy street below.

A tingle went up my spine.

Gabriel Kral.

My lover. My prince. And the heir to the Kral Syndicate.

Then I froze. Backed up.

But Stefan and Martin had ranged themselves behind me, a solid, immovable wall.

My hands fisted at my sides. "You're not Gabriel," I rasped as the man turned to face me.

2

GABRIEL

My brother Rafe and I glared at each other, slit-eyed.

"Well?" I smirked. "Is that the best you've got?"

We were alone in my private gym, stripped to the waist. A training fight, but with real knives—switchblades long enough to plunge into a vampire's heart, although the blades we used were stainless steel, not silver. Even a deep wound wouldn't kill us, although it would hurt like a mofo.

Rafe prowled around me, torso damp with sweat, and then lunged, knife out.

I twisted aside. The blade drew a thin red line across my ribs. I pivoted, slammed an elbow into his kidney—and with my other hand, jabbed my knife into his back beneath his rib cage. Not deep enough to do any real damage, but enough to draw blood.

Rafe grunted and dropped into a forward roll, springing back up to face me. "Got you," he taunted, his gaze flicking to the blood on my abdomen. His fangs lengthened.

"That papercut?" I snorted and glanced down at where the thin line was already healing over. "You'd be dead if this was silver." I brandished my blade at him.

Rafe danced around me, searching for an opening. "Like hell."

I crouched, instinctively peeling my lips to show my fangs. This

might be a mock fight, but that didn't mean we didn't take it seri-
ously. Winning was in our blood.

Father had made sure of it. Me and my two brothers had been
home-schooled, with half our day given to boot-camp-style training:
martial arts, street fighting, and how to handle the special silver
switchblades that were the most efficient way to stake a vampire.
His three sons might be dhampirs—half-vampire, half-human—but
he'd honed us like weapons.

Rafe feinted—and I leapt, deliberately overshooting him. Mid-
stride, I flipped the blade in my palm and slammed the base into
the back of his head. He stumbled forward and dropped to his
knees.

I grabbed his chin and yanked back his head. "Give." I touched
the sharp point to his throat.

He snarled and gripped my wrist. I dug my knee into his back to
block whatever evasive maneuver he was planning. Last week, when
I'd gotten him in a similar hold, he'd managed to toss me over his
shoulder. I was damned if he'd do it again.

On a nearby ledge, our phones buzzed in unison. I stilled,
breathing hard, and released my brother.

"That's Father."

Rafe nodded and came to his feet in a single fluid motion.

I strode to the ledge, tapped the screen. "He wants me down-
town ASAP."

"Same," Rafe said, looking at his phone. "Wonder what bug he's
got up his ass now?"

I jerked a shoulder. "Hell if I know."

But we duly headed for the showers. When the Primus of the
Kral Syndicate summoned you, you obeyed. Even if you were his
sons.

No, especially if you were his sons.

Ten minutes later, we were tricked out in suits and ties. Father
was old-fashioned that way. Business was conducted in the proper
attire.

The private gym was directly below my penthouse in the apartment building I owned on the Upper East Side. We ignored the

elevator to jog the eight flights down the service stairs to the underground garage.

"I'll drive," I said.

Rafe pulled out a quarter. "Flip you for it."

I snatched the coin in mid-air. "I win," I said without looking at it. Being the oldest of three brothers had its privileges—and besides, my Jaguar, my rules.

"Prick," he said amiably. But he settled his long body into the sleek silver coupe's passenger seat.

I dropped my sunglasses on my face before exiting the garage. Beside me, Rafe did the same. It was evening, but the sun still hovered above the horizon, enough to bother our sensitive eyes. A dhampir could tolerate more sunlight than a vampire, but our eyes were adapted for darkness, not light.

I turned the Jag south toward Greenwich Village.

"Have you heard anything from Zaq?" Rafe asked. "Or is he still in Syria?"

"He left three days ago." Our middle brother had been in northwest Syria on a humanitarian mission. "I got a text when he landed in Paris. Said he'd be back by last night."

"So I guess he got the summons, too." Rafe grinned. "After we find out what Father wants, maybe we can grab us some pretty thralls and go out. Just the three of us."

I nodded. It had been a while since we'd all been in the same city.

"Unless you have plans," Rafe added.

"No. I'm free."

"And hungry, I bet. Blood-wine only goes so far. And when's the last time you got laid?"

I cut him off with a hard look. "I drink when I need to. As for who and how often I fuck, that's none of your damn business."

"Sure, dude," Rafe muttered, but dropped the subject.

By the time we arrived at the syndicate's anonymous brownstone in the Village, night had fallen. Even this quiet, treelined street buzzed with the special energy that was Manhattan after dark.

I pulled into one of the spaces reserved for our top people, and we exited the car.

A curvy woman in a short summer dress dragged her boyfriend to a halt. "That's them," she hissed. "The Dark Angels."

"Yeah?" He raised a brow, trying to appear unimpressed, but I sensed his spike of fear.

He kept walking, but she'd already whipped out her phone. "Can I have a photo? Please?"

"Not now." I went to move past her.

Rafe grabbed my arm and flashed her a grin. "Just one, sugar." To me, he muttered in a voice too low for humans to hear, "We're the face of the syndicate, remember? Father's orders. Make nice with the humans."

I ground my back teeth. "Right."

Somehow, we'd become media darlings—the three Kral brothers. The syndicate's Dark Angels.

We were a goddamn hashtag, for fuck's sake.

I blamed my mom. She'd insisted on naming us after angels: Gabriel, Zaquiel and Rafael. It was her little rebellion against the vampire world. An angel, after all, is a creature of light—a bright, shining being. A vampire's complete opposite.

"Awesome." The curvy woman shoved the phone at her escort and inserted herself between us. "Let me guess. Gabriel"—she twinkled up at me—"and Zaquiel." She winked at Rafe.

My mouth twitched up. But nothing fazed my youngest brother.

"I'm Rafael, darlin'," he said without losing his grin. "The good-looking one."

I snorted, but in fact, of the three of us, Rafe was the most classically handsome, with the sculpted face of those pretty-boy gods you see in museums.

She chuckled and put an arm around both our waists. "I'm Ceci, and that's Connor."

I set an arm on her shoulders and stared unsmiling at Connor. On the other side, Rafe did the same thing, only he smiled.

Connor scowled and took three photos in rapid succession.

"Here." He shoved the phone at Ceci and waited, arms crossed, while she told Rafe thank you—three times—and then with a flirty wave at me, continued on her way with Connor.

When he sent a last scowl over his shoulder, I showed him my fangs. I understood why he was pissed, but I didn't take shit from humans.

He gulped and sped up, dragging Ceci with him.

I smiled and jogged up the brownstone's steps. "Oh, Rafael," I said in a mocking falsetto. "You are *too* irresistible."

"Go fuck yourself," Rafe suggested. "Besides, she was just as interested in you. That whole dark-and-broody thing sucks them in."

I snorted. "Should've staked you when you were a baby."

The doorman was a wiry, world-weary New Yorker. "Good evening, sirs," he said as he opened the steel-and-silver reinforced door with perfect timing.

"Evening, Dino." I strode into the stately marble-and-bronze lobby, Rafe at my heels. A Kral soldier pushed the button for Father's private elevator.

My brother glanced around. "No Zaq."

"Late," I replied. "As always."

We exchanged a wry look. Like our mom, a New Orleanian down to her scarlet toenails, our middle brother ran on his own relaxed time. According to Mom, he'd even been late to his own birth.

The elevator descended three floors to a secure area carved out of New York bedrock. We passed through another two layers of security before reaching Father's inner sanctum.

Tomas Mraz, his lieutenant and righthand man, waited in the outer room to let us in. A big blond Slovak, Tomas had grown up with my dad in the Carpathian Mountains, and had been turned at the same time. When I was a kid, the blunt, ever-smiling Tomas had reminded me of a Teddy bear, until I was brought into the syndicate and saw him slice a man's throat without losing the grin.

The lieutenant wasn't smiling now. "Gabriel. Rafe. Go in. He's been waiting for you." He jerked his head at the study.

Inside, Father was pacing the antique red-and-gold carpet, his lean frame clad in one of his usual hand-tailored suits. At three centuries, he was still young for a vampire. His face was unlined, his dark eyes clear. But his short black hair was ruffled like he'd been dragging his hands through it.

Rafe and I exchanged a glance. Karoly Michal Kral was never ruffled.

Father turned to us, his relief palpable. "You're here."

I frowned. "What's wrong?"

He scraped a hand over his face. "It's Zaquiel. He's missing."

My stomach tightened. "You're sure? It's not the first time he's gone A.W.O.L."

Zaq hated the syndicate, would resign in a heartbeat if Father allowed.

"I'm sure," Father said grimly. "He hasn't been seen since Monday."

"Hell." Rafe's black brows lowered. "Could the Syrians have him?"

"No. We've traced him to Paris. He disappeared sometime after landing at de Gaulle."

"I can vouch for that," I inserted. "He texted me from the airport. At least, that's where he said he was."

"He was. The surveillance cameras recorded him talking to a middle-aged female with big sunglasses and brown hair, and then— nothing." Father spread his long, elegant hands.

"Fuck." I squeezed the back of my neck, tried to think beyond the fear gripping my gut. "Okay. Dark glasses. Could she be a vampire?"

"Or a dhampir?" Rafe added. "Or it could just be part of her disguise."

"If she's even a *she*," I muttered.

"I haven't ruled anything out," was my father's reply. "But if she's a vampire or dhampir, she's not in our database."

I frowned. "So not a member of one of the larger covens." We kept extensive files on the major covens and syndicates, but there were always small nests of vampires who preferred to fly under the radar.

"Could be a rogue," Rafe pointed out.

"Or Slayers, Inc.," I added.

Rafe's eyes met mine. Not all slayers were human. In fact, dhampirs made the best slayers. We were almost as strong and fast as vampires, and had a vampire's enhanced senses.

Father's smartphone buzzed. He glanced at it and stilled.

"What?" I asked.

He wordlessly turned the screen toward me and Rafe.

One down.

Beneath the message was a photo of Zaq, his wrists in silver cuffs attached to a dirty concrete wall. He stared defiantly at the camera, his T-shirt ripped, a scruffy beard covering his cheeks and jaws.

I zeroed in on the bruise blooming on the side of his neck. In the center were two tell-tale puncture wounds. Some SOB had fed from him without bothering to heal the wound.

"It was sent on his own phone," Father said.

My nostrils flared. Scarlet hazed my vision, and my fangs slid out. For a few moments, I was pure predator.

Beside me, Rafe snarled, "Those thrice-damned bastards." I didn't have to look at him to know his vampire was dominant right now, too.

My father's gaze locked on mine. He wasn't calm—far from it—but the icy rage I saw brought me back to myself.

I had to stay in control. Zaq's life might depend on it.

I drew a slow breath, retracted my fangs. "You'll trace the message."

"For what good it will do. They've probably destroyed the phone already." But he opened the door, handed the phone to Tomas. "I want to know who sent this, and from where. Highest priority."

The big blond lieutenant glanced at the screen. His bushy brows climbed. "Right away."

"And Tomas? This has to be kept a secret. No one else can know."

Tomas gave a curt nod and closed the door again.

I eyed my father. "Tell me something," I asked, tight-lipped. "When did you first suspect Zaq had gone missing?"

"Early yesterday morning. He was supposed to check in when he landed in New York."

"So you've known for thirty-some hours that something's wrong."

Father's spine straightened. His black eyes narrowed in a look that would've sent his minions running for cover.

I stared back. It was an old argument between us. He was supposed to be grooming me to take his place as the Kral Primus, yet I was continually left out of the loop on important developments.

Beside me, Rafe shifted uneasily.

"I *knew* nothing," Father bit out in cold, precise phrases. "In fact, I believed that this was another of your brother's stunts, or that he was indulging in his tendency to play white knight for humans."

I heaved a breath. "Fair enough."

"But," he admitted, "perhaps that was a mistake. I've heard rumors of a coup attempt."

Yet another thing my father hadn't bothered to tell me. "Who?" I demanded.

"I don't know." He sank into the big black armchair behind his desk. "The rumors are just that. Nothing concrete. Whispers in the fucking night."

He slammed a fist onto the desktop, rattling a box of Cuban cigars and toppling the sole family photo, the one taken at Mardi Gras back when me and Zaq were teenagers.

I leaned forward to right the photo. We all looked at it.

My father stared coolly at the camera, seemingly bored, but he had my pretty, dark-haired mom snugged up to his side. She in turn, had an arm draped over my shoulders. Eleven-year-old Rafe had wormed his way between me and Mom. He flashed his trademark cocky grin, his neck smothered in cheap plastic beads. On my other side stood a grinning Zaq, his T-shirt powdered with sugar from too many beignets, his brown hair streaked from the sun and looking like it hadn't seen a comb in days.

Fury clamped hot fingers around my throat. Zaq was the good one, the kind-hearted Kral. Hell, he'd given away most of his trust fund to poverty-stricken humans, saying, "They need it more than me."

He didn't deserve to be a pawn between my father and the vampires who wanted to take him down.

I met Father's eyes. "I'll leave for Paris tonight."

"No." He leaned back in his chair. "You will conduct business as usual. The other syndicates would love to know someone found a hole in my security, and even some of our own people might try to take advantage of it. No one but you and a few of our top men can know Zaquiel's gone missing. *No one.*"

I slapped my hands onto the desk's polished mahogany surface. "With all due respect, I'm not going to sit on my ass here in the States while Zaq is pinned like an insect to a goddamned wall."

"I'll go," inserted Rafe.

"No," my father and I barked at the same time. Rafe scowled but subsided.

I opened my mouth to argue further but Father held up a hand. "Hear me out."

I straightened. "Go ahead."

"They'll expect me to send you or Rafe to France. They may even be counting on it, which is why you're staying here. You'll go out, be seen, handle any routine business. Tomas will be staying in New York to advise you. Here." He handed me a burner phone. "I'll contact you on this—it's secure. But don't try to contact me. I intend to go completely dark." His face hardened. "I believe someone here at headquarters is behind this, either working on their own or with another coven."

"A mole?" Rafe breathed.

"Yes."

I stared down at the phone, trying to absorb that not only was Zaq a prisoner, my father suspected someone close to us was behind it. "You're going to Paris?"

Father nodded. "It's a start. Perhaps I can find something our people in France missed."

"I see." My mouth twisted. I knew why Father was going, and not me or Rafe. We were dhampirs. In his eyes, we'd never be strong enough.

My brother stirred. "Take me to Paris. I'm one of our best trackers."

Father shook his head. "That's why I'm sending you to Montreal. I can't be sure the Tremblay Syndicate isn't a part of this. Victorine Tremblay would love to take out my sons."

My fingers constricted on the burner phone. "The blood feud." *Of course.*

The blood feud between the Kral and the Tremblay Covens dated back two centuries, although in the past decade, a fragile peace had held.

My father nodded grimly, but Rafe went still as a hunted animal.

"Zoe Tremblay," he said flatly.

Two summers ago, something had happened between the two of them. Something Rafe refused to talk about, even to me and Zaq.

"Did you think I didn't know about you two?" Father asked.

My brother lifted a shoulder, let it drop.

"She's her mother's second-in-command," Father continued. "Use her."

"Bad idea," Rafe returned. "Victorine Tremblay told me personally that if I ever touch Zoe again—if I even breathe the same goddamn air as her daughter—she'll consider it a deliberate act of war against the Tremblays and will respond accordingly."

"So you did touch the daughter," Father said.

"That's not the point," Rafe gritted.

Father waved a long-fingered hand. "Find a way around Victorine. Use a glamour on the daughter...or that famous charm of yours."

I regarded my dad incredulously. "You negotiated the end to the feud yourself. Now you want to risk starting it up again?"

"If I'm right, it's they who have broken the truce. The Tremblays have close ties to the French vampires. Victorine's own sire is an enforcer in the Paris Syndicate. Take me and my sons out, and Victorine is perfectly placed to step into the power vacuum that would open up." Father trained a cold stare on Rafe. "This isn't up for discussion, Rafe. Your brother's life may depend on what Zoe can tell you. If Victorine is part of this, we need to know. Please," he added.

My brows crawled toward my hairline. I could count on one hand the number of times I'd ever heard Father say *please*. And never to one of us.

"Jesus." Rafe plowed his fingers through his black curls, then gave a grin that was all sharp teeth. "Okay. Sure. I have some unfinished business with the woman anyway."

"Good. Sit down, both of you." Father indicated the chairs in front of his desk. "Tomas and I have ten minutes to brief you, then I'm off to France. Rafael, I've made arrangements for you to fly to Montreal."

"What about Mom?" I asked as we seated ourselves.

"She's safely at Black Oak Manor with Giles"—one of his top enforcers—"and a couple of my best people."

I nodded. Karoly Kral might be a cold bastard, but my mom was his heart. He'd drive a stake through his own chest before letting anyone hurt her.

"She knows about Zaq?"

"Not that he's been kidnapped, no. Just that he's run into some trouble and I'm investigating." Father pressed the intercom on his desk. "Tomas?" he said in Slovak. "You can come in now."

The big blond lieutenant entered. "They know?"

Father nodded. The two exchanged a few rapid sentences in Slovak and then switched to English to explain to us exactly how this was going to go down.

When they were finished, Father steepled his fingers beneath his chin and examined us. "Any questions?"

Rafe and I shook our heads, and we all rose to our feet.

Father clasped Rafe in a hug. "Check in with Tomas as soon as you make contact with the Tremblay female."

"Zoe," he corrected, tight-lipped.

Father raised a dark brow. "As you say. No unnecessary communication," he continued, speaking to all three of us. "Gabriel's in charge, but if you have any issues, contact Tomas, not me. And use burner phones and your code."

Rafe and I nodded. When sending and receiving from a burner phone, it was standard Kral procedure to identify yourself with a short string of letters and numbers known only to the inner circle.

"You two go." He nodded at Rafe and Tomas. "I have something to say to Gabriel."

He waited until the door closed behind them before turning to me. "You wanted a chance, son. This is it. As soon as we get your brother back, I'll announce that you've been promoted to oversee the two southeastern covens. Meanwhile, you have my permission to act on my behalf—within reason, of course."

The southeastern covens covered a good two-fifths of Kral Syndicate territory, stretching from Maryland to Louisiana. Excitement gripped me, but I kept my face as stony as his.

"Thank you, sir." I stuck out my hand.

He clasped it and hung on for a few seconds longer than necessary, his way of showing me affection. Rafe and Zaq got the occasional hug, but I was the Kral crown prince.

I had to be hard, emotionless. Controlled.

"We *will* get Zaq back," I vowed. "And don't worry, I'll keep things running here. You won't be sorry you left me in charge."

A thin smile. "See that I'm not."

ॐ 3 ॐ
MILA

In the dim light, the vampire's eyes shone pure gold, like polished coins set in the smooth brown of his face. Wolf's eyes. He had the lean, hard muscles of his kind; something about being turned does that to them.

"So you're Camila."

At the satisfaction in his voice, the fine hairs on the back of my neck stood upright.

Never show fear.

I straightened my spine, drew back my shoulders. "What do you want? Where's Gab—?" I halted.

A cold smile. "Did you think the prince had sent for you?"

My stomach bottomed out. Because okay, a part of me *had* hoped that Gabriel had sent for me. The part that had cried a little every day since I'd snuck out of town with only my backpack and a suitcase full of clothes.

"Then what's this about?"

The vampire pursed his lips. "You haven't seen your family for— how many years?"

"Three," said Martin.

My interrogator nodded. "You haven't even kept in touch."

A sick dread coated my throat. "So? We don't get along. Is that a crime?"

"I think you get along just fine," he returned silkily. "I think you've stayed away to protect them. You'd do anything to keep them safe, wouldn't you?"

I stared back without speaking.

He glided across the room to a large desk and tapped a key on a computer, rotating the screen so I could see it. Photos of my family scrolled past.

I couldn't help it. I moved closer, eyeing them hungrily.

Mom, with her messy brown bun and wry smile. Dad, with his dark, expressive eyes and curly black hair.

And Joey, all grown up now, a younger, skinnier version of my dad. My kid brother had turned twenty-one last birthday, and I hadn't even sent him a card.

I wrenched my eyes away. "What do you want?"

"Your cooperation."

My scalp tightened in warning. "To do what?"

He nodded at Stefan and Martin. "Wait in the drawing room. You may feed, if you wish."

"Yes, sir." They left, closing the door behind them.

The vampire waved a hand at a couch. "Sit, please."

I sat, aware of how defenseless I was. You couldn't hear the air conditioning, but it must've been set on Arctic blast, because goose-bumps popped up on my bare arms and legs. My fingers literally itched for my switchblade. Maybe I'd end up dead, but at least I could do some damage first.

He inclined his head. "Allow me to introduce myself. I'm called Andre." He seated himself in a nearby leather armchair.

"Andre." I nodded back, as if keeping things polite meant I'd walk out of here a free woman.

His eyes narrowed. "So the reports are right. I can't tell what you're thinking. I can't even tell if you're afraid. You're like a clear pool."

I hitched a shoulder. It was true, as far as I knew, although Gabriel was the only supernatural I'd ever tested it on.

"Not that it's worth anything," I muttered. Maybe vamps couldn't read my mind or emotions, but they could still compel me to obey them.

"That's where you're wrong. If you hadn't disappeared like that, we'd have hired you three years ago."

"As what?" My chin jutted as I recalled the beautiful, empty-eyed thralls in the other room. "I won't be some vampire's blood whore."

He waved a blunt-fingered hand. The big ruby in his thick gold pinky ring glinted blood-red.

"Of course not. That's for humans without your gift. No, you've shown initiative, intelligence. You've even developed some rudimentary fighting skills. Not many humans could've gotten past Martin's guard. Most importantly, you've attracted the interest of the crown prince. That makes you very valuable in my world. Do you know that ever since you, Gabriel will only drink from dark-haired, dark-eyed women?"

My stomach twisted. I hated to think of Gabriel with any woman but me.

"Who the fuck are you?" I demanded. "And I don't mean Andre, or whatever you're calling yourself this decade. Are you from a rival syndicate? Because if you are, you might as well kill me now. I won't be used to hurt him."

I'd left as much for his sake as for mine. I'd be damned if I'd be dragged back and used against him.

For a man, Andre's lips were full, sensual. They turned up in a small smile. "You know I can compel you."

My lungs compressed. "You can try. But I also know it takes a helluva lot of energy to compel a human for more than an hour or so, especially when she resists with everything she has. And I *will* resist you."

"Ah." He nodded. "But there are other, just as effective methods to gain cooperation." His gaze flicked to the PC.

My fingernails dug into my bare thighs. An icy sweat prickled my nape. But I made myself stare back coolly.

"However," he continued, "I prefer my humans happy."

"I'm not *your* human."

A shrug. "Your degree is in agriculture. After you left Maryland, you apprenticed at an organic farm, and since then, you've worked at farms whenever you can. Tell me, Camila, what could you do with a million dollars?"

My jaw dropped. My secret dream was to open a sustainably managed flower farm. A million dollars would go a long way toward making that dream a reality.

But not at the cost of Gabriel's life—and how the hell did this vampire know so much about me, anyway?

I leaned forward, speaking slowly and distinctly. "I won't hurt him. Not for any amount of money."

"You don't have to hurt him, darlin'. Just distract him. That should be easy enough." He looked me up and down. "He craves you, and I think you aren't unwilling."

My lip curled. "So you can do what?"

"That's not important." Wolf-gold eyes burned into mine. "Think about it. No more running, and maybe you could convince Gabriel to make it permanent. If not, by this time next month, you'll be a rich woman."

I hesitated. I'm not ashamed to say I was tempted. Not by the money—if I'd asked, Gabriel would've bought me a farm. Back when we were together, he was always trying to give me expensive jewelry and clothes.

But I was tired of running. Tired of always looking over my shoulder, wondering if this would be the day the syndicate would finally catch me.

And I'd have Gabriel. A deep ache squeezed my chest.

It was too good to be true, like a fairy godmother had snatched me up and granted my every wish.

Which is why I shook my head. I might have left Gabriel, but I'd never stopped loving him. I was damned if I'd let this devil in a sleek gray suit entice me into betraying him.

"No." My nails dug deeper into my skin. I knew that I wouldn't leave here alive. Andre couldn't risk me going to Gabriel and telling him something was up.

Andre eyed the tiny red crescents on my thighs. His nostrils flared and a vivid, electric blue shimmered around the edges of his irises. The look he turned on me was pure predator.

Too late, I recalled you never let a vampire see blood, even a tiny amount.

"Are you sure?" he murmured.

My throat had closed up. Somehow I pushed the word out of my mouth. "Yes."

"I'm sorry to hear that." He rose and opened the door.

A terrible premonition slithered down my spine. I jumped to my feet.

"Mila!" It was Joey, face ashen beneath his tan.

❦ 4 ❧
GABRIEL

I leaned against the hammered copper bar of Ruby's Speakeasy and took a sip of blood-wine. The music in the Kral Syndicate's exclusive underground club was thick with the pounding beat of hard, sweaty sex. Paintings of vampires and humans in various erotic combinations hung on the walls, and candles in red glass votives flickered on small black tables. In the speakeasy's nooks and crannies, the plush couches had been claimed by vampires and their thralls.

Three days had passed with no news about Zaq. Three days in which I hid my worry for my brother behind a cool exterior while managing the syndicate's many concerns. These days, most of our businesses were legal, if not completely aboveboard. Casinos up and down the East Coast. Exclusive clubs and trendy restaurants. A media group that owned everything from magazines to TV stations. Hell, even a major New York investment bank.

I'd worked twelve-hour nights, often staying up past dawn. With Tomas's help, I was staying on top of things. My father would be proud when he finally returned.

If he returned.

I tightened my grip on my wine glass.

It was as if he'd fallen along with Zaq into some fucking black hole. What was going on? And how long was I supposed to wait before I said the hell with it and went looking for them?

I didn't even have Rafe to discuss things with, because of Father's prohibition against unnecessary communication.

Two of the syndicate's newest thralls sidled up on either side of me, both dark-haired with olive skin and full, kissable mouths. One of my men must've sent them over.

"Hello, Gabriel." The one on the left raked bold black eyes down my body. "You look...lonely."

I hesitated, but Rafe had been right. It had been too long since I'd fed from a warm human throat. The music throbbed in my groin, the insistent beat reminding me it had also been too damn long since I'd had a woman.

Vampires looked down on dhampirs as weak half-breeds, but in my opinion, I had the best of both worlds—a vampire's powers and enhanced senses, and yet I lived and breathed just like a human. If necessary, I could go long periods without drinking blood, although fresh blood amped up my vampire half, making me more powerful and extending my already long life by centuries. It also made me damn near irresistible to a human.

Too bad it hadn't worked on the only human I'd ever really wanted.

My lips twisted.

The thralls lost their smiles, edged away.

She's never coming back. And you need blood and a good fuck.

I set the wine glass on the copper bar and reeled the two women back in.

"Not lonely. Waiting for you."

They smirked, playing the game. The thrall with the bold eyes pressed closer.

I racked my brain for her name. "Krystal. Can I buy you a drink?"

"I'd like that." Her smile said she'd like that and more.

The thrall on my right slid her hand beneath the collar of my silk shirt. A sharp nail toyed with my nipple.

Her name I knew. "Gina. What can I get you?"

Even white teeth closed around my earlobe. "Something cool... and wet."

I don't apologize for drinking from thralls, or using their soft human bodies. We pay them well, and they're free to leave whenever they wish. If some stay longer than is good for them, they can't say they haven't been warned.

It's no secret that a human can get addicted to the high of being fed on. A blood high, they call it. I'm told it makes the sex incredible.

"Can do. Two mojitos," I told a server in a tiny black dress and steered the women toward a nearby alcove.

Krystal nuzzled my neck. "I've always wanted to do one of the Dark Angels."

I turned my head to smile down on her and stilled.

Mila Vittore. Twenty feet away, staring at me like I was a ghost. It was as if my craving had conjured her out of the speakeasy's dark corners.

My already slow-beating heart thumped, a single hard knock against my chest. How many times in the past three years had I thought I'd seen Mila only to be disappointed?

It's not her. She's never coming back.

I'd made my peace with that. I'd kept tabs on her. At any time, I could've sent men to bring her back, but I'd honored her decision to leave. A Kral keeps his promises.

Besides, this woman looked different. Thinner, harder.

My Mila had a wild cloud of chestnut hair, not a chic updo. My Mila wouldn't have been caught dead in that short, tight-as-sin red dress and strappy high heels. And my Mila would never have set a toe in a vampire speakeasy.

Still, I couldn't help staring. The sound of the crowd faded away. I didn't even notice I'd loosened my grip on the thralls.

The woman's dark, soulful eyes snagged on mine. Her mouth rounded in a soft *O*.

And everything I thought I knew about Mila was turned on its head.

29

5

MILA

Gabriel Kral.

A thrum went up my spine, spread out to my belly. Even my fingers and toes tingled.

He hadn't changed in the three years since I'd last seen him. Same long, powerful body. Same raven hair and peaked black brows. Same brilliant green eyes, like emeralds set in the strong planes of his face.

Two curvy women were stuck to him like Velcro. Andre had told the truth. From the back, the women could've been me—not now, but a few years ago, before I'd lost twenty pounds. They hung onto his biceps, nuzzling his neck, rubbing their breasts against his arms.

My mouth flattened. If he wasn't careful, they'd drool on his shark-gray Armani suit.

But he was relaxed, smiling...until he glimpsed me across the club. The smile faded. A brief word to the thralls, and they moved on to another man.

Gabriel stalked across the club to me. He'd always reminded me of a panther. Lean. Graceful. Purposeful. Every movement controlled, predatory.

The crowd parted for him like he was royalty—which I suppose he was.

I straightened, made to shove my hands into my pockets. Except the sleeveless red bodycon dress didn't have pockets. I left my hands on my hips, hoping I didn't look as awkward as I felt.

He stopped a few feet away and inhaled slowly, as if testing it was really me. His gaze raked down my body before returning to my face. The heat in his eyes made me gulp.

"Mila."

My whole body clenched. Air backed up in my lungs.

I can't do this.

But I had to.

"Gabriel." I coolly inclined my head and slipped past him to the bar. "A beer," I told the bartender.

"Of course. Which one?" She indicated the row of craft beers on a shelf above her.

I hitched a shoulder. "Whatever you—"

Behind me, a dark voice murmured, "She'll have the honey beer."

The bartender didn't wait for my okay, just opened the bottle and poured it into a tall glass. When the crown prince spoke, you obeyed.

"You'll like this." Gabriel handed the glass to me himself. "It's got ginger, too."

My heart squeezed. He'd remembered. That I liked not just honey beer, but ginger. The day we'd met, I'd just eaten a couple of ginger snaps. From then on, Gabriel said, whenever he smelled ginger, he thought of me.

Oh, God. I can't do this.

I wrapped my fingers around the icy glass. My lips felt hot, dry. I ran my tongue over them. His gaze tracked the movement, and I stilled.

A long finger touched the bottom of the glass, tipping it toward my mouth. "You're thirsty. Drink."

I obediently sipped. It was good, sharp with a hint of sweetness. "Mm," I said with genuine pleasure.

He regarded me unsmilingly. He was too close, his wild green scent wrapping around me like a seductive scarf. My stomach tightened with yearning. My nipples beaded against the satin scrap they'd given me as a bra.

I set the beer down and inched closer, desperate to press myself against him, to ease the ache.

His gaze flicked to the hard tips, lingered. He traced a finger up my cleavage and over my collarbone before closing a hand around my nape, lightly controlling me. At that firm touch, my knees melted.

I set a hand on his chest. Even through the suit, I felt his heat.

His mouth was so beautifully shaped; sculpted, with a full lower lip, his sexy scruff the perfect frame. "Why are you here, Mila?" His thumb caressed the side of my neck.

I blinked—and recalled the tiny mic masquerading as my left earring. Andre was listening to ensure I stuck with the script.

I stiffened. Gabriel tightened his grip on my neck, keeping me where I was.

I forced myself to meet his eyes. "I missed you." That was the God's honest truth.

Gabriel scrutinized me. "Really."

"Honest." My free hand twisted in the tight red skirt, pulling it even higher. I was a lousy liar and I knew it.

But I had to lie like a champ. Joey's life depended it.

"Hm." His fingers stroked my nape. "I missed you, too. But then, I wasn't the one who left without a goddamned word."

I stared at him. Was that hurt I heard in his voice? But his face was as forthcoming as a blank sheet of paper. Even his eyes were blank now.

His mouth came closer, hovered over mine. "They got to you, didn't they?" he said against my lips. "What did they promise—a million? Two?"

My mouth dropped open. "No!"

"Don't lie to me."

He was the crown prince now, his mouth a stern line, his eyes emerald chips of ice. It was like facing his father. I had to fight not to cringe from him.

I lifted my chin. "I'm not."

He shook his head in disgust and turned away.

"No!" I grabbed his sleeve. "Wait, Gabriel—"

A vampire was instantly at my back. Cool fingers wrapped around my bare upper arms. "Should I toss her ass out of here, boss?"

He gave a curt nod without looking at me.

"Gabriel," I whispered. "Please."

The vampire pried my fingers from Gabriel's sleeve. I watched in despair as he slipped into the crowd.

Two vampires held me now. When I tried to shake them off, their grip tightened.

"Come quietly, babe," the one on my right said. "You don't want any trouble."

"Or maybe you do," said an amused voice in my left ear. "I'm sure we can...accommodate you."

I froze. "No. I don't want any trouble."

"Good girl."

They hustled me toward the front door. I twisted to look over my shoulder at Gabriel, but his back was toward me.

I opened my mouth to call his name, shut it again. Nausea welled up in me.

I can't do this.

I could still stop this. Let him walk away, allow security to hustle me out of the dark club.

No one but the two of us knew that three years ago, Gabriel Kral had offered me the blood bond. He'd even sworn his half of the oath. It was only left to me to accept. Once I did, he was honor-bound to protect me.

If you'd have told me that one day, I would use it against him, I'd have said I'd die first. But I thought of Joey and made my mouth form the words.

"Gabriel Kral, I accept your blood bond."

His spine snapped straight. I hadn't spoken loudly, but I knew he'd heard.

I hurriedly said the rest, "And bind myself to you in return. To be yours, and yours only, for the rest of my life."

The vampires released me and backed off. A murmur went through the speakeasy. One by one, people turned to stare at me, the vampires on the couches rising to get a better look.

Gabriel swung around. A thin blue halo encircled the emerald of his irises. I gulped, excruciatingly aware I was facing his vampire half.

The speakeasy was completely still now except for the throbbing music. He prowled toward me.

"Be sure, Camila." His eyes bored into mine. "There's no going back."

No.

I forced my fingers to unclench from my skirt. "I'm sure." The short sentence came out as a rasp. I cleared my throat, tried again. "I want this, Gabriel."

"Then let it be so. Camila Vittore is now mine," he added with a cool look at the avidly watching crowd.

All around the speakeasy, eyebrows shot up. The thralls sent me envious looks, then pasted smiles on their faces and congratulated us. Some of the vampires joined in, but most remained silent, eyeing me like snakes behind a glass wall sizing up prey they'll never taste.

"Come." Gabriel hustled me toward the exit, the two guards on our heels.

"Wait." I dug my heels in. "My purse—I left it with security."

"You won't need it."

He started up the steps two at a time, dragging me with him until I stumbled in the high heels. He cursed but slowed to a more human pace.

We came out on a chic little block in the East Village. New Yorkers dressed in the latest summer fashions strolled by, unconcerned that this street was owned by the Kral Syndicate.

I'd had time to study the organization while I was on the run, and I'd come to see what a genius Gabriel's father was. Karoly Kral had brought vampires out into the open, welcomed humans at his clubs. Not only that, he hired humans at obscene wages and pumped money into politics so that local officials would do almost anything to land a Kral casino or nightclub for their city.

In return, vampires moved freely in the human world, and their syndicates had their pick of humans willing to be thralls in return for the generous pay and the high of being a vampire's blood toy.

And the Kral Syndicate? It was now the wealthiest, most powerful vampire syndicate in the Americas, maybe even the world.

The bodyguard to my left raised his hand, and a limo down the street purred to life. In the three days Andre had spent preparing me, the temperature had remained high. The sticky air pressed on my skin, but I shivered as I waited on the sidewalk next to Gabriel.

He still held my bare upper arm. At my shiver, his grip tightened.

"You can't change your mind," he gritted, low-voiced. "The bond has been accepted, witnessed."

I jerked my chin in acknowledgment.

Oh. My. God. What have I done?

Andre had said all I had to do was get close to Gabriel. "I just want information," he'd told me. But it didn't take a genius to guess how he intended to use that info.

I glanced around, desperate for a way out—and saw Martin on the sidewalk across the street, a pretty thrall on his arm.

I froze. Fear crawled, spider-like, down my nape.

Martin and Stefan had spent the past three days "training" me, just the three of us in a windowless basement room. Touching me: my face, my neck, my breasts. Whispering that if I didn't obey Andre to the letter, they'd do that and more. Speculating what a good little blood slave I'd make... And the only thing stopping them from doing the same—or worse—to Joey was me.

The blond vampire sauntered past, his attention seemingly on the thrall, but I knew better.

My hand went to my throat. Tonight, right before I'd been dropped off a few blocks from the club, Martin had licked me right over my jugular vein. "Remember we have Joey," he'd murmured, then politely helped me out of the taxi.

Gabriel's gaze followed mine to Martin. He gripped the back of my skull and turned my head so that I was looking at him. Displeasure came off him in hot waves.

"And Camila? Don't even think of running. This time, I'll drag your ass back before you get five feet."

I moistened my lips. "I don't know what you mean. Why would I run?"

"No?" His fingers dug into my nape. "Well, know this. The blood bond means you're mine. Tonight. Tomorrow. Next month. Next year. It's permanent, a contract recognized in both the human and vampire worlds. Run, and you'll just make me angry. And trust me, cher, you don't want to make me angry."

The limo pulled up to the curb. One bodyguard opened the door for us while the other sat in the front with the driver.

Gabriel released me. "After you," he said with an icy courtesy.

I climbed inside.

6

GABRIEL

I settled my long limbs onto the opposite end of the seat from Mila. The driver pulled into traffic, followed by two other limos of the same make and color. One turned left, one went straight, and we went right—a sample of the increased security I lived under these days. Precautions I'd already grown to hate, even though I understood the need. If it was up to me, I'd take my Jag out to the island instead.

Mila swallowed, the sound loud in the small space. But her face was serene. A mask I ached to rip off to find out what she was really thinking.

What did she want?

I'd meant what I'd said. The blood bond was permanent. Now that it had been invoked and accepted, only I could break it, which as far as I was concerned, made it forever.

And she knew that damn well. Three years ago, I'd explained exactly what it meant before I'd sworn my half of the oath. She'd said it was what she wanted, too...and then run.

Now, in accepting the blood bond, she'd put herself under my control. This was more than a thrall contract. A thrall had choices, could leave when the contract was up. But Mila would be mine, and only mine, for as long as I wished.

I'd be lying if I didn't feel a dark thrill.

My woman. My blood toy.

Mine.

I'd loved Mila—once. Hell, I'd spent the first year after she'd left angry and depressed. But I'd understood. I was the crown prince, my father's heir. The various vampire syndicates around the world were our version of the human mafia.

I'd told Mila straight out that if we bonded, it was for forever. A Kral simply couldn't allow his women to go free. It was as much for their own safety as the syndicate's.

And besides, a vampire didn't share his toys, and where Mila was concerned, I was very much a vampire.

But now she was back, and I wanted to know why.

I eyed her moodily. She shifted the tiniest bit under my scrutiny.

I'd hungered for even a glimpse of her, and now I had her alone in this small, enclosed space with only my driver and a Syndicate soldier on the other side of the sound-proofed partition. Even racked with suspicion, I couldn't help drinking in every detail.

The etched silver hoops in her ears. The way the crimson dress dipped low over her breasts to show soft, bitable curves. The strong, intriguing muscles of her legs. Her tangy, very feminine fragrance.

Her gaze jumped from the dark street outside the window to the men in the front seat and finally to me. Her fingers knitted together on her lap, but she maintained that serene mask.

In that moment, I'd have given half my fortune to sense her emotions. I wanted—no, *needed*—to know what she was feeling. But she was as unreadable as a field of new snow.

"Where are we going?" Her voice was huskier than I recalled, another reminder that she'd changed in the years we'd been apart. Back then, she'd always seemed so young to me, so fresh-faced— hell, the day we'd met, she'd just turned twenty-one. I was only four years older, but it had seemed more like ten.

Now she was a woman—a woman who'd turned up at a damn convenient time.

Because if my father's enemies had searched the world for the one woman guaranteed to slip under my guard, her name would be Camila Vittore.

You won't be sorry you left me in charge.

My jaw hardened. "Somewhere we can be alone," I replied.

"Oh." Sooty black lashes swept down, concealing her eyes. "Good."

I eyed her. "Are you afraid of me?"

I already knew the answer. I might not be able to sense her emotions, but I knew Mila, and that tense body and too-serene expression said she was anxious, uncertain.

Good. Let her suffer. She deserved it for running like that.

Her chin lifted. "Should I be?"

"You tell me."

She shrugged and looked out the window.

Several beats passed in which she sat stiff and composed as a queen going to her execution. I sighed and relented. The vampire part of me took a dark enjoyment in her fear, but another, better part—Father would sneer that it was the human in me—felt a curl of shame. Once, this woman had been my whole world.

I pressed a button and soft music filled the interior. Another button, and a minibar slid out from the console in front of us.

"Would you like a drink?" I asked.

She licked her full red lips, and my cock went from half-mast to a full salute. "Yes, please."

I swallowed against a vivid image of her naked and on her knees, saying *yes, please* in those same husky tones.

Later.

"Beer?" I gestured at the bottles. "Or wine?"

"You have anything stronger?"

I raised a brow. The Mila I'd known had stuck to beer, wine, and the occasional sweet, slushy drink.

"Whiskey?" I showed her a bottle of single-malt scotch, and at her nod, poured two fingers worth into a Glencairn whiskey glass.

As I handed her the glass, our fingers brushed. Her breath sucked in.

So she wasn't as unmoved as she appeared.

39

She tossed down a hundred dollars' worth of scotch in a single gulp, and then wheezed. Her face flushed.

I stifled a smile even as pain twisted through me, sharp and sudden.

There you are.

That was my Mila. Half-tamed, impetuous. A wild child who dressed in cut-offs and bare feet and crooked daisy-crowns, not chic little dresses and elegant hairdos.

She shoved the glass at me with a scowl. "What is that stuff —gasoline?"

I eyed the pretty heat in her cheeks. Beneath the smooth skin of her throat, a vein throbbed.

My fangs lengthened. *Mine.*

Gods, I wanted to taste her, to drink from that hot, succulent vein.

She stared back, dark eyes wide, a rabbit facing down a wolf.

I dragged my gaze away. Took the whiskey glass from her and set it on a tray in the mini-bar.

"No," I said, rough-voiced, as I poured myself a large glass of blood-wine. "It's a limited-edition scotch from a brewery we own in Scotland. Next time, try sipping it."

"Oh." She chewed her lower lip. "Actually, now I kind of like it. I feel—." She shook her head.

"What?"

Her sleek updo was already showing signs of wear. I tucked a wayward strand behind her ear, amused in spite of myself. The woman was the polar opposite of most of our thralls with their perfect faces and surgically enhanced bodies.

Mila turned her head to rub her cheek against my hand, then went rigid when she realized what she'd done. But she didn't pull away.

"What do you feel?" I prompted. I fingered the hairclip, itching to remove it for the sheer rush of seeing her silky brown curls tumble down around her shoulders.

But I hadn't forgotten the men in the front seat. I could wait until we were alone.

"Hot," she whispered without looking at me. "I feel hot."

I stifled a groan. Need churned in me like a savage, white-capped river.

It was only the thought of Zaq—chained with silver and at the mercy of some sadistic vampire who couldn't even be bothered to heal the wounds he'd inflicted while feeding—that made me withdraw to my side of the limo.

I sipped my blood-wine, deliberately focusing on its rich, slightly saline taste.

The woman ran. Hid from you for three fucking years. So desperate to escape you that she lived in tiny, roach-infested apartments and drove a beater car.

Even if she wasn't a plant, she was only here now because she wanted something.

Mila withdrew again, toeing off the high heels and curling up on her side of the limo to stare out the window. We crossed the Williamsburg Bridge.

She jerked to attention. "Where are you taking me?"

I set my finished glass on the tray and closed the mini-bar. "Why do you care?"

Something flickered in her eyes. "I want to know. What's so strange about that?"

Suspicion formed an ugly ball in my stomach. "You're mine now," I reminded her softly. "You go where I tell you to go."

Her full mouth compressed. The words *Fuck you* formed on her lips, but she bit them back.

My suspicion ratcheted higher. Since when did Mila hold back? She was one of the most honest, straightforward people I knew. If she was happy, you knew; and if she was pissed off, you knew that, too.

As the limo wound its way through Brooklyn traffic to the Long Island Expressway, I took out my laptop to handle a few Syndicate issues that had cropped up during the night.

Questions burned in my mind. But I could wait until we got to my locked-down, secluded beach house.

Mila wasn't going anywhere.

7

MILA

I slanted a glance from beneath my lashes at Gabriel. In the limo's dark interior, the light from his laptop screen cast his face into sharp relief.

He looked very much his father's son. A ruthless, top-of-the heap predator. And so damn sexy you just didn't care.

I curled up in my corner, staring out the window—and was thrown back five years to the day we'd met.

It was the summer after my junior year in college. That afternoon, I'd gone hiking in a state park on the Chesapeake Bay. When I lost the path, I wasn't worried; I'd grown up in these woods. Getting lost in them was my favorite hobby. I simply had to walk toward the bay, then follow the shoreline south to the park entrance.

To the west, the sun had begun its lazy slide down the sky. Keeping it behind me, I headed east for the bay. But when I emerged from the trees, the bay was still a hundred yards away, and I was on the edge of a large, lush garden.

It was like I'd stepped into a dream. I stared around me, entranced by the wild tumble of flowers. Peach-colored roses and sweet-smelling lavender. Spiky blue salvia and magenta coneflowers.

Honeysuckle and black-eyed Susan and other flowers I couldn't name, all touched with gold by the setting sun.

Small stands of trees shaded the winding paths, and in a nearby stream, water flowed around moss-covered boulders. Several hundred feet away, a stone mansion perched on a cliff above the bay like a great gray hawk, its windows glowing faintly through the tall oaks surrounding it.

I'd heard of Black Oak Manor, of course, but the rich people who owned it didn't mix much with the locals. The three sons didn't even attend school—they had tutors instead. I knew their last name was Kral, and that was about it.

But the locals knew to stay away from Black Oak. Come too close, and security would hustle you away with a sharp warning. Nobody was stupid enough to try it a second time.

I'd started inching back into the forest when a movement to my left made me whip around, heart pounding. In the shade beneath a wisteria-draped pergola stood a man dressed all in black from his T-shirt to his close-fitting jeans. Even his hair was as black and shiny as a raven's wings.

When he stepped out of the shadows and into the slanting gold haze, it seemed like part of the dream.

I caught my breath. He had a face like a fallen angel, seductive, sinful. Later, I'd learn that his dad was Slovak, his mom French Cajun. He had his dad's high cheekbones and long-lidded eyes, and his mom's proud, even features. But that sensuous mouth was all his own.

"You're trespassing," he said in a voice like dark brown velvet.

"I'm sorry. I got lost and—crap, I'll just get going." I inched backwards. "I promise I'll never come back."

He put out a hand. "Don't."

I stilled. From the roses nearby came the hypnotic hum of bumblebees, and from the Chesapeake came the far-off whine of motorboats crossing the bay.

"Don't—?"

"Don't leave." He strolled closer. In the dusky light, his irises were the same bright green as a new spring leaf. "You like gardens?"

"I like this one." I waved an arm at the colorful blooms, talking fast and nervously. "It's like a faerie garden. Something magical— like it exists out of time. You know what I mean?"

He glanced around. "I never really thought about it. Come." He tipped his head at a path through the flowers. "I'll show you around."

I nibbled my lower lip. "I'd better not. I don't want you to get in trouble."

His smile creased his right cheek. "It's okay. I live here."

"You're not with security?"

"No. It's my mom's garden. She's right inside." He nodded at the mansion.

"Holy shit." I'm sure my eyes went round as saucers. "That's *your* house?"

He held out his hand. "Gabriel Kral."

I took it. An electric jolt shot up my arm. I blinked. His face didn't change, but I somehow knew he'd felt it, too.

"Or I can show you the way out of here." He smirked, but not nastily. No, it was a wicked, dare-you-not-to-run-away smile.

I grinned back. I never could resist a dare. "I'd love to see your gardens. And my name's Camila, but everyone calls me Mila."

"Mila." He repeated my name slowly, as if tasting each syllable. "I like it."

He reached for my hand again. This time, I was prepared for the jolt. He interlaced his fingers through mine, and proceeded to give me an impromptu tour. By the time he called an Uber to take me home, he knew all about me—that I was an ag major, that I dreamed of someday owning an organic flower farm—and I'd agreed to meet him for coffee that Friday.

It took me a whole month to realize he wasn't human. Karoly Kral was too canny to plaster his name on his hotels and casinos, and this was before the Dark Angels had become a thing. It's not like I didn't know vampires and dhampirs existed, but they were rich and powerful, and lived in New York penthouses or French chateaus or Singapore high-rises.

They didn't wear shorts and baseball caps and hang out with smart but awkward twenty-one-year-old women.

Sure, Gabriel was different, but in a good way. His family obviously had money, but he didn't make a big deal about it. Panty-melting good looks. And so into me I could hardly believe my luck.

By the time it dawned on me I was seeing a man with fangs and superhuman powers, it was too late. I was crazy in love with him.

❦

G abriel closed his laptop and put it away.

My heart sped up. Would he touch me?

Did I even want him to? He was angry, suspicious. Not that I blamed him; if I were him, I wouldn't trust me either. If he put his hands on me, would I be able to handle it without being torn apart by guilt?

But oh, it had been so long...

I shot him another glance. He met my eyes. His grass-green gaze seemed to penetrate clear to my soul.

I shifted on the seat. Why had I pestered him about where we were going? It wasn't even necessary.

The mic in my left earring was matched by the GPS tracker in my right earring. The security at Ruby's had examined the earrings, but they were apparently state of the art, because while the vampire on duty had taken my purse, she'd allowed me to wear the earrings into the club.

Which meant Andre and his thugs were probably right behind us.

The scotch sat heavy in my stomach. My mouth felt as dry as sand.

I licked my lips. "Do you have any water?"

He touched a button, and the minibar slid out again. "Help yourself."

"Thanks." I selected a bottle of Evian and gulped half of it down before stowing it in the cupholder beside me.

The minibar was more like a minikitchen, with a couple of

45

refrigerated compartments filled with drinks, ice, and sliced lemons and limes. Other compartments held both cold and warm snacks.

I fiddled with the bottles, checked out every compartment. Gabriel's head rested against his seat, but I felt him watching me from beneath partially closed eyelids.

My skin prickled. The small space seemed to shrink even further. His heady scent was everywhere, teasing my nostrils, dredging up memories I'd tried to forget.

I took a slow breath and closed the mini-bar.

We were in Queens now. It was close to midnight, but the expressway was packed with cars heading out to Long Island. According to Andre, Gabriel owned a beach house in Montauk that he never took his women to. Andre had been sure Gabriel would take me to his Upper East Side penthouse.

Was it good or bad that he was taking me to his beach house instead?

I hugged my knees to my chest, digging my bare toes into the buttery leather seat.

The Krals kept a low profile, but they hadn't become so powerful by playing nice. Karoly Kral was one of the most ruthless men in the world, and Gabriel was his eldest son and heir. And I was at his mercy.

I gripped my legs harder and buried my face in my knees.

I was in *un bel pasticcio*—a nice pie—as my Italian nonna used to say, a polite way of saying I was in deep shit.

Worse, Joey had been dragged into it. I didn't know if I could ever forgive myself for that. Anguish squeezed my chest. By now, my parents must be frantic with worry. If only I could text them, let them know he was okay. But Andre hadn't given me a phone, and even if he had, I wouldn't have used it. He'd made it clear that Joey's freedom—and maybe his life—depended upon my complete cooperation.

We pulled off the highway. I set my bare feet back on the floor and sat tall, fingers interlaced on my lap, face smooth and unconcerned.

You can do this.

We passed through several small, pretty towns before reaching the outskirts of Montauk. My nape tingled with the certainty that we were being followed. But I didn't dare sneak a look behind us— not with Gabriel's watchful gaze taking in my every move.

A short while later, we turned onto a private drive. The property was surrounded by tall black fencing topped with barbed wire. At a word from the driver, the gate opened as we approached, then slid shut behind us. As we continued up the driveway, we passed two wolf-like dogs and a pair of leather-tough vampires, all four pairs of eyes shining in the dark.

No wonder Andre was searching for a way through Gabriel's security.

We passed through a hedge of boxwoods taller than me and halted in front of a cedar-shingled beach house. The moment the door locks popped, I was out of the limo. I couldn't see the Atlantic, but I could hear it crashing somewhere beyond the house. To the east, a lighthouse flashed, and the air was heavy with brine.

On the dark road, a car drove past. I cast an uneasy glance through the boxwoods, but if it was Andre, he was too smart to slow down.

The wind off the ocean tugged at my updo, teasing out more strands of hair and whipping them around my face. I swiped the strands away from my mouth, but they immediately whipped back. I'd left my shoes in the limo, and somehow, in scrambling out, I'd ripped a hole in my dress over my hip.

Gabriel rounded the limo. I slapped a hand over the rip.

He looked down at me expressionlessly. "Hold still." He removed a long hair from the corner of my mouth.

"Thanks." I gave him a tentative smile.

He considered me for a long moment, then his gaze went to someone standing behind me. "Airi. This is Mila. She's not to leave the grounds without permission. When she's outside the house, you'll put a guard on her at all times. See that security is informed."

I glanced over my shoulder. The bodyguard from the limo had been replaced by a woman with short, water-straight black hair and the dark, tip-tilted eyes of a Japanese ancestor. Like the other guards, she wore a crisp black uniform with a silver wolf embroidered on the pocket over her heart.

"Of course." Airi bent her head over her phone to send the message. Her short hair swung forward to reveal a snarling wolf tattoo.

I swallowed queasily.

For three years, I'd been hounded by Kral Syndicate enforcers. Now, I was surrounded by them.

Gabriel gripped my upper arm. "Inside." He marched me up the front steps.

The door opened as we reached the top of the steps. A large woman in a gray dress waited in the foyer, her wiry salt-and-pepper hair in a bun, her skin a smooth light brown.

A grin split her face. "Welcome home, M'sieur," she said in a Cajun accent. "And you, Mam'selle."

"*Bon soir*, Lougenia." He smiled back.

I blinked. For a few seconds, he'd turned into the old Gabriel, not the steely-eyed syndicate prince who'd ridden silently in the limo with me for over two hours. Then he glanced at me and the prince was back.

He moved his hand to my lower back, a not-so-subtle statement of ownership that sent a tingle up my spine. Heat pooled in my core, my body remembering how good it had been between us.

I mentally shook myself. *Don't be an ass, Mila. That was then, not now.*

And I was here to help bring him down.

Guilt filled my mouth, an acid, hopeless taste.

"This is Mila," he told Lougenia. "She'll be staying with us for a while." To me, he said, "Lougenia is my housekeeper. If you need anything, she'll get it for you."

The housekeeper gave me a warm smile. "Don't hesitate to ask, sugar pie. Anything at all." She glanced back at Gabriel. "She'll be with you in the master suite?"

My muscles locked. Because however ready my body was for him, the rest of me was all tangled up: terrified for Joey, and almost as terrified for Gabriel. His security was good, but Andre had a secret weapon—me.

Plus, there was Gabriel's coldness. Could I have sex with a man who so obviously distrusted me? Hell, I wasn't even sure he *liked* me anymore.

Underneath it all was the constant awareness that Andre or one of his people were listening to every word we spoke. I was afraid to even ask too many questions in case it gave him some crucial piece of information.

Gabriel felt my tension, of course. He couldn't read my emotions, but my taut body gave me away. He frowned down at me, his fingers tightening around my waist.

Sadness clogged my throat. I knew he thought I didn't want him, and I hurt for us both.

"Put her in the rooms next to mine," he said in clipped tones. "She'll need the basics—a toothbrush, hairbrush. And clothes—she didn't bring any luggage. Shoes, too," he added with a glance at my bare feet.

Curiosity flickered across the housekeeper's broad face, but she simply dipped her head. "Very good, M'sieur. If the young lady will come with me..."

The foyer was all tile and polished wood, with a high ceiling and a brushed-steel chandelier. It opened into a living room with wall-to-wall windows, that like the foyer, was built on clean, open lines, with glossy modern furniture and more brushed-steel fixtures. Cobalt vases stuffed with wildflowers—sky-blue cornflowers, cheerful daisies, ferns, Queen Anne's lace—perched on the slim steel-and-wood tables.

Lougenia explained that the beach house was on a cliff, its main rooms in a straight line so that they all had a view of the ocean. "This is the upper level," she said, leading me past the living room down a hallway a good twenty yards long. "There are four suites on this level. The kitchen is on the lower level along with the dining room. There's a gym down there, too, and a more formal room for entertaining. Not that M'sieur Gabriel ever has anyone out here to entertain."

"No?" I gazed around, head spinning. It was so big, and maga-zine-perfect.

"He doesn't come here often. He bought the house three years ago and then..." She moved a sturdy shoulder in a shrug.

We passed two closed doors before stopping at a third. "This is your suite, and the master's rooms are there." She nodded at the closed door at the end of the hallway.

As we entered my rooms, I sucked in a breath. I'd half-expected a small, bare cell. This was anything but. It wasn't a suite; it was an apartment, big and gorgeous, with white walls and a polished maple floor. The furniture was pure beach house: a large, comfortable-looking couch and chairs in a blue-and-white striped fabric.

"This is your bedroom." Lougenia opened the door to a cozy-looking space with the bed set into a nook with sloped ceilings. This time, the colors were reversed, with the walls sky-blue and the bed made with an embroidered white coverlet and a mound of plump white pillows. The side facing the ocean had a large bay window with a window seat that invited you to curl up and dream.

"And the bathroom is here." The housekeeper indicated an open door on the opposite side of the bedroom.

I poked my head inside. There was both a walk-in shower and a tub the size of a small pool. Fancy soaps and creams were arranged on a tray on the granite counter, and a small table held a large vase of sunflowers. I fingered a fluffy towel, feeling like I'd been plucked out of my real life—the one where I had to steal food to survive—and dropped into a fairy tale.

From the doorway, Lougenia's smile was satisfied. "It will do, Mam'selle?"

"Oh, yes." I beamed at her. "Thank you."

She shrugged a beefy shoulder. "It's as M'sieur requested. Now," she said, bustling into the bathroom, "everything you need tonight is here." She opened a linen closet to show all the supplies anyone could need for a month's stay—brushes, toothpaste, shampoo, lotion, and so on.

"You'll find a bathrobe in the bedroom closet," she continued, "and if you give me your size, I'll have your new clothes here by morning." She cast the red dress a dubious look. "You'd like more dresses like that?"

I winced. "God, no. A pair of shorts and a couple of T-shirts are fine." I glanced toward the dark bay window and the ocean I could hear beyond. "And a bathing suit, if it's not too much trouble."

"Of course. The currents in the ocean here are too dangerous for swimming, but we have a pool on the grounds. What about shoes?" she asked as we returned to the living room.

"Sneakers, please, and maybe a pair of flipflops?" I gave her my sizes and she noted them on her phone. "Oh," I said, "don't forget underwear."

Something made me turn my head. Gabriel stood in the open doorway, watching me through hooded green eyes.

My breath snagged.

My fairytale prince had arrived, and he was nothing like the stories we tell children.

"Thank you, Lougenia," he said without taking his gaze from mine. "You can go to bed now. Mila won't be needing you until the morning."

The housekeeper nodded and headed for the door. Gabriel moved aside to let her pass, then put his hands on the door jamb, blocking me in the suite with him.

I moistened my lips. My stomach chose that moment to growl.

"Lougenia?" He glanced over his shoulder. "Bring Camila something to eat."

"Very good, M'sieur. I'll send it right up."

Then she was gone, and I was alone with Gabriel. I took a few steps back. He shut the door and followed me, step by step, with that lean predator's grace.

He drew a slow breath. "You're afraid." This time it wasn't a question.

My hands gripped my skirt, inching it higher. His gaze flicked to the tear over my hip. When I glanced down, I saw skin and a scrap of the tiny satin panties they'd given me—black satin with little red hearts, like it was freaking Valentine's Day.

"No," I lied.

I adjusted the skirt, trying to cover myself, but instead, I somehow made the tear even larger. If I kept this up, I'd be standing before him wearing nothing but a few tattered scraps.

And damn if that didn't make my inner thighs tingle.

Down, girl. The bad vampire is looking at you with darkness in his eyes.

"Hm." He shrugged out of his suit jacket, dropped it on a chair.

I scowled. "What's that supposed to mean?"

A shrug. "Maybe you should be afraid. That's why you ran, isn't it?

I pressed my lips together. Why should I care what he thought? But it stung, that he believed I was such a coward that I'd run rather than tell him straight out that I wouldn't accept his blood bond.

"Believe what you want." I swung around, not sure where I was going. I just wanted to get away.

"Answer me, Mila." His eyes shimmered ice blue, and suddenly, he was right in front of me, blocking my way.

8

GABRIEL

Mila looked like a goddess in the lipstick-red dress. A long-legged, earthy, incredibly fuckable goddess.

I stalked forward, drawn by something as powerful and unbreakable as the moon's lure for the tide. She gulped and dug her fingers into the spandex skirt, tearing it further.

My gaze locked on the flirty red-and-black panties. Had she worn those for me? My dick pressed painfully against my zipper.

She hurriedly smoothed down the dress—and made the rip larger.

My lips twitched. I pressed them together.

I was *not* going to be amused by Mila.

I was *not* going to notice how, now that we were beneath the living room's bright overhead light, I could see she was not only thinner, but hollow-eyed from exhaustion.

Most of all, I was *not* going to give into the tenderness that kept tugging at me, especially when she muttered, "Stupid dress," under her breath.

"Answer me," I repeated in a soft, *obey-me-now* voice. I stepped closer, deliberately invading her space. I was six inches taller and a good seventy-five pounds heavier, and I wanted her to understand just who—and what—she was dealing with.

Her eyes widened, but she squared her shoulders and stared back.

The gods help me, that pleased my vampire half. Easy prey is boring.

"No," she gritted. "I didn't leave because I was afraid."

"Then why?"

She shrugged a slender shoulder.

My jaw tightened. I was the Kral crown prince. Very few people —vampire, dhampir or human—dared stand up to me, and for someone to shrug off a flat-out demand was almost unheard of.

But this woman—this *human*—dared. She stared up at me, her lush mouth set in stubborn lines.

I ground my back teeth. I could compel her to tell me the truth, but I couldn't quite bring myself to do it. Because the day I compelled Mila to do anything was the day I'd lose her for good.

Oh, maybe I'd have her body and her blood, but I'd seen what happened to those thralls bound to power-drunk vampires who used compulsion more than absolutely necessary. I'd have an empty-eyed shell of a lover.

The ocean breeze had done its work on her updo. Wavy chestnut wisps framed her face, and the clip looked like it would fall off any second.

I brought my hand up. She flinched, which bothered me on some primal level, even though my darker side wanted her afraid.

Wanted her to suffer for leaving me without even a fucking goodbye.

Still, I gentled my voice. "Take it easy. I just want to—."

I undid the clip, letting the rich brown waves tumble down. I dropped the clip on the coffee table and combed my fingers through the silky tresses, working out the tangles and arranging it around her shoulders.

All the while she stared at me, a tense crease between her eyes. I smoothed the crease away with my thumb.

She heaved a breath and relaxed a fraction, and something inside me eased as well.

"C'mere." I urged her closer until her forehead rested against my chest. Gathering her hair, I moved it aside and stroked her nape.

She was so tight, a wire stretched to the breaking point.

Guilt snaked through my belly. Was she that afraid of me?

I gently squeezed the flesh on either side of her neck.

"Relax, cher." My mom was part Cajun, and it tended to come out when I was with children, but almost never when I was with women.

Unless the woman was Mila.

"I can't," she muttered against my shirt.

"Yes, you can." I worked my fingers up her neck, pressing and circling, and then back down and out along her shoulders.

"Easy for you to say," she grumbled, and my lips twitched in spite of myself.

But her breath sighed out. Her hands came up to rest, butterfly-light, on my chest.

My heart clenched. "That's it. Relax."

Her fingers spread out on my chest. They were warm, the nails cut short. She stroked the thumbs over my nipples. When I caught my breath, she stiffened and curled her thumbs into her palms as if she hadn't meant to do it.

I continued to massage her neck and shoulders until she relaxed again.

A knock on the door made her start. She pushed at my chest. Reluctantly, I let her go.

It was Airi, the head of my personal security. "I have the food, sir," she said through the closed door.

I took the tray and waited for the door to shut again before tapping a control on the wall to activate the security system. A precaution, even though Airi or another enforcer would remain on guard in the hall all night, and the entire compound was wired with a high-tech system so expensive only billionaires could afford it. In addition, Tomas had assigned extra soldiers to prowl the grounds 24/7.

I set the tray on the coffee table. Lougenia was a fucking treasure—she'd prepared an assortment of sandwiches, fresh fruit and tender young vegetables. She'd even included two glass flutes and a split of champagne chilling in a bucket.

Mila stood near the window, arms wrapped around herself.

I indicated the couch. "Sit."

She cast a longing glance at the food, but shook her head. "Let's just get this over with."

"Get this over with?" The guilt receded, replaced by anger. "Don't play the victim card. You came to me, remember? Now, sit."

Mila worried her lower lip. She had such a beautiful mouth, soft and full, with a sexy upward tilt at the corners.

"Gabriel," she said. Just my name, nothing else.

"What?"

She opened her mouth, closed it. "Never mind."

She took a seat on the far end of the couch. I moved the tray so that it was in front of her and sat down, my thigh touching hers.

She stilled. Her gaze lifted to my face, then skittered away. "I suppose I am hungry." She reached for a succulent-looking strawberry.

I grabbed her wrist. "I'll feed you."

Her chin jutted. With her other hand, she snatched up the strawberry and brought it to her mouth.

I plucked it from her fingers. "The rules have changed, Mila. First rule is, I'm in charge now."

She squeezed her thighs together, and her pupils darkened. No fear now. Instead, I scented arousal. I didn't bother to conceal my smile of satisfaction.

"Open." I brought the plump red fruit to her lips.

Her gaze went from the strawberry to my face, and then those soft lips parted.

Watching her eat was pure torture. The juices coated her lips, making them shiny and red...like she'd look after taking me in her mouth.

I swallowed hard and fed her another. She ate it slowly, deliberately, her gaze locked on mine the entire time.

I forgot this was meant to be a lesson in who was boss now.

Instead, I fed her another strawberry. And another. By the fourth, I was iron-hard.

A muscle in my jaw worked. Was she playing me? Or was she as caught up in the moment as I was?

I couldn't read her, and it was driving me insane.

It didn't help that my dick didn't give a damn either way. It strained mindlessly against my pants, eager to bury itself inside her tight, wet heat.

I could almost see Father shaking his head in disgust. *"Control, son. That's what separates the primus from those he rules. A primus is always in command, especially of himself. From control comes strength and from strength comes power."*

I tore my gaze from hers. "Champagne?" I asked.

When she nodded, I popped the cork and poured us both a glass.

"Thank you." She accepted hers with a longing look at the sandwiches, cut into triangles and arranged on their own plate. "What are those?" She pointed to a trio of miniature shrimp po'boys.

"A New Orleans specialty." I brought the small, fried-shrimp-stuffed roll to her mouth.

She took a taste and closed her eyes with pleasure. "More, please."

I fed her another po'boy, followed by curried chicken on wheat bread. I continued feeding her between sips of champagne until she'd eaten most of the sandwiches, then had a few myself.

She finished her champagne and set the flute down.

"More?" I lifted the bottle.

"No, thanks." She stifled a yawn. The tendons of her neck stretched.

I stared, arrested, at all that smooth, delicious flesh. The hunger rose up in me—for both blood and sex. Even for a dhampir, it could be almost unbearable at times.

She brought her hand to her throat. "Are you—tonight?"

"Am I what?"

"You know."

"Going to feed from you?"

Beneath her fingers, a pulse jumped. My mouth watered. I could literally taste how good Mila would be, savor the warm rush of her blood as I sank my teeth into her throat at the same time I stroked into her hot cunt.

She nodded wordlessly.

Control, Gabriel.

"No." My voice sounded harsh in my ears. "You're tired. Go to bed."

"Oh." Her swallow was audible. "Okay. You sure? I mean, a deal is a deal..."

Was she relieved or disappointed? I couldn't tell.

But I did know that if I stayed much longer, I was going to push her down on the couch and rip the rest of that snug excuse for a dress off her—and when I did, I wanted a woman who wasn't about to keel over from exhaustion.

I rose to my feet, pulling her up with me. "Go."

I turned her toward the bedroom, but couldn't resist bringing my mouth to the turn of her neck. Inhaling her honeyed scent.

A tremor went over her—and then, very slowly, she tilted her head to the side. Exposing the tender skin beneath her jaw.

My breath punched in my lungs. My fangs lengthened.

In the thirteen months we were a couple, I'd never fed from her —just taken a tiny sip here and there.

At first, I hadn't wanted to scare her off. For the first time in my life, I had a woman who treated me like just another guy, and I liked it. We had sex—I wasn't a damned monk—but the summer we'd met, she'd only just turned twenty-one. She might have been of age, but she seemed so fucking young. I'd believed it was the honorable thing to do, a way to prove to Mila that she was more to me than simply another human.

Now it seemed incredible that I'd never taken more than a few small tastes. Maybe if I had, she wouldn't have run.

Darkness slithered through me. Moving her hair aside, I scraped my fangs over that soft, exposed spot, careful not to break the skin.

Her breath sped up, and her eyelids lowered. "Gabriel. Please..."

My throat hummed in a low, pleased growl. I *would* have her, writhing beneath me and begging.

Taking anything I wanted to give her and pleading for more.

Screaming my name until her voice broke.

But not tonight.

"Get some sleep." I straightened and smacked her round ass. "And Mila?"

"What?"

"You *will* tell me. Anything I want to know." I turned and strolled to the door.

I deactivated the security and went out, shutting the door behind me. The security reactivated immediately after.

Mila's outraged gasp was audible through the closed door.

When I chuckled, Airi eyed me strangely.

"Guard her with your life," I snapped at the enforcer, and entered my suite.

❧ 9 ❧
MILA

I glowered at the locked door, equal parts angry and aroused. For a few minutes, I'd forgotten everything but Gabriel. His scent. His hard body. His magical, knowing fingers.

My muscles had been lax, my pussy wet for him.

When he'd scraped his teeth down the side of my throat, I'd nearly come out of my skin.

And then he'd left me, the prick.

I don't know who I was more upset with, him or myself. One thing I knew: I was damned if I'd tell this cold-eyed stranger why I'd left.

Even if he did make my lady parts sit up and beg.

My dress had hiked up. I jerked the skirt down, tearing it past all repair. With a feral snarl, I dragged the thing off and shoved it into a waste basket before stomping into the bathroom.

The soaking tub was actually a big jacuzzi. I blew out a breath. *You're in.*

That was the important thing. If Gabriel wanted to play with me, well, I couldn't blame him. And I also couldn't pretend I hadn't liked it.

I took a quick shower to wash off the makeup and my own nervous sweat, and then filled the tub, adding bubble bath for good measure. I lowered myself into the hot water and turned the jets on low. As they purred to life, a sigh of pure pleasure escaped my lips. I sank deeper until the bubbles reached my chin.

For a few minutes, I just lay there. It made no sense, but for the first time in a long while, I felt safe.

I knew it wouldn't last. Gabriel's security seemed solid, but Andre was an old, powerful vampire. He'd find a way inside.

Not tonight, though. Andre hadn't told me much, but I'd heard enough to guess the plan was to attack Gabriel in his Manhattan penthouse.

So for now, I was safe, and so was Gabriel.

I swallowed sickly. I fingered my left earring, wishing I dared remove it and its mate. They were soldered on, but a pair of wire cutters would do it.

But they had Joey.

Andre had tied my hands as surely as if he'd snapped a pair of steel cuffs on me. I couldn't even write Gabriel a note.

"We'll know if you do," Andre had warned.

I wasn't sure *how* he'd know, unless he had someone on the inside—or maybe they were monitoring me via Gabriel's security system? But I couldn't take the chance.

I cast a bleak look in the direction of Gabriel's suite and got out of the tub. My relaxed feeling had evaporated along with the bubbles.

Back in the bedroom, I turned the lamp on low. It had been a long time since I'd slept without a nightlight. Too many monsters lurked in the dark.

Curling up in the big bed, I stared at the sky-colored wall, sure I wouldn't sleep, even worn out as I was. But for too long, my nerves had been stretched to the breaking point, and my belly was full. The combination made me heavy-eyed.

I rolled onto my other side. This time I faced the windows. The blinds were closed, but somewhere far below, the ocean threw itself against the rocks, over and over, in a hypnotic rhythm.

My eyelids drifted shut. I felt again Gabriel's hands on my shoulders, massaging me, long-fingered and sure. Touching me exactly where I most needed it.

Sorrow stabbed through me. I'd missed him so much. It hurt, to have him be so cold.

But his kindness hurt even more, because I didn't deserve it. I didn't know how or when Andre would attack, but he would. And then Gabriel would fight Andre to the death rather than allow him to hurt me.

It was time to face facts. I didn't have to do a thing to help Andre. Just my being here endangered Gabriel.

My accepting the blood bond had made things even worse. Gabriel was honor-bound to protect me now.

God, I hated myself. Hot tears pricked my eyes.

You did what you had to do. It was Gabriel or Joey. At least Gabriel has a fighting chance.

But knowing that didn't do a thing to relieve the guilt eating me from the inside out. I moaned and pressed the heels of my hands to my eyelids.

Outside, the ocean heaved and sighed. Gradually, my breath slowed to match it.

When I was sure I wasn't going to cry, I took my hands from my face and resolutely closed my eyes. I might not be able to sleep, but I needed to rest.

❧ 10 ❧

GABRIEL

I spent the rest of the night working in the study off my
bedroom. Near dawn, my father finally contacted me on the
secure phone, a cryptic text that was pure Karoly Kral.

The objective is in good health but the way forward is obscure.

I scowled at the message. What the hell was that supposed to
mean? It was like my dad was channeling his inner Yoda.

But I gathered that Zaq was alive and unharmed, which meant
Father had discovered where he was being held. For once I was
grateful for my inhuman, cold-as-ice father. If anyone could rescue
my middle brother, it was him.

Still, I wanted more information. I was about to text him back
when I received a second message.

Do not attempt contact.

I growled but obeyed. He'd probably already destroyed the
phone he'd contacted me with anyway.

I reached for my own smartphone, itching to let Rafe know the
news, but he was still deep undercover in Montreal. Finagling a

meeting with the Tremblay princess was going to take cleverness. But getting her to talk to him? That was going to take a king-size dose of his famous charm. From what Rafe had said, he and Zoe had struck sparks off each other the size of Mount Vesuvius. Then things had gone bad. Very bad.

Zoe Tremblay had a rep for being as coolly vicious as her mom. He'd be lucky if she didn't turn him over to Victorine herself.

That left my mom. With Father away, she'd be keeping a human's hours, but it was almost dawn, and I'd promised to contact her as soon as I had any news about Zaq, day or night.

She answered on the second ring. "Gabriel? You have news?"

"Yeah. Father's making progress." I was careful not to say too much, both for security purposes and because it was an unspoken rule in our family that Mom was kept out of Syndicate business.

"Thank the good Lord. Is he—coming home soon?"

I heard the hesitation. What she really wanted to ask was, *Are* they *coming home soon?*

"I don't know," I admitted.

"Still, that's good news—that he's making progress. What about you? You're okay?"

"I'm fine. You know Tomas. I can't take a piss without a body-guard trying to hold my you-know-what."

She chuckled. "Poor baby. I feel like I'm on house arrest myself. Lord forbid I try to leave the grounds. I'm like a mother duck with a posse of hard-ass, scowling ducklings. Your father's orders, bless his heart. I understand, but..."

"I'm sorry," I said, although on Mom's safety, my dad and I were in complete agreement. "It's only until we figure out what's going on."

"Don't worry. I just put my nose in the air and act like a movie star."

My mouth twitched. I could just see my beautiful, dark-haired mom—who was as down-home as they get—sashaying about like a bored Hollywood A-lister.

Toeing off my shoes, I leaned back in my chair and propped my feet on the sleek black desk. "I'll send you a pair of sunglasses."

"Cat's eye," she returned without missing a beat. "With rhinestones. Big, glittery rhinestones."

I grinned. Knowing my mom, she'd wear them, too. "You got it."

"Now, why don't you tell me what's wrong?"

I took my phone from my ear and stared at it. The woman was a witch. "It's not what you think. Everybody's fine. I promise."

"Then what is it?"

I hesitated. Mom wouldn't be pleased to know Mila was back.

It wasn't that she hadn't liked Mila. It's that she knew as well as me that my father would never accept anyone but a vampire as my mate. I'd hidden Mila from my parents for as long as I could, although I'm sure my father's spies had informed him I was banging a human. Father wouldn't have cared if I'd kept Mila as a thrall, but once he'd realized she meant more to me, he'd asked—no, commanded me—to bring her to dinner.

It hadn't gone well.

Father had been barely civil to Mila, and after she'd left, he'd called me into his study to chew me out. "You know better than this, Gabriel," he'd said coldly. "You're the crown prince. It's your duty to mate with a vampire, to keep our line strong."

My fingernails had dug into my palms. I'd been within a hairsbreadth of planting a fist in the center of his lean, tight-lipped face. "*You* didn't."

"You dare?" he'd hissed.

"To tell the truth straight to your face? Hell, yeah."

His ebony eyes flashed blue, but I glared back. I was damned if I'd back down.

"That was different," he said. "I'm a vampire. I knew my blood would breed strong sons."

I drew a slow breath. A kick to the gut couldn't have hurt any more. "And my blood wouldn't?"

A wave of a long-fingered hand. "You're not a vampire."

My jaw hardened. "That doesn't make me weak."

My fangs had lengthened. If my mother hadn't entered the study at that point, I think I would've either attacked my father, or walked out and never returned.

"Gabriel?" Mom asked now. "What aren't you telling me?"

I expelled a breath. "It's Mila. She's back."

"What do you mean, she's back?"

"I mean she's here. With me. Not in this room, but—with me." I pinched the bridge of my nose. Gods, I sounded lame even to myself.

"I see." A pause. "Are you sure you know what you're doing?"

Hell, no. "Yeah. If you mean do I trust her, no, I'm not sure. But I'm being careful."

"Just where is 'here'?"

"The beach house. I figured it was the most secure place for us both while I figure out why she's come back after all this time."

"I see."

I winced. That made two *I sees* in a row.

"I know you didn't want me to mate with her. But this is different."

She sighed. "It's not that I didn't want you to mate with her. It's that I don't want your kids to go through what you and your brothers did."

I straightened. My feet hit the floor with a thud. "What d'you mean?"

"You think I didn't know how the vampire spawn bullied you? I hated it." Her swallow was audible. "Just hated it. But your father refused to let me interfere. He said if we did, they'd never have any respect for you. That the only way you could survive in his world was to be tougher than them."

My nape tightened in memory. Zaq, Rafe and me had had targets painted on our backs from day one. The worst had been the coven gatherings, where the other spawn picked on us unmercifully until we were big and strong enough to fight back.

"Jesus. He's even more of a prick than I thought."

"Careful." Mom's voice hardened. "That's my mate you're talking about."

I scowled. I was damned if I'd apologize, but my quarrel wasn't with my mom. "Look, don't worry. I've got things under control."

She inhaled. I could almost see her rubbing her forehead like she did when she was worried or upset. "You sound just like your father. He won't like this, you know."

"I'll handle him. Mila's here, and she's staying until I figure out what the hell's going on. She accepted my blood bond."

"I see." This time the pause was so long I thought she'd ended the connection.

"Mom?"

She heaved a breath. "Just promise me you'll give her a choice. A thrall contract is one thing. Mating with a vampire—or a dhampir— is something else. And will you be happy with a human mate?"

I glowered at a painting on my study wall. "Who said I still want her as my mate? She's my thrall. The blood bond just means my contract with her is exclusive. She's a source of fresh blood, and that's all. End of story."

Okay, maybe the fresh blood came with hot, mind-blowing sex, but I was *not* going there with my own mother.

"Oh, cher," Mom replied in a *men-are-clueless* tone, and changed the subject.

We talked another few minutes, then I said goodbye and opened my laptop again. The first thing I did was order a half-dozen rhinestone sunglasses sent to Mom in Maryland. Next I purchased clothes and shoes for Mila, having gotten her sizes from Lougenia before she went to bed. The last thing I bought was a gold chain blood-bond bracelet from the syndicate's own jeweler.

By then, dawn had reached its glowing fingers through the blinds. I closed them and rubbed my tired eyes.

Mom was right. Father was going to be pissed off—no, furious. And all the work I'd put in to prove I was a worthy heir would go right down the drain.

My jaw set. I'd figure it out. Somehow.

Because I wasn't giving Mila up.

I turned to leave, then sat back down at my desk. I couldn't sleep without assuring myself Mila was still there, even though there was no way she could've gotten past the vampires prowling the grounds, not to mention my Czechoslovakian wolfdogs, an intelligent, loyal, and menacing mix of German Shepherd and Carpathian grey wolf.

I brought up the house security system on my laptop. A couple of taps and I could see Mila, curled up in the center of the big bed, her dark hair spread out on the white pillow, the sheet pulled up to her chin. The bed dwarfed her, making her look more like a waif than ever.

She muttered something in her sleep, shook her head. Her breath quickened, and the mutter changed to a whimper.

"No, no, nonono..."

My chest tightened. I wanted to go to her, take her in my arms and comfort her. But I remained where I was, afraid it was me who haunted her dreams.

"Promise me you'll give her a choice."

I dragged a hand down my face. The hell with that. Three years ago, I'd given Mila a choice, and look where it got me.

This time, it was different. She'd come to me, accepted the blood bond. Sworn she knew what it meant.

That didn't make her my mate. The mate bond was a unique, soul-to-soul link, while the blood bond was basically a thrall contract, even though it was an exclusive and unbreakable one.

No, the blood bond didn't make Mila my mate.

But it did make her mine.

I blew out a breath. It wasn't that easy, and I knew it. The woman was so thick with secrets, I could practically see them, like a sticky web entangling her.

She sighed and stopped moving. I waited until I was sure she was okay, then closed my laptop.

I'd asked her why she'd left, and she'd refused to answer. But that had been my heart—and my hurt pride—talking, not my head.

Because the more important question was, why had she come back?

11

MILA

I woke to sunlight pouring through the bedroom doorway from the living room. I automatically reached for my phone to check the time, then remembered I didn't have one.

I looked around for a clock. But the bedroom, while comfortable, was furnished with just the basics: a nightstand, a lamp, a tall dresser, a single chair. It was more like an upscale hotel room than a residence. Even the painting over the bed was pretty but impersonal: a beach scene with a lone white Adirondack chair shaded by a striped umbrella.

I made a pit stop to wash up, then pulled on a fluffy blue bathrobe to explore.

In the living room, I got my first view of the Atlantic. My breath caught. The house projected out over the cliff. Outside was nothing but blue sky and the ocean far below, an intense turquoise that shaded to indigo farther out. It crashed against the rocks, wild and free.

I set my palms on the window and pressed my nose to the glass, drinking it in.

Gabriel knew I loved the ocean. It was like he'd bought this house with me in mind.

Yeah, right. I gave myself a shake and turned away.

Still no clock, but a knock on the door told me someone knew I was awake. "Your clothes are here, miss."

A click and an electronic beep, and the door swung open. A golden-haired woman waited on the other side, dressed in the same black uniform—slim black pants, button-up shirt embellished with a snarling silver wolf—as the rest of Gabriel's security force. Not a vampire, though; they'd be asleep now.

She wasn't any friendlier than the vampires, though. She gazed at me, unsmiling, over the stack of boxes in her arms. "Where do you want them?"

I reached out. "I'll take them."

"As you wish." She dumped them into my arms and bent to pick up another pile.

"Wait," I blurted, juggling the boxes. "These...they're all for me?"

Scorn flickered over her fine-boned features. "Of course." She stacked five shoeboxes inside the living room next to the door.

"Thank you," I said, and got a stiff nod in return.

She dropped several intriguing bags next to the shoeboxes and straightened. "When you're ready, Lougenia said to tell you brunch is in the dining room. Your door will be unlocked during the day."

She pulled the door closed with a decisive click.

"Well, screw you, too," I muttered, then forgot her to take in my loot.

Color me shallow, but I love presents, and I hadn't had a gift in three years. No Christmas gifts. No birthday gifts. Hell, I hadn't even been using my own birth date. Not that I'd let anyone get close enough to learn it anyway.

I set my own packages down with the rest and knelt, not opening anything at first, just shaking the boxes one-by-one and examining the labels before turning to the bags. I didn't recognize a single store name, but I could tell they were from trendy little boutiques that don't bother with price tags. Because if you have to ask, you can't afford it.

I wasn't surprised Lougenia had gotten everything delivered so fast. The Kral Syndicate probably owned half the shops, and if they didn't, the owners would have fallen all over themselves to do Gabriel Kral a favor.

Scooping up an armful of packages, I took them to the bedroom and sat on the bed to open them.

Lougenia—or someone—sure had good taste. One box was filled with cute little shorts, and another held a dozen pretty T-shirts and tanks in a rainbow of colors. I also found button-up shirts, dress pants, yoga pants, two hoodies and four swimsuits ranging from a bright yellow one-piece to a tiny red bikini. There were even a couple of sleepshirts.

My next trip yielded several flirty summer dresses that I could actually see myself wearing, and the shoes, all five pairs of them: running shoes, sandals, flip-flops, and two pairs of high heels.

The last bags held sexy bras, panties and nighties so sheer they'd make a porn star blush.

"In your dreams, Kral," I muttered as I dug around until I found a few exercise bras as well. But I couldn't help fingering the slinky red mesh romper with the crotchless panties and picturing how Gabriel's eyes would heat if I wore it for him.

My stomach growled, reminding me that I'd missed breakfast. In fact, from the height of the sun, it was closer to lunchtime. I pulled on shorts and a roomy orange button-up shirt with big blue flowers, then shoved my feet into the flip flops.

My hair was in wild tangles around my face. I brushed it and pulled it back into a ponytail, securing it with an elastic band I found in the bathroom.

The hall was empty except for another guard, this one a lean feline of a man with close-cut brown curls. Like the golden-haired woman, I couldn't tell if he was dhampir or human, but at least his smile was genuine.

"Good morning, miss. I'm here to take you to the kitchen."

He turned to go, but I said, "Wait. Is Gabriel up?"

"Not yet."

I glanced at Gabriel's door. "What time is it, anyway?"

"A little after eleven."

I blinked. I hadn't slept that late in years.

"What time does he usually get up?"

"I couldn't say, miss. But if there's something I can help you with, let me know."

"No. I'm fine." Just itchy to see Gabriel.

"Then if you'll come with me?"

I followed him back to the foyer and through a door down to the lower level, where I found Lougenia bustling around the kitchen. Like the rest of the beach house, the kitchen was comfortable, almost casual. Somehow I'd figured all vampires lived in Gothic manors complete with heavy velvet curtains, antique furniture and flickering iron sconces. Black Oak Manor had been kind of like that.

But the kitchen and the adjoining dining room were clean, airy spaces with off-white cabinets, maple floors and sea-colored walls.

"There you are." Lougenia gave me an easy smile. "You must be starving. Here." She handed me a glass of orange juice. "I have brunch ready for you."

She led the way into the light-filled dining room. My guard faded back into a shadowy corner. Maybe he was a vampire after all, although the windows had a bluish-green tint to protect sensitive skin.

"I wasn't sure what you like." Lougenia gestured at a large maple table heaped with enough food for a family of four.

My stomach growled. "I'm not picky."

I sipped my orange juice and grinned at Lougenia. "Oh, that's good. You must've squeezed it fresh."

"Sure did," she returned, pleased. She nodded at the nearest chair. "Sit yourself down, then. I'll bring you another glass."

"Thanks," I said as I took my seat. "And may I have some coffee, please?"

"Coming right up."

I ate some of almost everything: eggs, bacon, home fries, and a Belgian waffle topped with blueberries. I considered the pancakes but decided I'd had enough, although I couldn't resist the fresh cantaloupe.

When I was finished, I carried my plate and silverware into the kitchen, but Lougenia snatched them out of my hands. "That's my job," she scolded.

I lifted my shoulders in apology. "I'm not used to having someone wait on me, and besides, I wanted to tell you how good everything was."

A smile lit her broad face. "Tomorrow I'll make my mama's famous shrimp étouffée and grits."

I grinned back. "Bring it on."

Leaving the housekeeper to her work, I carried my coffee mug to the balcony outside the dining room. The wind tore at my hair and clothes, and far below, the surf threw itself against the rocks.

I was so used to being wound tight that being tense felt like my natural state. But now, I raised my face to the wind and the sun. I drew a deep breath, let it out.

My shoulders eased away from my ears.

Right here, right now, I was happy...at peace.

It wouldn't last. It couldn't last.

I could almost hear the seconds ticking by. Whatever Andre had planned, it would happen soon.

But for these few moments, I let myself enjoy it.

❧ 12 ❧

GABRIEL

I found Mila on the balcony, looking like a wildflower in the bright clothes, her face lifted to the sun, her hair in a careless ponytail. Already, a few strands had escaped to whip around her head.

My breath punched in my chest. She was so beautiful, so vibrant. A sunlit sprite too good for a dark creature like me.

She looked so at home, just as I'd pictured when I'd purchased this house three years ago. I'd planned on surprising her with it as a mate-gift. There was even a meadow she could use to start her flower farm.

I watched her for long minutes, hidden in that shadowy dimension where vampires can't be detected, before returning to the physical world. Opening the sliding door, I stepped outside.

I could tell the instant she sensed me. Her spine straightened, her face lowered.

My mouth twisted. *She didn't come back for you.*

It was so obvious she had a hidden agenda. But I could wait. Sooner or later, she'd tell me the truth. Mila was too open, too honest, to keep a secret for long.

She finished her coffee and set the mug on a round black patio table. By the time she turned to me, she had a smile on her face. A smile that almost looked real. "Morning."

I inclined my head. "You slept okay?"

A small shrug. "Yeah." She waved a hand at her outfit. "I wanted to thank you for the clothes."

"You like them?"

This time, her smile was genuine. "I love them. Lougenia has good taste."

I nodded noncommittally. The hour I'd spent ordering her clothes had been worth it. It satisfied something primal in me, seeing her dressed head to toe in an outfit I'd chosen.

And I couldn't wait to see her in that blood-red romper-thingy.

Mine.

Fingering the gold bracelet in my pocket, I prowled closer. "Everything fits?"

"I think so. Yeah."

"You don't know?"

I stopped a foot away from her. She gazed up at me, brown eyes wide. "I didn't try everything on."

I captured a strand of wavy dark hair between my fingers. "What about the nightgowns? And that red romper?"

She moistened her lips. "What about it—them?"

"Did you try the romper on?" I pictured her leaning over a chair, bottom turned up with those crotchless panties framing her pretty sex, and went instantly hard. But I kept my face expressionless, enjoying how her heart sped up as if she were picturing the same thing.

"No. Not yet. But I'm sure it—they're—fine." She gulped. "Everything's fine, I mean."

"You'll tell me if there's a problem."

"Okay. Sure." A pulse fluttered in her throat.

I snaked an arm around her waist and set my mouth to that tempting flutter. Not to drink, just to tease us both. I wouldn't feed from her until she was stronger, but that didn't mean I couldn't touch her.

Her throat muscles worked beneath my lips. I nudged the shirt away from her shoulder and trailed kisses over her collarbone. She smelled clean and fresh.

"Would you like to see the beach?" I moved my mouth to the soft golden skin beneath her jaw and sucked—hard.

Her breath hitched. Her heart sped up, the rapid beat a counterpoint to the boom of the surf.

"The beach?"

"Mm-hm." I nibbled on her earlobe. "Down below, there's a private beach. Nobody can reach it except us, and the local boaters know to keep away."

Her hands came up between us. But not to push me away. No, her fingers curled around my shoulders, pulling me closer. Round, firm breasts pushed against my chest, the tips hard.

Without looking away from her, I set my sunglasses on the table next to the mug and moved my mouth to hers. She opened her lips...and melted into me.

Lust punched up my spine. She wanted me. That part, at least, was no lie. I could scent her desire, a honeyed female spice. Hear her pounding heart.

I slid a hand between her thighs. Even through the shorts, I felt her heat. I undid the button of her waistband.

She moaned and slid her fingers into my hair. Sucking on my tongue. Nipping my lips.

I eased her zipper down, caressing her mound through her panties. With my middle fingers, I teased her clit, rubbed her plump folds.

Her groan was raw, needy. "God, I missed you," she said against my mouth.

I stilled, recalling two things. We were on the balcony, in full view of my bodyguards—and she couldn't have missed me as much as she claimed, or she wouldn't have stayed away for so long.

I withdrew my hand. She pressed closer, undulating against my hard, very ready cock.

I tightened my arm around her waist, urging her up against me. The only thing between us were a few layers of material—my T-shirt and board shorts, and her thin summer clothes. Her leg came up, twining around mine. Her flipflop fell off, and warm toes caressed my bare calf.

Holy Dark Mother, it felt good.

I took the kiss deeper, eating at her mouth, sliding my tongue over hers. Letting her feel my hunger before backing off in small increments, rubbing my lips over hers, pressing kisses to her eyes and her nose. Finally, I gripped her arms and set her away from me.

"No." She whimpered my name and tried to squirm closer again. "Don't go."

I took a choppy breath.

Her eyes opened. They were dark, dazed. "Please, Gabriel."

My fingers flexed on her arms. "There's a bodyguard on the other side of that window," I said in a rough voice. "Unless you want him to see me pull down those shorts, bend you over the rail and fuck you, then we need to chill."

"Oh." She glanced at the window and flushed. "Yeah."

Her elastic hair band had fallen onto the balcony floor, leaving her hair in a wild mass around her shoulders. I picked it up and handed to her.

She took a deep breath, then her face shuttered. I watched as she coolly zipped up her shorts and redid her hair.

Her smile was even more cool. "I'd like to go to the beach now."

I stared down at her. The wildflower was gone, an ice-cold lily in its place. And damn, I hated that it had been me who'd made her retreat behind that emotionless façade again.

"Gabriel?" She arched a dark brow.

"One thing first." Removing the bracelet from my pants pocket, I clasped it around her wrist. It was slim but unbreakable, with three tiny gold daisies in the center. I engaged the special clasp to ensure it couldn't be removed.

Her gaze flew to mine. "What's this?"

"A symbol of our blood bond. All the blood-bonded thralls wear one."

"I see," she said flatly, then ran a fingertip over the delicate flowers. "You got me daisies." Her throat worked. "A daisy chain. You remembered."

Our eyes met. For a heartbeat, we were both back in that summer meadow the day she'd turned twenty-two.

As the sun slid beneath the horizon, she'd danced barefoot through the tall grass in a tiny T-shirt and cut-off jeans, hair in a thick braid that fell halfway down her back. Heat shimmered around her.

I picked a handful of daisies and wove a lopsided crown to set on her head.

She laughed up at me. "I'm a princess. And you're my prince."

"Always." I wrapped my fingers around her nape and reeled her in for a kiss. She smelled like the meadow, fresh and sunny. The white daisy petals glowed like pieces of moonlight against her dark hair.

Now I tore my gaze from hers.

"The bracelet can't be removed," I said in a hard voice, and opened the sliding door. "The beach is this way."

We were on the lower level. The staircase to the beach was accessed through a door at the other end of the building. We headed down the hall, a dhampir enforcer trailing us. We passed the gym, empty now, with the vampires asleep in their underground lair and the two dhampirs on site handling security.

A set of wall-mounted shelves held suntan lotion, caps, towels and beach blankets. I offered Mila a cap, but she refused it, so I set it on my own head before grabbing a blanket and a couple of towels.

The door to the outside was solid steel reinforced with silver strips to repel vampires. I touched a palm to the sensor and the door unlocked with a soft snick.

The dhampir enforcer made to follow us, but I halted him with a look. "Wait up here."

I wanted to be alone with Mila, and no one was going to reach the beach without his knowledge. And if they came by boat, I had a secret passage carved into the cliff that no one but my brothers knew about.

"You're the boss," he said with a shrug, and took a stance on the concrete landing just outside the steel door.

The beach was sixty feet below in a cove hemmed in on three sides by jagged rock outcroppings. I led the way down the steep metal staircase. During high tide, the beach was reduced to a strip of sand and pebbles, but right now it was a large expanse, broken only by a heap of boulders to our right.

As we stepped onto the sand, Mila turned to me, eyes wide. "You really *do* have your own private beach. No one else comes here?"

"Nope. It's just us."

"That's insane!" She dropped her flipflops next to the stairs and ran straight into the ocean. A wave slapped against her legs, nearly knocking her over. She merely laughed and opened her arms, the bracelet gleaming on her wrist.

"It's cold!" She spun to face me, the water up to her thighs.

I smiled, relieved to have my wildflower Mila back. Toeing off my sneakers, I joined her.

"Careful. There are some strong undercurrents along this part of the coast."

"Lougenia told me." Her reply ended in a yelp as another wave crashed into her, splashing her to the chest. She giggled, arms spread wide like she was embracing the whole world—ocean, sky, sun.

Maybe even me.

My heart constricted. I gripped her hand as the ocean sucked at our feet. The next wave was the largest yet. It slammed into us, soaking us both to the skin. She would've gone down if I hadn't snagged her by the waist and moved us both closer to the shore.

She chuckled and swiped a hank of wet hair from her face as I set her back down again. "Why didn't you warn me? I would've worn a bathing suit."

My mouth curved. "Maybe I wanted to get you out of your clothes."

She stilled. We stared at each other. My blood surged, slow and hard, in my veins.

Then she grinned. "I always did like how you think."

She jogged back to the beach blanket. I remained where I was, the ocean churning around my calves, while she unbuttoned her shirt and dropped it on the blanket. Next she peeled off the shorts, leaving her in a blue exercise bra and matching boyshorts.

My fangs pricked my gums. Yeah, she was thinner, but the woman still had some sweet curves.

She ran past me into the surf, executing a clean dive into the next wave. So much for my warning about the currents.

I didn't love the sun, but I could tolerate even bright sunlight for an hour or two. Leaving on my sunglasses and cap, I pulled off my T-shirt and joined her.

She splashed me in the face and dove under. I was after her in a flash, capturing her by the ankle and pulling her to me for a hard, salt-flavored kiss.

We played in the waves until I turned to look at a boat motoring by a little too close. Behind me, Mila fell silent. I glanced over my shoulder to see her staring at the snarling wolf tattoo on my right shoulder blade.

Fuck. Just when she'd finally started to relax around me.

She moved closer, touched the tattoo. "That's new." Her fingertip followed the midnight swirls over my skin, outlining the wolf's snarling mouth and sharp fangs. "When—?"

"A few months after you left."

"Why?"

I sent her a hooded glance. "I think you know."

It was the official emblem of a made enforcer in the Kral Syndicate, although I'd been bloodsworn not to speak about that with an outsider.

"Mm." She brought her hand back to her side.

I turned around again. "You have a problem?"

Yeah, I sounded belligerent, but she knew what I was...who I was. Once, she'd said it didn't matter, that she loved me anyway.

I was proud to be a Kral enforcer. My father had built a powerful organization from one small coven. We had a strict code of honor, one he insisted everyone followed to the letter. A Kral

Syndicate member didn't lie, steal, or cheat—unless you lied to, stole from, or cheated us. And we only killed when absolutely necessary.

Mila exhaled. "Well. Congrats, I guess."

I jerked my chin in acknowledgement.

"No." She shook her head at herself. "That sounds like I'm not happy for you. I am—truly. It's what you wanted, what you worked for."

"Thanks," I said, but the playfulness had gone out of the afternoon.

She pushed her hair off her face—she'd lost the hair band in the water—and glanced around. A shiver went over her too-thin body.

I swore under my breath. I should've remembered how run down she was. "You're cold. Let's go back to the beach."

I swept her into my arms and headed back to the beach. She stiffened. Not much, but enough so I noticed.

But as I stepped out of the surf with her, she twisted so her arms were around my neck. Long legs twined around my waist. Even with the cold water, I'd been half-erect as we played. But now, with her soft sex pressed against me, I started to lengthen.

She nibbled on my ear. "Warm me up, Gabriel."

At her husky tones, I went rock hard.

She gave a hum of satisfaction and undulated against me. "Nobody can see us here, right?"

"Mm-hm." The enforcer above knew better than to watch us.

"Good." Her tongue traced my earlobe. "It's okay if you want to fuck. I had an injection."

My brows snapped together. I pulled back to scrutinize her face. "Why?" I told myself I wasn't jealous, just possessive.

A shrug.

I tightened my grip on her. "You weren't with anyone else while you were gone. So why get an injection?"

"So you *were* watching me."

I tangled my fingers in her wet hair and pulled back her head so I could see her eyes. "Answer me, Mila."

A shadow crossed her face. "I—had a couple of times where I

was afraid a guy would—you know. So I got the injection, just in case."

"Gods." I squeezed my eyes shut. "Give me their names."

"I...can't."

I glared down at her. "I. Want. Their. Names."

She heaved a breath. "I don't know their names. Or if I did, it was just first names."

"Gods." Fury rose up in me—at Mila, for running and making herself vulnerable, and at myself for allowing it.

I was grasping her hair too tightly. I forced my fingers to release their grip. "So that's why you took those self-defense courses."

Her breath sucked in. "Were you spying on me the whole fucking time?"

"Not the whole time. I just checked on you now and then." Setting her on the sand, I wrapped a towel around her shivering form. "But I should've been, if this was the sort of shit you had to put up with. Did you think I wouldn't worry about you? I wasn't even sure if you'd been kidnapped."

Her gaze slid from mine. "I left a note."

"Yeah, you did," I said evenly. "A goddamn note after thirteen months together. You said you loved me, and you didn't even have the balls to say goodbye to my face."

She chewed her lip, gave a small shrug. "I hate goodbyes."

"Don't give me that." I gripped her shoulders. "You owed me more than that." The hurt she'd dealt me made me snarl in her face. "Was the idea of accepting my blood bond that bad? You had to run from me like I'm some kind of monster?"

She seemed to wilt in my arms. Then she lifted her chin and pulled the striped towel more tightly around her.

"You know I don't think that. I *never* thought that. I may wish you'd been born someone else—someone normal—but I never thought you were a monster."

"No? Then why did you leave?"

She shook her head. Her soft lower lip trembled.

I swore. "Don't you fucking cry. I swear, I'll turn you over my knee if you pull the tear-thing on me."

Her chin jutted. "I'm not," she snapped as a fat tear rolled down her cheek...her too-thin cheek. She gave another hard shiver.

I let out a few choice words and pulled her into my arms, towel and all.

Gods, I was an ass. Not for having it out with her, but for doing it now, when she was clearly not up to it. "Take it easy," I muttered. "It's all right."

She burrowed her head into my shoulder. "No," she said, so low I barely heard her. "It's not all right."

I tipped her chin up and rubbed my lips over hers. "Then tell me, Mila. Tell me what's wrong so I can make it right."

She pressed her lips together and shook her head.

My insides twisted. Why wouldn't she trust me?

"Have it your way, then." I went to pull away, but she released the towel to grab me.

We were both damp and sticky from the salt water. She wrapped her hands around my shoulders and pressed up against me. The bra and boyshorts were so wet, she might as well have been naked. I felt every curve and line of her.

My cock swelled even more. I gripped her round bottom. The towel fell the rest of the way to the sand.

"Please," she whispered.

I dragged off my cap and dropped it on the beach, followed by my sunglasses. "Please, what?"

She raised on her toes to set her lips to my ear. "Please fuck me." A husky murmur. "That's what I want. You. Right here, right now."

Heat balled at the base of my spine. I slid a hand into her wet boyshorts, palming and squeezing her ass.

Why not?

I wanted her. Bad.

And we were alone on my private beach with an enforcer guarding the only access. The only boats I'd seen in the past half hour had been fishing boats taking tourists out to try their hand at catching tuna or other game fish, and the captains knew to stay far away from Gabriel Kral's cove. The motorboat I'd seen had already disappeared around Montauk Point.

I searched her face. Did she really want me, or was this just another ploy? Gods, I wished I could read her like I could other humans.

"Gabriel, please." Her fingers dug into my shoulders. "Stop teasing me."

Oh, yeah, I liked hearing her beg.

"Shh." I cupped her throat with my other hand. A light, barely there pressure.

She could've easily escaped me. But she remained where she was, tense and quivering, as I rubbed my thumb over the pulse jumping beneath her jaw.

My eyes went vampire, increasing my focus so that I saw every detail of her face. The amber striations in her deep brown eyes. The slight chapping of her full lips. The trail the single tear had left on her creamy olive skin.

Her eyes widened, and I knew she saw the blue ringing my irises. Her own pupils darkened, heated.

My other hand was still on her ass. I slid a finger deeper between her cheeks to where she was hot and wet. Her breath sped up.

My blood flamed. "You want this."

Her throat moved beneath my fingers. "Yes," she breathed. "God, I want it. So much."

"All right, then. But we do things my way."

She blinked. "What d'you mean?"

I didn't speak, just reeled her back in.

❧ 13 ❧
MILA

Gabriel's kiss was slow and open-mouthed. The unhurried kiss of a man who knows a woman is his, and that he can do anything he wants with her.

He slid his tongue over mine, tasting, sucking, nipping. Encouraging me to taste and nip him back. One hand was on my butt, his fingers warm and strong. The other remained on my throat.

I swayed into him.

He'd always liked to play with my throat. It was a power thing for him, I think. He wanted me to trust that he wouldn't hurt me. Or maybe it's that for a vampire, the throat and neck are extra erotic.

It got so just the touch of his fingers on my throat could get me hot, and today was no different. His grip was so gentle, yet controlled.

Heat pooled in my belly, between my thighs. I skimmed my hands over his broad shoulders and down the sculpted muscles of his back, learning him all over again. He was bigger than I remembered, harder.

The wind swirled around us. The sun beat down on my skin. And still he kissed me until I clung to him, weak-kneed and wanting.

He halted long enough to spread the cotton beach blanket on the sand. He laid me down on it, and then his powerful body covered mine.

Strong fingers cupped my face. "You're warm enough?"

"Hot. Boiling." I pulled him closer, kissing him with all the desperation in my heart, his gold bracelet heavy on my wrist.

It can't be removed.

I flashed back to the night he'd sworn the blood oath to me. I'd been excited, nervous, a little afraid. Still, after thirteen months together, I'd been sure we could make it work.

But within twenty-four hours, it had all come crashing down...

Don't think.

I wrapped my arms around him as tight as I could, twining a leg around his hip to urge him closer still.

He was all lean, hard heat, his skin dusted with sand and salt, his short dark hair mussed from the ocean and my fingers. He smelled like the outdoors, sharp and masculine.

When he broke the kiss, I whimpered and tried to pull him back.

The corner of his mouth lifted in a maddening smirk. "Easy, sweetheart. There's no hurry."

He lifted onto his hands and knees to crouch over me. His hands moved knowingly over my body. Electric sparks shot from my breasts to my thighs. I shivered with sheer pleasure, and he frowned.

"Let's get these wet things off." He helped me out of the bra and boyshorts, then removed his own shorts and lay back on top of me. Now it was just skin to skin, the two of us warming each other.

He licked his way across my breasts. He hadn't shaved, and his stubbled jaw abraded my tender skin in an exciting way. Sharp teeth scraped over my nipple.

I braced for a bite, but instead, he sucked on the tightly furled tip. I went hot, then cold, my body overwhelmed with sensation.

I bit my lip and dug my nails into his back, trying not to cry out, aware that Andre or one of his men were probably listening.

Gabriel gave my nipple another hard suck and then moved to

the other one. His mouth closed over me, warm and wet. Pleasure arrowed straight to my clit.

I couldn't hold back anymore. I bucked and moaned, a soft, needy cry.

He put a hand on my hips and pressed me back to the blanket. Hovering above my body so that I could feel his cock, a slight, teasing pressure when I wanted all of him.

He licked the underside of my breast. "You want me."

I slid my fingers into the heavy silk of his hair, stroked his nape. "You know I do."

"No, I don't know that." He stilled to look up at me. "You left, remember." His voice was expressionless, but a muscle worked in his jaw.

My chest squeezed. I'd known I'd hurt him, but I was just beginning to understand how much. "I'm sorry."

There are some things you just can't apologize for. Gabriel must have thought so, too, because he ignored me to continue, "I used to think about what I'd do if you came back. Picture all the ways I'd punish you."

"I'm sorry," I said again. "But you know it was for the best."

A low growl. "Best for who, damn it?"

I opened my mouth, but he set a hand on my lips. "No, don't answer. You'll just lie to me, and I can take anything but that."

Hurt stabbed me. I sucked in a breath.

You, I said in my mind. *It was best for you.*

His eyes shuttered, but he didn't apologize, just released my mouth and resumed kissing my breasts.

Pleasure danced over me. God, I ached for him. But not like this.

I turned my head to stare out at the ocean. "Fuck you," I said wearily.

He gave a dark chuckle that rippled straight to my core. "Oh, you will fuck me, Mila. Any way I want." He slid a hand between my legs, testing my wetness. "You're ready now, aren't you?"

I stubbornly set my mouth. Lord, this was messed up.

Me lying to him.

Him wanting me even though he didn't trust me.

And Andre listening to it all.

But a few yards away, the ocean ebbed and flowed hypnotically, the breeze off the water teasing my damp nipples. Above us, seagulls wheeled and screeched, white shadows against the bright blue sky. It was so wild and beautiful out here, like we were the only two people in the universe.

And I wanted him, so bad. Three years I'd been alone, afraid even to have a drink with another man because I didn't know who to trust—and besides, I didn't *want* anyone but Gabriel.

Let him be suspicious—he had a right to be. He could even punish me, because I had a feeling I'd enjoy his kind of punishment.

"Very ready," I rasped in a voice that didn't sound like me at all— and lifted my arm from my eyes to pull him closer. He captured my wrists in mid-air and pressed them to the blanket on either side of my head.

His thumb caressed the gold bracelet on my left wrist. Both our gazes went to it.

It can't be removed.

When he'd clasped it around my wrist, I'd felt so owned, and not in a good way. No, I'd felt like a body, a thrall—not a person.

And yet, he'd remembered that I loved daisies...

Gabriel's gaze returned to mine. "I want you to leave your hands there on the blanket. Understand?"

Don't think.

I gave a jerky nod.

"I could hold you down," he continued. "But I want you to restrain yourself."

Excitement shivered over my skin. My heart sped up, my nipples tightened even further. "And if I don't?"

"Then I get up and walk away."

I glanced pointedly at his cock, flushed and heavy above my mound.

"Oh, I can do it," he assured me. "Control is something that was pounded into me from a young age." When I flinched, he added,

"And no, my father didn't hit us. He didn't have to—he's very good at getting his point across."

His mouth moved lower, trailing hot kisses down my neck and around my breasts. "Yes or no, Mila?" A leisurely lick to the underside of my breast.

Pleasure seared through me. I struggled to get the next words out, but I needed to know. "So you'd let me go. Just like that."

"Mila." Remorse flitted over his good-looking face. "I thought you understood—you can't leave now."

"Oh." I blinked. I *had* understood, but hearing it stated straight out was...daunting.

But what did it matter? I probably wouldn't get out of this alive anyway.

Sorrow pressed on my chest, a heavy, smothering weight.

He released my wrists to raise back onto all fours. "I warned you that the blood bond is forever. But it's not just the bond, it's that everyone in the Ruby saw you accept it. We're connected now, Mila. To the vampire world, you're an extension of me. If you leave this time, you'd be dead or enslaved in less than a week. But everything else? That's up to you. We can fuck or not. It's your choice."

I swallowed hard, then reached for him.

If it was up to me, I'd choose Gabriel. Always.

He caught my hands and sat up, thighs bracketing mine, and pressed a kiss to each palm. Taking his time, like I was something precious.

Tears stung my eyes. I blinked them away.

He brought my left hand to his face and rubbed his cheek against it, his night beard a velvet rasp against my palm.

"Is that a yes?"

I rubbed my thumb over his cheekbone. "It is. Yes."

He gave a hum of approval before pressing my hands back down on either side of my head. "But we do it my way. Okay?"

My fingers curled into my palms, but I kept them where they were. "Okay," I replied. "Yes."

He gave me another kiss and then sat back on his heels again, gazing down at my naked body. The sunlight haloed his head, leaving his face in shadows.

Gabriel. My dark, seductive angel.

My breath hitched. For a long minute, he just looked, as I remained where he'd put me, hands on either side of my head, my legs stretched out along the blanket.

My breasts grew tight, heavy. A pulse beat between my thighs. There was something so erotic about being open to him like this, waiting for him to touch me.

At last, he began stroking his fingers up and down my body. Pleasure slid through me, warm and lazy. I floated on it, light as air.

He kneed my legs open and crouched between them. His mouth replaced his fingers. Kissing me everywhere—lips, neck, breasts, navel, the points of my hips.

When he reached my sex, he gave it a long, leisurely lick and then turned his head to nuzzle my inner thigh. I instinctively bent my legs, opening to him even more.

"There's a vein here," he murmured.

My mouth dried. "I remember."

He'd told me about it one moonless night in a cozy little cabin in the woods. By then, I was crazy in love with him. He could've done anything he wanted with me, but he'd held back.

That was the night he'd asked me to accept his blood bond, and I'd said no, that I wanted to think it over.

Teeth scraped over my sensitive skin. "You remember what else I said?"

I nodded wordlessly.

"Tell me," he said against my thigh. "What did I say?"

I moistened my lips. "You said it would feel incredible when you fed from me there. That it was how vampires bind their thralls to them. That it feels so good, the thrall will do anything to get it."

"You do remember." His tone was darkly satisfied.

When I lifted my head, I saw his incisors had lengthened. The vampire was showing his fangs.

I shivered with a mix of fear and excitement. This man was a predator in a sleek, hard-muscled body, and all that power, all that strength, was focused on me.

He scraped the tips over my other thigh. So carefully. But I jolted at the sharpness, and he licked the small wound.

"Shh. It's all right."

He continued playing with me. Sucking, nipping, licking, until I was dazed and moaning.

My fingers were knotted in my hair now, clenching and unclenching. It was the only way I could stop myself from reaching for him.

He kissed his way back up my body. "Keep your hands like that," he ordered. "I like how it lifts your breasts to me."

His teeth rasped over one soft curve. So delicately, I knew it would barely leave a mark.

And yet, he was marking me. Everywhere...

At last, his mouth reached the spot where I most craved his touch. He gripped my ass, his lips and tongue worked their magic on my sex, teasing and tormenting.

It was perfect, and then it was too much. I rocked my hips up to him, muttering broken pleas. The sun—the heat—was inside me now, searing my spine, lighting up my nerves.

I arched my back and whimpered his name as a climax exploded like a fireball through me.

I was still catching my breath when he thrust inside me, slow and firm. My sex contracted around him, drawing him deeper.

He gritted my name. "Mila."

"Yes." I twined my arms and legs around him, holding him close, as he stroked in and out of me. Long and hard and perfect.

A second shock of pleasure bore down on me.

He took my hands from his neck and, twining his fingers through them, pressed them above my head so I was stretched out beneath him.

His mouth moved against my ear, harsh, erotic whispers. Telling me to take him, all of him. That he'd never let me go now.

"*Mine*. My thrall. My woman."

My breath sobbed in. "Oh my god, ohmygod, ohmygod."

He nibbled his way down the side of my neck, sending heated sparks to my breasts, my clit. I angled my head for him, but he didn't feed, just kept his teeth on the skin above my carotid.

I wasn't sure if it was a promise…or a threat.

He swore on some dark god and then with a final firm, perfect thrust, stilled deep inside me, filling me with hot spurts.

My body constricted around his, and I came yet again in an explosion of light and pleasure that went on and on until I cried out. Calling his name. Begging him to stop, and in the next breath pleading for more.

Gabriel hung over me, chest heaving, and then rolled onto his back, bringing me with him so I was nestled against his shoulder. I heaved a sigh, wrung out and satiated, my body warmed from the sex and the summer sun.

For a time, the only sounds were the slap of the waves and the sound of our breathing. I combed my fingers through the wiry dark hair on Gabriel's chest.

Gradually, his last words penetrated my relaxed, happy haze.

Mine. My thrall. My woman.

Was that all I was to him?

I closed my eyes and rolled onto my back, facing the sky. On my wrist, the slim gold bracelet seemed to press into my flesh.

Stop it. You have no right to be hurt. You left him, remember? Not the other way around.

I'd told myself that I'd done it for him. His parents had made it clear that I was a liability, that Karoly Kral had had a hard enough time just getting the vampire world to accept his three dhampir sons as his heirs. As the crown prince, Gabriel was expected to choose a vampire mate. If he blood-bonded with a human, or worse, mated with one, he'd constantly be fighting off challenges.

But now I wondered if maybe I'd run away as much for me as for Gabriel?

Because he was right; deep down, I'd been afraid. I'd loved him—so much it hurt—but the blood bond was a serious commitment, especially with the man who'd one day be the Kral Syndicate Primus.

Accept the bond, and my life would never be the same. Accept it, and I'd never be free.

Gabriel rolled on his side to face me. He traced my lower lip with his finger before continuing down the center of my throat. I turned my head and attempted a smile, but my expression felt as stiff and artificial as a china doll's.

"It's not money, is it? Not this time." The finger moved down my breastbone. "They got to your family."

My smile faded. I stilled, heart pounding in my ears. For a few minutes, I'd forgotten Andre or one of his people might be listening. Hopefully the pricks had gotten an earful.

Jesus, I was terrible at this. Gabriel was too smart to fool for long, which actually gave me hope. Still, I couldn't admit it, not with them listening in.

I opened my mouth. Closed it.

"Shh," he murmured. "You don't have to say anything. But it's the only thing that makes sense."

I shook my head. "No. You're wrong."

He set a finger on my mouth. "No lies, Mila. Give me that much, at least."

I thought of Joey and moved Gabriel's hand away. "I'm not lying." The words tasted sour in my mouth.

He eyed me without speaking before rising to his feet and holding out his hand. "Time to go back. I have work to do."

"Yeah." I took his hand, even though the cool, impersonal way he offered it—like I was just another throw-away thrall—slashed at my heart.

I turned my back on him and dragged on my dry clothes. The damp underwear, I balled up and shoved into my front pocket.

With his dhampir speed, Gabriel was still dressed before me and waiting by the stairs, the towels and beach blanket tucked under his arm. I snatched up my flipflops and dashed barefoot up the stairs. Maybe I couldn't outrun him, but I had the satisfaction of hearing him blow out a hard breath as he jogged up after me.

He left me on the lower level with Lougenia, saying, "Feed her up," like I was a stray kitten who'd followed him home. To me, he said, "I have to go to Manhattan. I'll be back in a day or two."

Dismay rolled through me. If he left, would Andre pounce? I grabbed his arm.

"Take me with you."

Cool green eyes scrutinized me. "I have to work, Mila. You'd just be in the way."

That made me scowl. "I can entertain myself."

He gave Lougenia a look, and she excused herself to go back to the kitchen.

Gabriel took my chin. "You willingly bound yourself to me, Mila. That means what I say goes. If I say you stay behind, then you do. No arguments."

"That's not what—" I clamped my mouth shut.

Shut up, Mila. Or Joey's dead.

I released his arm, dropped my gaze. I felt so fucking helpless. Warn Gabriel about Andre, and Joey would be forced into blood slavery. But keep silent, and Gabriel might be staked as soon as he left the grounds.

"You're right," I said tonelessly. "I'm sorry."

He studied me for another few seconds that felt like hours, until I raised up on my toes and brushed my mouth over his. "I'll miss you, okay?"

"Mm." A long arm snaked around my waist, pulling me up against him. Warm lips traced the shell of my ear, sending rivulets of heat down my spine. "When I get back," he murmured, "you can show me just how much you missed me. I want to see you in that red thingy."

I nodded as he released me. But as he turned to go, I couldn't stop myself from mouthing, "Be careful."

His brows drew together. He gave a slow nod, as if something had just become clear.

But all he said was, "Get Lougenia to show you the pool. But don't go back to the beach without me—it's too isolated down there." He released me. "That's an order, by the way. And you're not to leave the grounds. A security guard will be with you at all times."

"Yes, sir," I muttered.

He chuckled and headed upstairs. A few minutes later, I heard the thrum of a helicopter.

۞

According to Lougenia, Gabriel owned the largest private property in Montauk. In addition to the beach house, the compound included a five-car garage, a large pavilion for entertaining outside, and a bunker-like lair with no windows that I assumed was home to Airi and the other vampires.

After lunch I took a path along the cliffs, trailed by the curly-haired guard from that morning. Sturdy daisies, sandwort and beach grasses dotted the cliff edges, and the scent of Pygmy pines and junipers filled the air. Flocks of twittering birds feasted greedily on the shadbush's blueberry-like fruit.

Far up the beach were couples and family groups with colorful umbrellas blooming like tropical flowers on the sand. But on this private path, the only person other than me was a man whose name I didn't even know. My step hitched. I'd been alone for so long. Family outings seemed a lifetime ago.

I squeezed my eyes shut, missing my family with my whole heart: my mom, my dad, Nonna, and especially Joey. We'd been close, despite the four year difference in our ages. I'd never thought of him as an annoying little brother because he was so much fun.

Hatred for Andre stabbed through me. What kind of low-down snake drags a twenty-one-year-old kid into something like this?

I dug my fingernails into my palms, hurrying along the cliff until I was practically running. *Hang on, Joey. Help is coming. You just have to hang on a little longer.*

The path turned inland, ending at a quiet pond nestled in a shady woods. I sat on a bench by the pond, watching the wood ducks paddle in circles.

Trying not to think. Trying to just be.

My guard stood ten yards away. I pretended to ignore him, but

95

even though he was quiet as a cat, it didn't work. I was too aware of him watching me.

With a sigh, I got up. "Can you show me the swimming pool?"

"Of course. You passed it on the way here." He led the way back to where the pool was concealed in a stand of trees overlooking the ocean.

When the guard tried to follow me inside the black steel fence, I sucked a breath through my teeth and spun to face him. "What's your name, anyway?"

He blinked twice, the only sign I'd startled him. "Paco."

"Camila." I held out my hand. "Nice to meet you, Paco."

His brows climbed toward his hairline. He looked at my hand like it was a concealed weapon, but shook it. "Nice to meet you, Miss Camila."

"Well, Paco," I said. "You think you could wait out here? I promise, I won't scale the fence and escape."

He hesitated, then inclined his head. "As you wish. I'll be right here." He faded into the trees just outside the gate.

I heaved a breath, and headed inside.

Like everything else about the beach house, the pool was one of a kind. Four different pools had been carved out and connected to look like a waterfall spilling down the hill, with each pool pouring into the one below, ending in an infinity pool that jutted out over the Atlantic. Drought-tolerant plants like yucca, purple coneflower, black-eyed Susan and spiky Russian sage were arranged in colorful drifts around the teak furniture, and a cabana at one end held everything from towels to cold drinks. There was even a bookcase stuffed with paperbacks and magazines.

True to his word, Paco left me to enjoy the pools alone. I swam laps in the infinity pool until my muscles screamed for mercy, and then slathered on suntan lotion and stretched out on a chaise lounge with a stack of magazines.

I flipped through a garden magazine, but for once, even flower porn couldn't distract me, although an article about a lush Savannah estate came close.

I knew the books wouldn't be much better. I set the magazine on my stomach and stared up at the sky.

If Gabriel had wanted to torture me, he couldn't have picked a better way. I would've done almost anything rather than stay behind, worrying that this was the day Andre would make his move.

I told myself Gabriel could take care of himself. He'd been trained by vampires, for God's sake. And I'd seen for myself how good his security was—and that was just the visible security.

But these are vampires. They're faster, more powerful, than dhampirs.

God, I missed my blade. I could live without a phone, but my hand literally itched for the knife's comforting weight.

I tossed the magazine to the concrete and jumped back into the pool.

Dinnertime came. I showered and changed into one of my new summer dresses before heading for the dining room.

This time, I had company; the two dhampirs who had been on duty that day, and Lougenia herself, who after cooking dinner, was off for the rest of the night, although she couldn't help directing the twenty-something woman who had taken over for her in the kitchen.

Lougenia had us all laughing about things she'd gotten up to as a girl in New Orleans. It turned out that she'd known Gabriel as a baby—her mom had worked for his mother's family, and the Krals had been frequent visitors to Rosemarie's parents' home in the French Quarter.

I egged her on, eager to hear about Gabriel's life as a kid. It was no surprise to hear he'd been very much the big brother: responsible, disciplined and very protective of his two younger brothers.

"He'd even take punishments for them," she added. "But in return, he expected their loyalty, and they gave it to him. He's a natural born leader. Not that he couldn't be a devil sometimes."

I blinked. "Gabriel?"

The older woman's dark eyes crinkled around the edges. "Oh, yes. It's the quiet ones you have to watch. Not that he was bad—he never hurt anybody with his tricks. Still, there were times he was the despair of his mama. She worried that he'd never be—." Lougenia shot a look at the two dhampirs and halted. "'Course, you'd never know it now," she smoothly continued. "M'sieur Gabriel works hard enough for five men. And he's so good with his mama—calls her almost every day."

The dhampirs nodded agreement, and I was pretty sure they weren't just sucking up for my benefit. They'd seemed genuinely shocked to hear that Gabriel Kral had ever been less than perfect.

Lougenia's helper appeared then, and the conversation moved to other things as she cleared away our dinner plates and brought out dessert. Vanilla ice cream—and a plate of ginger snaps still warm from the oven.

My lungs seized.

Lougenia beamed and offered me the cookies. "I baked these especially for you. M'sieur Gabriel's orders. He said they're your favorites."

"Thank you," I said over the boulder-sized lump in my throat. "They are."

I helped myself to one. It was delicious, sweet with a spicy bite. But I could hardly swallow it down.

"You like them?" she asked.

"Oh, yes." I managed to smile at her. "They're so good."

"Have some more." She set the plate before me. "And how about some ice cream?"

I'd lost my appetite, but I couldn't say no. She seemed so pleased with herself. So I ate a couple more, along with a scoop of ice cream.

But when I got back to my bedroom, I sank onto the bed and dropped my head into my hands.

Picturing that quiet, controlled boy who'd taken punishments for his younger brothers...and the man he'd grown up to be, the man with an enforcer's tattoo and dangerous eyes.

The made man who suspected me of being a spy, yet still remembered to order my favorite dessert.

An acid guilt ate at my stomach.

Oh, Gabriel. What have I done?

❧ 14 ❧

GABRIEL

Tomas Mraz rapped once on my office door, then entered without waiting for an invitation. "That woman must go." For once, his smile was nowhere to be seen.

I'd gone straight to my office at Kral headquarters—one floor up from my father's—and plowed through the work waiting for me. Tomas had appeared as soon as I sent my personal assistant home, having finished the most pressing business.

I didn't bother to ask who Tomas meant. By now, every member of the Kral Syndicate would've heard that Karoly Kral's eldest son and heir had formed a blood bond with a human.

I rose to my feet. "The hell she does."

The big blond vampire faced me from across the desk, hazel eyes flat. "Then you are the ass," he said in his Slovak-tinged English. "Do you think she comes back because she loves you? And how is it that she knows you are at the Ruby—have you asked yourself that?"

"Of course. That's why I'm keeping her close. Send her away, and she'll only disappear again. This way, I can find out who she's working for."

That made Tomas pause, but only for a moment. "Then you

know you must eliminate her," he said in his blunt way. "This woman, we all know she got under your skin."

I stared at him, uncomprehending. Then my heart jolted.

Kill Mila? No fucking way.

My vampire rose up, enraged, but when I spoke, my voice was as cold and hard as his. "That was three years ago. I'm smarter now. She's going to have to prove herself to me. And you of all people should know I'm not that easy to kill." Hell, the man had helped train me himself.

"I don't trust her," Tomas said stubbornly. "She was in Ohio a week ago, and suddenly she appears in New York. We don't even know where she has been the last few days. All I can find out is that a taxi let her out near the Ruby, and she came straight to the entrance like she knew you'd be there."

My jaw tightened. He was right—this didn't add up. But I'd take Mila and run before I'd let anyone harm her.

"Mila accepted my blood bond. She's mine now, understand? If anyone touches her—anyone at all—I'll show them no fucking mercy. I will send them to the final grave myself."

"Karoly won't be happy."

"Enough, Lieutenant." I slapped my hands on the desk. "I'm not a kid anymore. You will treat me as the Kral crown prince, which means while my father's away, I'm your goddamned boss—or you can get the fuck out of my office, and the building."

A flush suffused Tomas's square face. He straightened to his full height. "Karoly has ordered me to guide you."

I showed my fangs. This day had been coming for a long time. At heart, Tomas was a follower, the perfect second to my father. But he was also a vampire, and like a wolf pack, vampires craved a clear hierarchy, with the baddest, most ruthless on top. If I didn't establish dominance over Tomas now, I'd forever be the syndicate's third behind him and my father.

"But he left me in charge, which means you take your orders from me. Is that understood?"

The lieutenant dropped his eyes. "Yes," he muttered. "My apologies, sir."

I retook my seat. "Sit," I said in a hard voice.

Tomas sat.

I leaned back in my leather chair, pretending a calm I didn't feel. "Now, what do you have for me tonight?"

"I have been looking into who could have kidnapped Zaquiel. On Karoly's orders," he added.

I inclined my head. "And?"

"It could be any enforcer, of course. They are all dominant vampires."

"Agreed." Coups were a fact of life in the vampire world—within the covens themselves, and within the syndicates the various covens had formed. Again, like a wolf pack, the dominant vampires were continually jockeying for position.

"But," he continued, "the enforcers are all handpicked by your father, with my input. We give them the piece of the pie, allow to them more freedom than the other syndicates. So, I believe that they are loyal. It's the kapitáns that worry me. There are two or three who are perhaps...unhappy."

The kapitáns were the coven heads. They reported directly to my father or Tomas, and paid a tithe to the syndicate. Within their own covens, though, the kapitán was an absolute ruler.

"Who?" I demanded.

Tomas hesitated, and then reluctantly shared the names. "Desiree and Travis Johnson. And Yolanda."

The Johnsons were a mated couple who served as joint kapitáns of the Virginia-Carolina Coven, and Yolanda (no last name) headed the Florida Coven. All three were powerful vampires who'd been turned around the same time as my father. They could easily be planning a coup, either together or singly.

"Anyone else?"

He shook his head. "The Johnsons were in America when Zaq landed in Paris," he added, "but Yolanda was in Spain. She could've been directing things from there, but I don't believe any of them would work with the slayers. However..." He moved his shoulders in a European shrug. "I could be wrong. I will be happy to look into this."

I nodded. "All right. Let me know what you find."

"Of course."

I steepled my fingers beneath my chin in unconscious imitation of my father. "Have you tied his kidnapping to Slayers, Inc.?"

The elite group of hunters had long been tolerated by the vampire syndicates because they culled the worst of us, the vampires who'd gone so bad they were nothing but cold-blooded killers preying on humans. But in recent years, Slayers, Inc. had gone rogue, and the number of vampires being sent to their final grave had shot up.

Very few people knew this, but my father had been working behind the scenes to wrest Slayers, Inc., back under control. They were staking vampires for money and power now—and that couldn't be allowed.

Tomas's look was approving. "Your father asked this as well. I have looked into a possible connection, but I can find nothing."

"That doesn't mean they're not behind this."

"Agreed. I have run the new checks on all your people."

"They're clean." I'd had them vetted by two different organizations.

"It seems so, yes. But be careful."

"I will." I stood up and walked him to my door. "Keep working any angle you can find. I'll be returning to the beach house tonight. We can talk tomorrow night at our usual time."

He inclined his head. "As you wish."

I stuck out my hand to show there were no hard feelings, and we shook.

Tomas wished me a good evening and then paused, his hand on the doorknob.

"Speak," I said.

"It is possible that your Camila works for the slayers. After all, she's one of those humans who can hide their emotions from us."

My brow lowered. The hairs on my nape stirred. Tomas knew way too much about Mila. But then, my father would have extensive files on her.

"Impossible. I've been keeping an eye on her ever since she left."

Okay, maybe I'd lost her for a few days here and there, but I'd always located her again. "Slayers undergo years of training, but she worked at farms and low-end retail jobs, and when we first met, she was a college student."

"They are clever at placing their people."

"No," I said firmly. "Mila is *not* a slayer. It's just not possible."

He lifted a big shoulder, let it drop. "So she's not a slayer. For enough money, she could still stick the silver stake into you. You are sleeping with her, no?"

"*Enough.* Camila Vittore is *not* a slayer. But"—I tensed before reluctantly continuing—"it's possible they're using her."

"I'll see if I can find the connection. But you will be careful. Your father will string me up by the balls if something happens to you."

"I'm always careful." Hell, I'd survived three assassination attempts by the time I was twenty-five.

As soon as I was alone, I sat back down at my computer to poke around in Mila's background. It was easy enough to find out that her brother had gone missing. In fact, I wondered why Tomas hadn't already informed me.

The local paper had run a story on the missing twenty-one-year-old. I stared at the photo of Joey that came up on my screen. I'd only met him a few times. He'd been a teenager, an easygoing kid who never seemed to go anywhere without a pack of friends. The photo had been taken by the water. Joey aimed a cocky grin at the camera, his curly hair windblown, his arm around a pretty blond woman about his age.

My heart gave a single hard beat. *Of course.*

Mila would do anything for her family. Her brother was the key. Find him, and I'd discover who was behind this.

Normally my father would give a job this delicate to Tomas, but for now, I preferred no one else in the syndicate know about Joey Vittore. If this was an inside job, I didn't want to inadvertently feed intel to the man or woman. Instead, I contacted a small private firm that Father kept on retainer for jobs like this.

Fagan Security was owned by a married dhampir couple in Pennsylvania. The two had never joined the syndicate but were under Kral protection. Other than my father, they worked only for dhampirs and the occasional human.

Mariah Fagan took the call. I explained what had happened and hired her to start the search for Joey at double their usual fee. "But keep it quiet. No one but me knows we're looking for him —understand?"

"Got it," Mariah responded in her no-nonsense voice.

"I also want an around-the-clock team guarding his parents," I continued. "You already have their address. I want them kept safe, whatever it takes. But no contact with them. The Vittores can't even know you're there. Any questions?"

When she said no, I cut the connection, then deleted my search history and signed off my PC. Rising to my feet, I stared absently at a large black-and-white photo of the Manhattan skyline on the wall.

Someone was growling. Me.

My vampire was enraged. That Mila had been forced, maybe even compelled, to return to me. Underlying my fury was disappointment. It was as I'd suspected. Mila hadn't come back because of me, she'd come back to save her brother.

Tomas was right—I *was* an ass. I'd known something was off, yet I'd still hoped. You'd have thought I'd learned my lesson three years ago.

My fangs elongated. I slammed a fist into the photo. The glass shattered and the photo crashed to the black marble floor.

A knock sounded on my door. "Sir?" called one of my bodyguards. "Is everything all right?"

I drew a slow breath through my teeth, then opened the door so he and the other guard could see I was okay. "Everything's fine. But tell Dino to send down someone to clean up the mess—and have this photo reframed."

"Yes, sir."

I shut the door and turned back to the wall. For a long moment, I stared down at the broken glass. Rebuilding my composure, one stony block at a time.

A shard of glass had lodged in the back of my hand. I pulled it out and scrubbed the blood off in the bathroom attached to my office.

A janitor had arrived by then. My personal assistant had left for the night, so I waited until he'd swept up the mess before locking the office and heading up to the ground floor along with my bodyguards.

Outside, I climbed into the waiting limo and told the chauffeur to take me to our Brooklyn speakeasy. Usually, Rafe and I split club duty, but with him in Montreal, it had fallen to me. Karoly Kral believed facetime was the best way of ensuring your people stayed honest, and I agreed.

The club was on the river across from lower Manhattan in the trendy Brooklyn neighborhood of Williamsburg. It was packed with a mix of vampires, thralls, and hip young creatives, but not a single thrall ventured within a yard of me. Word about me and Mila had clearly shot like a rocket around our small, incestuous world.

A smoky-voiced singer took the stage. As she made love to the microphone, I told my bodyguards to have a drink and wait at a nearby table. I ordered a blood-wine and leaned against the bar, eyeing the nearest vampires. How many of them were part of this?

My brothers and I had had targets painted on our backs from the day we were born. At coven gatherings, we were ridiculed, pushed around. For some unknown reason, a vampire could have only one child with another vampire. After that, if either wanted more offspring, they had to seek out a human or a dhampir.

Most vampires chose to stop at one child. But if they wanted more, they impregnated a dhampir, so that their spawn were three-quarters vampire, giving them higher status in our world.

Only outcasts mated with a human...until my father had fallen in love with Rosemarie Fortier.

Through sheer, brutal will, Karoly Kral had forced first his coven, and then the entire Syndicate to accept his sons as his heirs. But that didn't stop the other vampires' spawn from beating the crap out of us behind Father's back.

My brothers and I had learned to stand up for ourselves, fast. We fought hard and dirty, using tricks we'd learned from my father and his enforcers. We even made up a few of our own. Looking back, the persecution we endured had a bright side. It made us tough, fierce fighters, men even the vampire world treated with respect.

And it forged Zaq, Rafe and me into an unbreakable team.

My fingers tightened on the wine glass. Damn, I missed my brothers. I hated being stuck holding down the fort in New York instead of tearing Paris apart looking for Zaq. Or barring that, watching Rafe's back in Montreal.

But I was the fucking crown prince. The Kral whose chief job was to act as stand-in for my father.

The singer met my eyes. Her lips curved in an inviting smile, her dark skin glistening under the single light, her copper-colored dress flowing over lush curves. Apparently no one had told her about Mila, but then, she was a human hire, not a thrall.

I raised my glass to her and waited until the song ended, then finished my wine and faded back into the shadows.

It was one in the morning, and I was tired of pretending to enjoy myself when I really wanted to be with Mila. I beckoned to my bodyguards and ordered them to inform my helicopter pilot I was returning to Montauk. Meanwhile, I sent Airi a quick text informing her that I was on my way back to the beach house. We took off forty-five minutes later.

The Montauk lighthouse was visible in the distance when my phone buzzed with a text from Rafe.

Dad's right. We have a mole. Trust no one.

My stomach knotted. In the darkness of the cockpit, I stared at the glowing screen.

It's not Mila. There's no fucking way she's a slayer.

But I couldn't help the ugly suspicions darkening my mind. She might not be *with* Slayers, Inc.—and she definitely didn't have the access to headquarters that the mole apparently had—but as I'd told Tomas, she could be working with the slayers.

Hell, this whole thing with Joey might even be a ruse.

The people behind Slayers, Inc. were smart—and very patient. They studied vampires obsessively, knew all sorts of tricks for inserting a slayer into the heart of a coven. The target never knew until they turned up staked.

As we swooped toward the lit-up helipad, I scowled at the dark ocean, then heaved a breath.

At least Rafe was okay. I typed a response.

Got it. How are things on your end?

A short pause.

I have the situation in hand. Will be in touch.

❧

I landed at in Montauk a little before three in the morning. As we touched down on the helipad fifty yards from the house, the two vampires prowling the grounds appeared, eyes gleaming in the dark. The wolfdogs, Daisy and Diesel, loped up behind them, panting eagerly.

I ruffled their short gray fur and listened to the vampires' report. Everything was quiet, with Mila safe in her suite for the night.

I'd left orders that Lougenia not be bothered, but she opened the front door herself. She'd even dressed in her uniform, although instead of her usual neat white tennis shoes, she wore fuzzy pink house slippers.

"Welcome, M'sieur." Her dark eyes searched my face. She hadn't been told Zaq was missing, but she'd seen the increased security, knew something was up. "Everything's all right?"

I jerked my chin in assent. "Go back to bed," I said gruffly. "You need your sleep."

"Yes, M'sieur. I just wanted to tell you that Mam'selle Mila ate good today. We'll put a few pounds on her before you know it," she added with a conspiratorial smile.

I glanced at the dhampir guard hovering behind her. "Leave us."

When we were alone, I squeezed Lougenia's shoulder. "Thanks. I knew you'd take good care of her."

"You go easy on her, now."

I frowned, but the woman had known me when I was in diapers. She crossed her arms over her ample chest and glared back.

I shook my head. "I'm away for half a day, and she has you wrapped around her little finger."

"That little girl has had a rough time. I just want to make sure you don't push her too hard. She needs to recover."

I stifled a sigh. My father would never tolerate this kind of insolence from his servants. But then, I wasn't my father—and Lougenia was more than a servant.

"Lougenia. I take good care of my thralls. You know that."

"M'sieur Gabriel," she chided as if I were still ten years old. "She's not a thrall."

"No?" I lifted a brow. Lougenia opened her mouth to say more but I took her by the shoulders and turned her in the direction of the kitchen and her private apartment. "Go to bed. Your little chick is safe with me."

She headed down the hall, but not before giving me a sharp, over-the-shoulder look. "You're worried about trusting her, but that's not the real question here."

"Fine." I folded my arms over my chest. "What's the real question?"

"Can you trust yourself?" And with that cryptic-as-fuck comment, Lougenia sashayed into the kitchen and through the door to her apartment, leaving me scowling after her.

I went straight to Mila's suite. Per my orders, a vampire stood guard outside the door. "You can go. I'll take over from here," I told the vampire, and let myself into the suite.

Mila's bedroom door was open. I cocked my head, listening, but although she murmured sleepily, she didn't wake up.

I removed my shoes and socks and left them by the door. The next to come off was my suit coat and shirt. I dropped them on the couch and walked on silent feet into her bedroom.

She was once again curled up in the middle of the bed. I eyed her hungrily, content just to be in the same room with her.

The nightlight cast a warm glow on her face, illuminating one soft cheek and pouty red lips. Her dark curls tumbled down her back and over one shoulder in a glossy waterfall I itched to plunge my fingers into.

I squeezed my nape. Gods, I was a fool for this woman. Even knowing she'd only come back because she'd been forced to, I still craved her.

I moved closer.

Compel her, whispered my dark side. *Make her tell you the truth.*

Mila whimpered, shifted her head from side to side. Suddenly, she let out a fearful yelp and jerked upright. Her gaze darted to me. She pressed a hand to her throat, the pounding of her heart loud in the quiet room.

I held out a hand. "Hey," I said, low and easy. "It's okay. It's me, Gabriel."

"You—oh." Her breath shuddered out. "I—I didn't think you'd be back tonight."

"I didn't have as much to do as I thought." To be honest, I could've done most of the work from here, but I didn't tell her that. The woman had too much power over me already.

I lowered myself onto the edge of the mattress. She wore one of the new nightshirts, the yellow one sprinkled with silly faces that I'd chosen because I'd wanted to make her smile.

"I'm glad. That you came back." She crawled onto my lap and pressed her lips to my throat. "I missed you." She snuggled closer, rubbing up against my bare chest, pressing kisses to my jaw, my face. "I was dreaming about you."

My arms came around her. I hadn't planned to stay, just check on her before going to my own suite. But somehow my hands found their way under the nightshirt. She had nothing on beneath but satiny, sleep-warm skin.

I grew instantly hard.

So what if I trusted Mila about as far as I could throw her? So what if she hadn't come back because she missed me like I did her—

a constant, empty ache at the center of my soul? Who the hell cared? Better the real thing than the pale substitutes I'd had to make do with.

After all, I was the one with the power now.

I was the one in command.

"Yeah?" I skimmed my palm over the curve of her ass. "Tell me about this dream."

❧ 15 ❧
MILA

My heart banged against my rib cage. My breath came in short, panicked bursts.

I *had* been dreaming of Gabriel, but the dream had turned dark. I was being hunted by vampires through the streets of Manhattan. They herded me into an alley with no exit.

Trapped.

I whipped around. Andre's eyes shown gold in the shadows, his fangs fully extended.

I gulped. Every hair on my nape stood on end.

"Mila," he chided. "You weren't supposed to leave Gabriel. You know what will happen to your brother." He reached for me—and I jolted awake.

The relief when I'd realized it was Gabriel, not Andre, in the bedroom was overwhelming. I'd crawled into his lap, needing him to touch me, hold me. Make me feel safe.

But I couldn't tell Gabriel about Andre, so instead I cast my mind back to the first part of the dream. The good part, where Gabriel had been doing hot, erotic things to me.

"My dream?" I traced my lips down the hard line of his jaw. He'd shaved, but already, black stubble had sprouted. "Let me think..."

"You seemed scared."

I hitched a shoulder. "You startled me. But I'm okay now."

"Good." His hand moved over my lower back in slow, easy circles.

My chest heaved. I cuddled closer, adrenaline still buzzing in me. Underlying his deep forest aroma was that sharp scent men have after working all day, even if it's just at an office—a little sweaty and stronger than normal.

It wrapped around me, warm, seductive.

I nuzzled his neck. "In my dream, we were back on the beach."

He made a throaty sound that was almost a purr. His cock twitched, pressing against my bottom. "You liked that?"

"Oh, yeah." I traced the peak of first his left brow, then his right. "It was hot...and you were doing dirty things to me."

His swallow was audible, but when he spoke, he sounded cool, in command. "Tell me about it."

He turned me so I straddled him. Between my thighs, his erection tented his zipper, pressing the smooth, expensive cloth against my bare folds.

Setting my hands on his chest, I kissed him. His muscles were defined beneath a dusting of dark hair. I ran my thumbs over his nipples, and his nostrils flared.

The adrenaline rush had gone straight to my core. I wanted, no, *needed* him. Taking me. Filling me.

"Well." I nibbled my lower lip. "You made me touch you...like this."

Easing his zipper down, I slipped my hand through the opening in his boxer briefs to finger his hot, hard length. His thigh muscles tautened. His eyes were black in the dim light, his pupils enlarged within the glowing circle of blue.

My lips curved. In this, we were equals. He wanted me as much as I wanted him.

I rubbed my thumb over the smooth cap.

Gabriel leaned back on his forearms and gave me a very male look. He'd never looked so much like a prince.

Dark, a little menacing.

The kind of man who expects to have his every whim satisfied.

"Were you naked?" A husky murmur.

I smiled. "In my dream? Yeah."

"Show me." A pointed look at my nightshirt.

I pulled it off and dropped it on the floor.

"And then what happened?" His low growl thrummed over my skin like rough silk.

"You were holding me down, like this afternoon." Pushing him onto the bed, I dragged off his pants and boxers before crawling up his long, powerfully-muscled body. "And your mouth was moving down my stomach..."

I nuzzled his lower abdomen down where his scent was strong and musky, rubbing my lips over the wiry hair at the root of his cock, nipping teasingly at the rigid length.

His stomach muscles jumped, but he folded his arms behind his head and gazed down at me from beneath hooded lids. "Tell me more."

"Why don't I show you instead?" I wrapped my fingers around his cock and brought my mouth to the head, licking around the rim, tasting the slit in the center. Pre-cum spurted onto my tongue, warm and salty.

"More," he said thickly.

"Like this?" I took the head into my mouth and sucked. With my free hand, I cupped his balls, rolling them between my fingers.

"Yes." His eyes slit with pleasure. "Do it. Just like that."

He kept talking. Telling me what to do to him in hot, graphic terms. My sex constricted and grew even wetter.

I slid my hand between my legs, fingering myself while I took him deeper into my mouth, sucking and licking. He was rock-solid now, the veins on his cock bulging.

"Are you touching yourself?"

I hummed an assent against his skin.

"Bring yourself back up here. I don't want you to come until I'm inside you." When I didn't obey immediately, he added, "Now, Mila," in a firm tone that sent an electric thrill straight to my clit.

I removed my hand from between my legs, but I took my time

releasing him, giving him a few last sucks while he watched, heavy-lidded.

His balls drew up tight. I sucked harder, but he speared his fingers into my hair. "Come here."

I slicked my tongue up his length one last time and moved back up his body. He gripped my upper arms, dragging me to him for a hard kiss. Then I was higher, hovering over his body, my legs on either side of his waist, while he suckled my nipples.

Desire flooded me in heated waves. My clit ached for his touch. I moaned and gripped his forearms.

He brought me back down, his strong hands easily controlling me so the tips of my breasts just brushed his chest.

"Kiss me."

I brought my mouth to his. His lips were soft and warm. He tasted of wine and something else, something primitive and very male. When I slid my tongue into his mouth, his incisors were longer than normal, their tips sharp.

My vampire was back, and the edge of danger only made me hotter.

His tongue met mine, sliding over and around it.

Then he was nibbling my jaw, my earlobe. Pressing kisses to my throat. Telling me how beautiful I was, how he couldn't get enough of me.

The world spun, and I was on my stomach. His hands came under my pelvis, lifting my ass. Long fingers spread my slick folds.

His tip nudged my opening, slid inside. He drew back his hips and thrust into me in a single slow, luscious stroke.

He cupped my throat, forcing me to lift my head higher, so I was stretched out beneath him, my legs on either side of his.

"You're so wet," he said against my ear. "So ready for me."

"Yes. Oh, God, please..."

He was long and thick and hard. I felt so full.

Captured.

Owned.

One hand stayed on my throat. The other moved between my clit and nipples, toying, pinching, stroking.

He withdrew partway and held himself poised over me. "I like my women to beg. Can you do that for me, Mila? Ask me real nice to fuck you?"

I hesitated, my fingers digging into the sheets. His *women*? But right then, I would've done anything he asked.

"Yes," I whispered. Then louder, "Fuck me, Gabriel. Please."

"Good girl." He thrust harder.

Pleasure slammed up my spine. "Please, please, please..."

My vision clouded over. Head swimming, I drew a jagged breath and arched my bottom up to take him deeper.

He slowed his thrusts, taking me to the edge and keeping me there until I was begging for release.

He slowed and then came up on his knees, pulling me up with him so I was on my hands and knees, too. He was still deep inside me, but no longer moving. His hands shaped my waist, the curve of my hips.

I clawed at the sheets. What did he want?

"Please," I begged. "Don't stop."

"I'm hungry, Mila." He moved my hair aside and kissed my nape. Prickles of heat danced up and down my spine. Sharp fangs touched the side of my throat. "Tell me I can feed from you. Because you're mine."

Mine. My thrall. My woman.

Doubt pinched me—was I just a body to him?—but I shut my eyes and focused on the sexy pain/pleasure of his fangs. Because I wanted this. Wanted to be his in every way.

I angled my head so he could reach the underside of my jaw. One hand cupped my chin while the other slid lower, feathering over my aroused, swollen flesh with excruciating care.

"Say it." A rough growl. "Say you're mine."

I quivered, excited beyond bearing. "Yes."

His teeth caressed my throat. His earthy green scent filled my nostrils.

Sensation arrowed to my center. My inner thighs tightened, and I bucked my hips, clenching around him.

He pulled out, the tip teasing my entrance. "Say it."

"Yes. *Yours.*" I released a jagged exhale. "Please, Gabriel."

"Ah, cher..." His body was over mine, around mine, in mine. "I won't take much. But I need to taste you. To feed from you."

"Yes. Now. Please..."

I'd thought I'd be scared, the first time he took more than a small taste from me. But I wasn't.

No, I wanted his bite, wanted him to drink from me.

His teeth punctured my skin. A sharp sting, followed by pleasure...waves and waves of it. A tidal wave of intensity that sucked me under and out to sea.

I was drowning, sobbing out Gabriel's name.

He groaned and pounded into me.

Lights burst behind my eyes, trilled up and down my body. He thrust one last time and stilled, sucking on my throat while I lay there, boneless and blissful.

I don't know how long he fed from me, but it wasn't long. When he finished, he licked my neck clean and rolled onto his back.

I collapsed onto the mattress and lay on my stomach, face turned toward him. Lost in wonder.

"That was..." I shook my head, unable to find the words.

"Mm." He kissed my cheek.

With a happy sigh, I snuggled up against him, idly stroking the hard ridges of his abdomen. He was warm, a little sweaty, his hair crisp under my palm.

"I think I missed this most of all." I toyed with a flat brown nipples. "Just spending time with you."

A grunt. "I'll get you some water." He eased himself out from under me.

"Thanks." I *was* thirsty—very.

I waited until he'd left the room, then sat up and ran my fingers over my throat. There was no blood, just a pleasurable tingle.

Gabriel appeared in the bathroom door with the water. "It's almost healed," he said as he handed me the glass. "There's something in my saliva that speeds up healing."

"I know. I'm just surprised at how fast it works." I drained the glass and set it on the nightstand.

"Would you like more?" he asked. So polite, like I was a friend, or just another thrall. Not the woman he'd just fucked into bliss.

My brow furrowed. Was something wrong?

I shook my head. "I'm good."

He brushed his fingers over my cheek. "Good night, then."

I grabbed his wrist. "You're not staying?"

"I don't think that's a good idea."

I released his wrist and brought my hand to my neck again. He'd fed from me. I could still feel him between my legs.

I'd felt so close to him, so wonderful. What was the matter?

The wonder seeped away. I wrapped my arms around my knees. "So this was just about fucking."

His face hardened. "What did you expect, Mila? We both know you didn't come back of your own free will."

I started to deny it, then snapped my mouth shut. I was tired of lying to him.

"Yeah," he said. "That's what I thought."

He curled his fingers around my nape and brushed a kiss over my lips, so gentle, hot tears pricked my eyes.

When he turned away, my gaze snagged on the black wolf tattoo. A reminder, if I needed it, of just who and what he was.

I dug my teeth into my lower lip. Stupid, stupid, stupid to let myself think this was anything more than a dhampir enjoying his newest thrall.

Gabriel let himself out of the suite, leaving me naked on the bed, hugging my knees.

I slept until almost noon, but when I woke up, Gabriel was still in his suite. The guard on duty said he'd left orders not to be disturbed.

Sharp hurt twisted my insides. *Stupid, stupid, stupid.*

I nodded coolly. "Thank you."

I downed one of Lougenia's amazing brunches without really tasting it, and then headed out to explore the beach house, trailed my lean, curly-haired guard. I'd tried to get more out of Paco than his name, but the only additional info he'd shared was that he was a dhampir, "Like the boss," he'd told me with obvious pride. The dhampirs, at least, were on Gabriel's side.

There were two other bedrooms, both unoccupied. Gabriel's security force apparently slept in the bunker I'd seen, or maybe in underground lairs.

The gym was occupied by two hard-faced, tattooed men, so I backed out and returned to my suite.

I worked out in my living room, practicing my self-defense moves and wishing again for my switchblade. However, pretty as my suite was, it was starting to feel like a cage, so when I finished my workout, I took another walk to the pond. Gabriel was still nowhere to be seen, so I spent the rest of the afternoon at the pool, swimming and reading.

Gabriel wasn't at dinner, either. After eating, I hung out with Lougenia for an hour before wandering onto the balcony. The sky grew heavy. Far out to sea, rain began to fall. It swept across the ocean toward me in a shining silver wave.

I raised my face to the cool droplets, letting them run down my face. Drinking in their clean scent. Catching them on my tongue.

I don't know how long I'd been standing there, allowing the rain to wash over me, when I felt someone watching me. I didn't have to turn my head to know it was Gabriel.

I wrapped my arms around myself. "Hello."

He moved up next to me, touched my wet T-shirt. "You're going to get cold."

I moved a shoulder. "It's a warm night."

He placed his hands on the rail. Together, we gazed at rain falling on the ocean. To the west, the setting sun painted the storm clouds a red-tinged purple.

Gabriel's fingers tightened on the rail. "You're not going to stay, are you?"

My head snapped around. "I can't leave. You said so yourself."

"That's right, you can't." A pause. "Unless I give you permission."

I stared at him. "Would you? Give me permission?"

"To leave?" His jaw worked. "I don't know. It depends on you, and why you accepted the blood bond."

My insides constricted. God, I wished I could tell him.

I shook my head and moved away, but he followed, clamping his hand onto mine when I tried to open the sliding door.

His body was warm against my back. I stiffened, even though what I really wanted was to lean into his heat. To surrender. I was so tired of running and hiding and lying.

"I know why you came back, Mila."

I set my forehead on the wet glass. "Stop it," I said through numb lips. "Please."

But he was relentless. "What I don't know is why you left in the first place."

I shook my head. "Don't do this. It was for the best, and you know it."

A furious growl. "No, I don't know it. You said you loved me, damn you. And then you were gone."

I tugged at the sliding door, even though my strength was no match for a dhampir's.

"Answer me." Gabriel spun me so that my back was against the plate-glass window. "Why did you come back?"

Anger flared deep in my belly. "Let. Me. Go."

"No." He gripped my chin, forcing me to look at his face. "I want the truth, damn it. Something's going on and I want to know what."

I shut my eyes. "Fuck you," I said wearily.

His fingers tightened on my jaw. Raindrops glittered on his dark hair. "Talk, Mila."

I tightened my mouth and glared back. To my disgust, tears stung my eyes. I blinked them away, but one escaped to run down my cheek.

Gabriel brushed it away with his thumb. I thought I saw a flicker of shame before he hardened his jaw. "Crying won't help."

I shrugged and looked past his shoulder. Caught in a nightmare with no way out.

He gripped my upper arms. "Talk, damn it. Was it the hundred K they gave you? Is that why you left?"

My eyes widened. "How do you know about that?"

"Did you really think I wouldn't find out?"

Right. This man was part of a syndicate worth billions. He could probably find out who my best friend in kindergarten was—and what she'd had for lunch today.

He tilted his head to one side. "I could compel you, make you tell me."

I inhaled sharply. It was the one threat I'd thought he'd never use against me. "You promised you wouldn't." My lower lip trembled.

His gaze flicked to it, then his mouth curled in a sneer. "That was before. When I trusted you."

I swallowed something sharp, bitter. Because he was right not to trust me.

"Fine," I gritted. "I took the money. But I only kept ten thousand of it, enough to get away. The rest, I gave to my family."

Ninety thousand dollars in crisp fifties, which I'd left stacked on the dresser beneath my goodbye note.

"Then why? I loved you. You said you loved me back. Why would you leave without a fucking word? I thought you'd been kidnapped. That—" He briefly closed his eyes. "I thought they'd got to you. The slayers, or another coven."

He released me and speared his fingers through his wet hair. "I thought," he said raggedly, "that you were dead—or a blood slave. Because why else would you disappear like that?"

I remained where I was against the window. "I'm sorry."

"Sorry? That's all you can say after putting me through hell?"

I exhaled. "I'm sor—."

He put a hand over my mouth. "Don't say it. Just...don't."

He waited until I nodded against his palm and then released me, stepping back as if he couldn't stand to be close to me.

"I had you traced, you know. I couldn't eat, couldn't sleep until I knew you were okay. When they found you at that farm in Tennessee, I had to see for myself that you were all right. I even came into that barn you were sleeping in, late one night. Just to make sure."

The barn had been made over into a dormitory for seasonal help like me. I'd felt safe, anonymous, among the mix of farmhands and interns studying organic farming like me. The best part was we all worked so hard that each night, I fell into bed exhausted, and didn't wake up until they rang the bell for breakfast.

I sagged against the glass. "I didn't know."

"I made sure no one saw me. But you weren't locked in. You were interning with a farmer, like you'd wanted. So I left."

"I'm—." I stopped myself from saying it that time. But suddenly, I was so cold. I shivered and wrapped my arms around myself.

He swore under his breath and, grabbing my hand, dragged me inside and through the dining room. The ever-present Paco had been replaced by a vampire. He regarded us, stone-faced.

I flushed, but Gabriel ignored him to tow me down the hall to my suite. Inside, he pushed me into the bathroom.

"Strip."

When I obeyed, he grabbed a towel and rubbed me down, and then bundled me into a bathrobe and marched me back into the living room.

He sat on the couch and crossed one leg over the other like the syndicate boss he was. Cool, in control.

Icy green eyes pondered me. "So. If it wasn't for the money, why then?"

I wrapped the bathrobe tighter around myself. My worry and exhaustion came to a head, and I just blurted it out.

"Because of you, damn it. I did it for *you*."

❧ 16 ❧

GABRIEL

Mila's statement caromed like a cannonball around my brain. *Like hell she'd done it for me.*

I'd initiated the blood bond with this woman. I'd intended to ask her to be my mate. And she'd left without a goddamned word.

My mouth twisted. She was still lying to me. A part of me wondered why I kept trying.

Then it hit me. I swore and came off the couch.

"It was my father, right? He got to you."

Her eyes slid sideways. "No."

"I don't believe you."

"Believe what you want." She stalked toward the bedroom. "I'm going to bed."

"The fuck you are." Snagging her arm, I whipped her around to face me. "We're going to finish this. Now. Tonight."

"Let. Me. Go."

She glared at me, her wet hair a rich brown tangle around her shoulders. The blue bathrobe had slipped down to reveal a softly curved breast. She noticed me looking, and snarled and yanked the lapels together.

But it was too late. We stared at each other.

The air changed, thickened.

She swallowed, a pulse beating in her throat. My gaze locked on its tempting flutter.

Last night, her blood had tasted sweet, tart, feminine. The essence of Mila. I'd had to force myself not to take too much, although after, I'd been ashamed I'd drunk from her at all. She'd lost that exhausted, fragile look, and I knew from Lougenia that she was eating well, but she was still recovering from her years on the run.

But now, looking at that hard, fast pulse, a vicious hunger gripped me. My fangs lengthened.

I was done trying to pry the truth from her. My gaze went to her wrist, where my gold bracelet glinted. She was here. She'd invoked the blood bond, sworn the oath. By our laws, she was mine.

"Fine." I swept her up in my arms. "You want to go to bed? We'll go to bed."

A few long strides took us into the bedroom. I dropped her on the mattress and followed her down, crouching over her. Instinctively, I tried to read her, needing to know the truth. But as always, she was frustratingly blank to me.

Outside, a heavy rain poured down. Night had fallen, leaving the room dark. I flicked on the bedside lamp. I could see her well enough, but I wanted her to see me, too.

"Gabriel. I—" She moistened her lips.

"No more words." I caught her face in my hands and gave her a hard kiss. "I can't tell whether you're lying or not, and you know what? I don't fucking care."

Her limbs relaxed. Her mouth remained stubbornly closed. It was as if she'd curled into herself, leaving me only her body.

I went rigid. She would *not* go passive on me.

"Kiss me back," I demanded against her mouth.

"Fuck you," she snapped—and speared her fingers into my hair. Her mouth opened. She sucked my tongue inside.

One long leg wrapped around my hip. The bathrobe fell open. She pressed against me. My already hard dick rasped against the zipper of my worn black jeans. I could feel the heat of her bare pussy through the material, hear the pounding of her heart. I ground myself against her and let my fangs slide out the rest of the way.

She explored them with the tip of her tongue. She didn't seem afraid, just curious.

My fangs weren't any more sensitive than my other teeth, but the touch of her curious little tongue, the idea that she was exploring the most vampire part of me, was so fucking arousing that I had to drag my mouth from hers.

I crouched over her. The bathrobe still covered her breasts. Jerking the lapels open, I captured her wrists in one hand and pressed them to the mattress above her head so she was stretched out beneath me.

Her chest heaved, causing her full, firm breasts to move enticingly. I used my free hand to pinch the nipples into hardness, then gave each a firm suck.

She moaned and squirmed beneath me.

I looked down at her. I'd never felt so much like a predator.

I wanted to possess Mila completely and forever. To *own* her.

The temptation to compel her was nearly overwhelming, but I fought against it. The vampire might hunger for total control, but the human knew it would be an empty victory.

Still, that didn't mean I wasn't going to take her, hard and long.

"I'm going to fuck you," I told her in guttural tones. "So deep you'll feel me in your goddamned soul."

"Oh, yeah?" Her words challenged me, but her eyes darkened, and I scented her spurt of arousal.

That was enough for me. I undid my pants and shoved them down to my knees along with my boxer briefs.

I slid my fingers between her thighs. She was slick, hot, her clit swollen. I toyed with the sensitive bit of flesh, enjoying the high, needy sounds she made.

She lifted her hips to mine. "Please, please, please..."

I wrapped my fingers around my cock and eased the blunt, sensitive head between her lips.

"*Gabriel.*" Her voice was sexy-rough. Tiny muscles tightened around me, drawing me deeper.

My lower back went rigid at the exquisite pleasure. Then I heard a single, furious bark—and the crash of breaking glass.

I stilled.

"Don't stop." She wriggled against me. "Please don't stop. I need—"

"Shh." I set my hand over her mouth. "Something's wrong."

It was agony, but I pulled out of her and rolled off the bed. For a moment, I stood there, hands on my thighs, sucking in air. Then I dragged up my boxers and eased myself back into the jeans.

Mila swung her legs off the bed next to me. "Gabriel?" she whispered.

"Put on your clothes," I returned, low-voiced. "*Now*."

"Got it." While she pulled on a T-shirt and shorts, I went to the head of the bed and the painting of the Adirondack chair. At least my erection had subsided enough that I could walk. I pried the tiny camera from its hiding place in the picture frame and ground it beneath my heel.

Mila had finished dressing. "Bring your shoes," I said.

She nodded and snatched up a pair of tennis shoes. I grabbed her hand, tugging her to the door. I removed the camera above it as well and set my ear to the wood.

Silence.

I pulled out my phone, opened the security app, and navigated through the various video feeds. This hall looked clear, although I saw someone creeping through the kitchen.

Hopefully, Lougenia had reached the safe room in her apartment in time, because there was nothing I could do for her now.

Where the fuck were the vampires on duty? Had some of them joined in the attack?

Using the app, I disabled the video cams throughout the beach house because I didn't know if I could trust my own goddamned security.

I put my mouth close to Mila's right ear. "There's a way out through my bedroom. Nod if you understand."

She nodded, her eyes dark, frightened pools in her pale face.

I extended my fangs to their full length—vampires fought dirty

—and eased open the door. A low shadow rushed at us. I dropped into a fighting crouch, but it was just Diesel. The wolfdog had somehow gotten in the house.

My jaw hardened as I straightened back up. Daisy was probably dead. Diesel wouldn't have left her otherwise.

I pulled Mila into my suite, Diesel pushing in after us. When the three of us were safely inside, I input the code to engage emergency security in my suite before hurrying with Mila into my bedroom.

Behind us, several deadbolts slid home, although a locked door wouldn't keep out a vampire for long. Even the laser beams set to slice through the body at knee, chest and neck could be circumvented if you were familiar with the system. But it should slow the intruders down long enough for us to escape.

Pulling Mila into the walk-in closet in my bedroom, I slapped a hand on the depression next to the light switch. A panel slid open behind a row of my suitcoats. I shoved my phone into the pocket of the nearest coat so it couldn't be used to track me, then removed a silver switchblade from a shelf.

"This way." I urged Mila into the hidden passageway beyond the coats.

She dug in her heels. "Give me a knife, too," she mouthed.

I hesitated—not because I didn't trust her with a switchblade, but because I didn't think it would do her any good against a vampire—but she stared back steadily.

"Please," she whispered.

I grabbed another one and handed it over. If it made her feel better, what could it hurt?

I jerked my chin at the hidden passage, then waited until she and Diesel were inside before shutting the panel behind me. We were in a narrow tunnel that lead down to the ocean and the speedboat I kept moored there. The darkness was broken only by miniscule dots of light on the walls about ten feet apart. When I'd had the passage built, I hadn't expected it to be used by a human.

Mila flicked open the shiny silver blade with an ease that probably shouldn't have surprised me, and peered over my shoulder.

"Stay close to me," I said. "This leads to a—."

She slapped a hand over my mouth, stopping me. "Don't tell me," she whispered.

I frowned. "You're bugged?" I mouthed.

She nodded and took my hand, guiding it to her left earring. "Mic," she mouthed. She brought my hand to her other earring. "GPS."

"Hell." We had to remove them. But maybe we could use the technology against the attackers?

The GPS had to go first. I gripped the silver hoop and gently but firmly twisted until the weld snapped.

"Trust me," I mouthed next to her right ear. I waited until she nodded before saying in a slightly louder voice, "They're searching the house now. We have to get to the helicopter."

Meanwhile, I snapped my fingers for Diesel, who'd pushed ahead to sniff out the passageway. He trotted back to look up at me expectantly. I twisted the silver earring around his collar and took him back into my suite. Mila followed, watching us from the bedroom door.

I disengaged the security and rubbed my cheek against Diesel's rough fur. "If you get out of this alive," I murmured, "you'll be eating steak for the rest of your life."

I eased open the door to the hall. The door to Mila's suite stood open now. "Go," I told the wolfdog in a low voice. "Heliport."

He whined, but obediently loped down the hallway.

I returned to my suite, silently closing the door and reengaging the security. Back in my bedroom, Mila had donned her sneakers. She stood with her arms wrapped around her middle, a big-eyed waif in a rainbow T-shirt and cargo shorts. The still-open switchblade glinted obscenely in her hand.

Guilt swamped me. This was all my fault.

I should've never shown myself to her, all those years ago in the garden. Security had been on their way to escort her out, but I'd told them to back off, that I'd handle it. But instead of ordering her off our property, I'd somehow found myself offering to show her the garden instead.

She'd been so entranced by the flowers, she hadn't noticed that all I could look at was her. By the end of an hour, I'd known I had to see her again.

I hauled her into my arms for a hard kiss. "Don't worry," I whispered in her right ear. "It will be all right. I have people looking for Joey."

Her head whipped up. Her fingers curled into my shirt.

"I don't care about me," she mouthed back. "But please, don't let them hurt him."

And just like that, I knew Joey had really been kidnapped. No one could fake that kind of terror. Her pupils were dilated, her heart racing, her scent sharp with fear.

Which meant Mila had been forced to spy on me.

Maybe it was a fine line, but it meant everything to me—that she hadn't *wanted* to help my enemies.

I tucked a strand of hair behind her ear. "He'll be okay," I mouthed. "I swear it."

She nodded, anxious yet trusting.

My heart squeezed. "He'll be okay," I repeated. "I promise."

I just hoped I could keep that promise.

I took Mila's hand, and together, we ducked through my suits and into the dark passage, which was basically a rough tunnel with no steps. In a couple places where it grew too steep, I'd had the workmen install metal ladders.

Mila gamely kept up, climbing down the two ladders like a cat burglar. Even though I had to move slower to accommodate her human reflexes, we were in the cavern in under five minutes. I slapped my palm on the control, and a door concealed in the rock slid open. Outside was a strip of beach separated by a high, rocky outcropping from the larger cove we'd visited yesterday.

The boom of the surf filled the small cave. Ten yards away, my speedboat was secured to a small dock, concealed in a V-shaped cove formed by the high black rocks.

It was time to get rid of Mila's other earring. I carefully twisted it off her earlobe and shoved it under a rock at the back of the cave.

We hurried, hand in hand, onto the wet beach. The rain had passed, and the sun had dipped below the horizon, leaving a muted orange shimmer on the dark sky. Long shadows stretched, finger-like, across the narrow cove, and to the east, the moon hovered, a slender silver crescent above the black water.

I shot a glance up at the beach house. The windows were dark, the whole compound shrouded in an unnatural quiet. But then, vampires fought silently, with stakes and silver blades, and they had incredible night vision.

I started toward the speedboat, then froze. The boat rocked gently, the ocean slapping against the hull. But something or someone was huddled on the deck.

I pushed Mila in the direction of the cave. "*Go.* Hide in the passage until sunrise."

But it was too late. A man leapt off the speedboat and stalked toward us with a vampire's easy grace. Two other vampires dropped like black bats from the top of the sixty-foot cliff, landing on the beach a few yards away. One man blocked the way to the passage—whether by intention or accident, I didn't know.

"Gee, boys," Mila said out of the side of her mouth. "Nice of you to drop in."

My lips quirked in spite of myself.

The vampires closed in on us from three sides. Mila edged closer to me.

There was a series of ominous clicks as they released their switchblades one by one. The long knives shone in the moonlight.

"That's Andre," she hissed. "The man who has Joey."

"Bastards." I released my own blade. It was Andre Redbone, along with two young vampires from his coven. Apparently, my little trick with Diesel and the GPS hadn't fooled them for long.

A cold fear skated over my skin. Three vampires against me, a dhampir—and I was all that stood between them and Mila.

"If you get a chance," I muttered, "take the speedboat and stay out to sea until daylight. I'll keep them busy."

Her swallow was audible. "I don't even know how to start it."

Holy Dark Mother. Could this night get any worse?

"Then you'll have to get to the passage," I rapped out. "But for now, get the fuck behind me."

❦ 17 ❦

MILA

Terror squeezed my lungs. I went motionless, staring at Andre like a mouse bewitched by a golden-eyed cobra. His fangs had elongated, and his irises were rimmed with vampire blue.

"Mila!" Gabriel reached out a long arm and swept me behind him. "Snap out of it."

I lurched backward, coming up short against the tall rocks behind me. It was the slap awake I needed. I gripped the switchblade and crouched beside him.

Inside, my mind was screaming. *Run. Get the fuck out of here.*

But where? I had no idea how to operate a motorboat, or any boat, for that matter. Unless you counted kayaking on the Chesapeake Bay.

And despite what Gabriel had said, the passage wasn't an option. I didn't know if any of his security force was still alive, and besides, a vampire could bring me down before I'd gone two yards.

"Dhampir." Andre stopped just out of Gabriel's reach, a sneer on his handsome face. "Stand down and the woman will live."

The other two vampires closed in, switchblades ready. Like Andre, they wore all black, making them nearly invisible against the cliffs hemming us in on three sides. It was too dark to make out their features, but I caught the gleam of blond hair to my right.

Martin.

And something about the way the man on the left moved made me sure it was Stefan.

I gulped. For a sickening moment, I was thrown back to those three days of "training" in the basement of the apartment building. I'd been allowed only a few hours of sleep at a time. Food and water had been rationed, leaving me constantly hungry.

Andre had made it clear that this would be my life if I didn't do exactly as he said. But I was used to being tired and hungry.

What had made those three days a nightmare were Stefan and Martin. The two vampires took turns browbeating me, telling me I was a weak human, and that Gabriel had never loved me. Reminding me they had Joey—and that they knew where my parents lived.

Worse, one of them was constantly in my room. I'd wake up to find Martin watching me like a hungry boy who'd been promised a piece of his favorite candy. Or Stefan would be sitting on my narrow cot, touching me: my face, my throat.

Especially my throat.

Andre had promised me to them first, they'd told me, and he confirmed it right before releasing me.

"They're young, and they can't get enough blood"—Andre had smirked—"and sex. But don't worry, do as you're told, and you'll be free to go along with your brother."

"You're dead," Gabriel told Andre now, his voice low and cold.

I gave myself a shake.

This time, you're not alone.

I had Gabriel, and my own weapon. I gripped the switchblade's handle.

Andre's fangs shone white in the darkness. "You think you can win against three vampires?"

"Maybe not, but at least I didn't send a human to do the job for me."

"A distraction." Andre waved a dismissive hand. "And it worked even better than I expected. You literally had your dick inside her when we broke through your security."

Gabriel's sharp breath was audible. "Bastard."

Hatred burned in me. My fingers clenched so hard on silver handle, I'm surprised they didn't dent it.

Andre's gaze flicked to my knife. "Try it," he invited, "and our bargain is void. My coven has been eager to meet your brother. Fresh meat is always welcome, and a young man like him will be especially sweet."

Martin and Stefan hummed their agreement.

Horror skittered up my spine. That bargain had been the only thing protecting Joey. I swallowed, nauseated at the thought of my kid brother enslaved by these evil pricks.

But I was through running, and I was damned if I'd watch Andre kill Gabriel right in front of me. I'd have to trust that Gabriel and his people would rescue Joey. I might be a slow, "weak" human, but I could still do some damage with the long silver blade.

But to do that, I'd have to get closer.

I lowered my gaze, let my shoulders cave in. Let Andre think he had me cowed. Meanwhile, I'd watch for an opening.

Gabriel sprang, feinting left and driving Andre and Stefan back. When Martin swooped in from the right, Gabriel was ready. He struck out, lightning fast, with his knife. The blond vampire shrieked and fell to the sand, hands clutched to his groin.

Gabriel didn't wait for him to recover. He struck again, shoving the long, thin blade up through Martin's rib cage into his heart.

Martin groaned and went limp.

Gabriel snarled. "Burn in the bright fires of noon."

His profile was outlined against the rising moon. It was like seeing a big cat from the side, his fangs long and white. Scary as shit.

The man wasn't even breathing hard.

That was my Dark Angel. My lips peeled in a feral grin. Maybe we had a chance after all.

Andre and Stefan came at Gabriel from either side. The fight became a blur of motion, all three men moving at insane speeds.

I crouched nearby, desperately wanting to help. But I couldn't even tell which one was Gabriel.

Then Stefan stepped back, circling behind Gabriel while Andre attacked him from the front.

Stefan stopped a few feet away from me, his body partly turned so I could see his back. His gaze on the two combatants, he barely spared a glance at where I was hunkered down against the rocks. He held his blade in front of him, its sharp point twitching right and left with the fighting men in a chilling dance.

I zeroed in on his exposed nape.

The teacher of one of my various defense classes had been a hard-eyed ex-Marine. He'd explained in detail why you never turned your back on a man—or woman—holding a knife. Sever the spine at the nape, and it was over, even for a vampire.

We'd practiced it: one person the attacker, the other the victim.

"If you decide to go for it, don't hesitate," the teacher had emphasized. "Give it everything you have."

A second ticked by, then another, while I stared at Stefan's nape. My breath turned icy in my nostrils. I'd never killed before.

But it was them or us.

I rose to my feet, slowly, stealthily—and lunged, bringing my arm up high and stabbing the blade with all my strength into the back of Stefan's neck. I yanked it down toward the spine.

He grunted and swung around, wrenching the knife from my hand. "You stupid...bitch."

His eyes were a foot from mine, a demonic blue-ringed brown. I stared at him, lungs working.

He raised his switchblade, and then swayed. Blood bubbled from his mouth. The knife dropped to the sand and he collapsed at my feet like a marionette with its strings cut.

I backpedaled until I hit the rocks. Someone was making a high, keening sound. I clapped my hands over my ears until I realized it was me.

My face felt wet. I scrubbed at it with my T-shirt, then stared at the dark stain.

Blood.

Oh, God. My stomach heaved. I fell to my knees and threw up on the sand.

When I looked up again, Stefan was moving feebly, and Andre had Gabriel down, his mouth latched on Gabriel's throat. Neither man had a knife. Gabriel tried to push Andre off, but the other vampire was stuck to him like a leech.

Gabriel's struggles grew weaker.

It was up to me. Dragging myself across the sand, I rolled Stefan onto his stomach. The switchblade was lodged firmly in his spine. I scrabbled in the sand for his own knife but couldn't find it.

Gabriel was barely moving now.

I grabbed the handle of the knife in Stefan's spine, closed my eyes and jerked. It didn't come out. It was caught on something.

Fuck, fuck, fuck.

Taking a sobbing breath, I straddled Stefan and wrapped both hands around the handle. The metallic scent of blood made my stomach heave again. Bile burned my throat.

I yanked again. This time, the blade released. I rolled Stefan onto his back. His eyes were closed but his hands clawed at the sand.

I raised the blade above my head and plunged it into his heart. He jerked, then stilled, his head lolling to the side. I smelled the smoke as his skin crumbled to ashes.

My gaze swung back to Gabriel and Andre. Gabriel caught my eye. He reached out a hand for the switchblade.

I licked my lips, nodded. I pulled the bloody knife from Stefan's still-disintegrating chest and crawled off him, holding it as far from me as possible.

"Oh God, oh God, oh God." I didn't know if I was praying or swearing.

I scrambled, spider-like, across the beach and put the switchblade in Gabriel's palm. His fingers closed on it. Sucking in a breath, he reared up and thrust it into the side of Andre's throat.

The vampire hissed but still didn't stop feeding until Gabriel gave him a hard shove. With a snarl, Andre released his throat.

Gabriel heaved Andre off him, and he fell to the beach. Gabriel crawled a few yards away and collapsed, panting, on the sand.

I crouched beside him, keeping a wary eye on the motionless Andre. What I really needed was a silver blade so I could stake the sonuvabitch. But the beach was too dark. I couldn't locate even one of the knives.

Andre moved first. He pulled the blade out of his throat and with a grunt, came to his feet, one hand pressed to the wound, the other gripping the knife.

His gaze took in the two disintegrating vampires before swinging to me. I rose to my feet and backed up, looked frantically around for a weapon. All I saw was a small rock. I bent and picked it up without taking my eyes from Andre.

His T-shirt was torn, the ragged black flaps fluttering in the wind. He staggered, caught his balance.

Gold eyes scorched mine. "That," he said, "was a mistake."

My mouth dried. My heart threatened to smash out of my chest.

I raised the rock. "Go. To. Hell."

Andre fingered the switchblade, eyeing Gabriel's prone body. With an animal-like growl, I threw myself on top of him in a pitiful attempt to protect him.

In the house above, lights came on. A searchlight swept over the beach, casting Andre's face in demonic relief. He swore and staggered toward the boat dock, gaining strength with each step. By the time he reached the speedboat, he was strong enough to leap aboard.

Panic gripped me. He was getting away—and he still had Joey.

"*No.*" I sprinted toward the dock as the motor roared to life. Without turning on the running lights, he cast off, swung the boat around and zoomed off.

A sob tore threw me. "No! Come back here, damn you. Take me instead!"

I hurled the rock at the boat, but Andre was already too far away. It sank, unnoticed, beneath the black waves.

Tears streamed down my face. I staggered into the surf. I was up to my waist before I realized what I was doing.

Behind me, Gabriel called out weakly. "Mila?"

I dragged my gaze from where the speedboat had disappeared into the darkness, and, still sobbing, turned to go back to Gabriel.

He was hurt. He needed me.

And right now, there was nothing I could do for Joey. "I'm sorry," I whispered. "So sorry."

"Mila?" Gabriel again.

I stumbled back up the beach and dropped to the wet sand beside him. I scrubbed away the tears. "I'm here."

His fingers opened and closed on the sand, seeking me. I took his hand in both of mine.

"You okay?" He tried to lift his head. "They're...gone?"

"I'm fine. And two of them are dead. But Andre got away—in your boat."

"Joey?"

"He—" I could barely push the words past the painful constriction in my throat. "Andre—he said he'd keep Joey as a blood slave if I didn't help him."

Gabriel swore and tried to sit up. He grimaced and sucked in a breath.

"No—stay." I grabbed his shoulders. "There's nothing you can do right now. The lights are on in the house. Help is on the way." At least, I hoped it was.

He let me press him back to the sand. "You sure...you're okay?"

"I'm fine." I took a steadying breath and focused on Gabriel. "But you—you're hurt. He was feeding on you."

"This?" Gabriel touched the wound on his throat. "It will heal. But—" His hand hovered over his stomach.

"What? I can't see anything, damn it." I was shivering so hard now, I had a hard time keeping my voice steady. "It's s-so freaking d-dark out here."

"Maybe...for the best."

"Damn it, Kral. You're scaring me here." I eased up his T-shirt—and gasped. His abdomen was covered with blood. I could see at least two deep, ugly slashes.

I leaned closer, fighting down terror. Because it looked like he was still bleeding. A dark pool soaked the sand beneath him.

PURSUED

The searchlight swept over our heads again. I knew they couldn't see us hunkered down in the cliff's shadow, but I was reluctant to show myself until I knew who'd won, Gabriel's people or Andre's.

Gabriel gave me a crooked smile. "Don't worry...I cut him... good, too. That's why...drank...my blood."

"Jesus." I sucked in a breath and glanced at the ocean. "Maybe I should clean your wound? Salt water is good for that, right?"

"I'll be all right." Gabriel's eyelids drooped. "Just...don't leave me. Promise?"

"Of course not." I took his hand. The fingers were ice cold.

It's just reaction. He's hurt, lost a lot of blood.

"Sorry," he said. "Should never...have...kissed you. Done anything...with you."

My stomach tightened. Something was very wrong.

"Stop it. It was me as much as you."

"Noo," he insisted, the words slurred. "I'm...shorry. Should've kept...away." His eyes closed.

"Gabriel!" I gripped his hand. "Stay with me. Please."

His fingers closed on mine. "Love you, Mila."

His voice was weak. Too weak, like he was trying to get the words out before it was too late.

I nuzzled the unhurt side of his face. "Maybe I love you, too. But if you leave me now, I'll hate you forever. Understand?"

He didn't say anything, but his lips curved.

"You don't believe me, do you?" Tears stung my eyes. "Well, you're right. I won't hate you, but I'll never forgive you."

The only sound was the waves slapping against the beach.

"Gabriel?"

No answer.

"Talk to me, damn it!"

I darted a look at the beach house. Should I get help? But what if the person manning the searchlight was one of Andre's vampires?

Gabriel groaned. His mouth worked like he was thirsty.

He'd lost too much blood. To heal, he needed to drink.

And I knew what I had to do. Even a few weeks ago, I might

137

have hesitated. For three years, I'd been on the run from the Kral Syndicate. A part of me was still wary of Gabriel's vampire side.

But right now, I was grateful I could do something to save him. Because Gabriel Kral was my everything, dhampir or not, enforcer or not.

I brought my wrist to his lips. "Drink."

He muttered something but didn't open his mouth.

I glanced at his abdomen. The blood still flowed sluggishly out, and the dark pool on the sand beneath him had increased.

How fast did a man bleed out, even if he was a dhampir?

My eyes went to the switchblade that Gabriel had stabbed Andre with. But it was dark with Andre's blood—vampire blood. I had no idea what that would do to me.

Gabriel's breath shuddered out...and didn't come back in.

My heart seized. I grabbed the switchblade, darted to the ocean and rinsed it with salt water, then hurried back. I set the blade against my wrist, gritted my teeth, and slashed open a vein.

"Drink." I touched the wrist to his mouth.

He lay still as death.

"Gabriel!" I shook his shoulder. "Wake up and drink, damn you."

Another few seconds ticked by. Then at last, his mouth moved against my skin. He took a tentative lick and swallowed audibly, as if it hurt even to do that. He took a second lick, then started lapping at my blood.

"That's it." I closed my eyes, dizzy with relief. "Take all you need."

He gripped my wrist, holding it to his mouth. His eyes were wide open now, shining in the dark like an animal's. His fangs had lengthened, too. The sharp points touched my skin, but he didn't sink them into my wrist, just sucked.

I glanced at his abdomen. The deep gashes were healing before my eyes.

My shoulders slumped. *Thank God.*

"That's it. Keep drinking. You're already getting better."

He licked my wrist, closing the cut, then released me. "That's... enough." His eyelids drifted shut.

I cleaned the switchblade on the wet sand and settled his head on my lap, tucking the still-open blade beneath my thigh.

"How do you feel? Is there anything else I can do?"

"No. But...hurts. Need...rest."

"Okay." I stroked his hair, wincing at the lump behind his left ear. "Damn. They really worked you over, didn't they?"

"Should be...dead. Good thing I had...secret weapon."

"And what's that?"

He turned his head to press a kiss to my palm. "You."

My stomach clenched. I resumed stroking his hair.

"Yeah," I said under my breath. "But *whose* secret weapon?"

Voices came from the cove on the other side of the rocks. I stilled, heart slamming, afraid to call out.

Two long, low shadows shot over the rocks. Gabriel's pet wolves.

Amber eyes narrowed on where I was crouched over their master. They growled in unison, a harsh, menacing sound.

I gulped and stretched out a hand, palm down. "Good dogs?"

They moved forward, sniffing my hand, and then to my relief, trotted over to examine the two piles of charred bones and ashes that were all that remained of Stefan and Martin. When they returned, they settled on either side of Gabriel. One nuzzled his face while the other let out an anxious whine.

His lips turned up. "Daisy. Diesel." He rubbed their muzzles. "Sit."

They dropped their hindquarters, panting softly.

Two vampires—Airi and a wiry brown-skinned man named Umar—appeared on the rocks above. They dropped to the sand on either side of us.

Gabriel pushed himself up on his forearms. For an agonizing moment, Airi and Umar considered the two of us. I moved my hand to the switchblade concealed beneath my thigh.

Then Umar held out a hand. "Can you stand?"

"Of course." Gabriel took the hand, and the two vampires helped him to his feet.

"He's hurt." I scrambled to my feet. "His stomach, and I don't know where else."

Gabriel draped an arm over my shoulder and squeezed, silently warning me not to say anything further. "I'm good."

He trained a look on the vampires. When he spoke, his tone was pure ice. "Let's get back to the house, and then you can tell me what the fuck happened."

❧ 18 ❧

GABRIEL

Something in a supernatural's blood reacts with silver. Worse, the metal weakens us. But thanks to Mila, I'd healed enough to fake a strength I didn't feel.

Airi and Umar helped me over the rocks, but I made my own way up the stairs even though with each step, my gut felt like it was being ripped open all over again. And already, the silver poisoning was making me lightheaded, feverish.

I clenched my jaw and bore it. Until I knew exactly how my security had been compromised, I couldn't risk anyone—especially the vampires on my staff—seeing how shaky the attack had left me.

Back in my suite, I downed a large glass of blood-wine. Mila looked on anxiously, her clothes bloody, her pretty face streaked with more blood and dirt.

Remorse fisted my heart. I hated like hell that she'd been dragged into this, but it was too late now.

I smoothed the backs of my fingers over her cheek. "Why don't you take a shower?"

"What about Joey?" She gripped my wrist, eyes bright with fear. "Andre's going to make him a blood slave. He said he'll give Joey to his coven."

"We'll find him," I promised grimly.

And then Andre Redbone was dead meat. This wasn't just about me and my place in the Kral hierarchy. By dragging humans into it —*my* humans—he'd crossed the line.

This was war.

"I think I know where he is," Mila said.

I stilled. "Joey?"

An eager nod. "In Manhattan—an apartment building on Fifth Avenue. That's where they took me. Joey was there, too. Andre let me see him. He was trying to be tough, but God, he was so scared."

A black fury filled my head. "Where, exactly?" I asked as calmly as I could.

"On Fifth Avenue, across from Central Park. They kept me in the basement."

I felt my eyes go vampire. I swore, low and vicious.

Mila blinked, heart rapping so hard I could almost feel it in my own chest.

"Damn it," I grated, too on edge from pain and anger to mince my words. "Don't you be afraid of me. You *know* I wouldn't harm a single fucking hair on your head."

She looked at me another moment, then brought a hand up to stroke my temple. "I know."

The light touch felt like a blessing. I nuzzled her palm, still on edge, but beneath was the peace she'd always brought me. I'd almost forgotten how good it felt, how *right*.

Like the world was a better place than I knew it to be.

I drew her into my arms, ignoring the pain that stabbed my abdomen. "You're safe now. I swear it on everything I hold holy."

She rested her head against my chest. "I know."

"All right, then." I blew out a breath. "So. Tell me about this basement."

She pulled away, thinking. "I can't tell you much—I was locked in a cell the whole time. But I can tell you there's no elevator to the basement. We took an elevator to the first floor, then went down another flight of stairs. There were six cells all together."

"Would you know the building if you saw it?"

"*Yes.*" Her whole face lit up. "I didn't see a building number, but it was just north of East Seventy-Sixth Street. And I had a good look at the front."

"That's all we need to look it up on Google Earth." I limped into my office and sank carefully into my chair, trying not to groan.

Mila laid a hand on my shoulder. "Let me do it."

I nodded and opened my laptop. As soon as I'd entered the password, she leaned over me to open the geolocation app, narrowing the search to Manhattan's Upper East Side. A short time later, we were viewing the buildings on Fifth Avenue between Seventy-Sixth and Seventy-Seventh Streets.

"That's it!" She zoomed in on a building near the corner of Seventy-Sixth and Fifth.

My jaw tightened. The building was owned by a member of the Louisiana Coven. Not Redbone, but Brenda McFadden, the vampire liaison between Louisiana and my father.

"You're sure?"

"Positive. I remember the orange trees." She pointed to the potted trees on either side of the walk.

That was good enough for me. I messaged Fagan Security to check it out. "Be careful," I warned. "We suspect it's a vampire nest."

"Will check it out ASAP," was the reply.

"Don't go inside—I'll handle the extraction. And I'm sending a couple of enforcers to take over security for the Vittores." With Redbone's back to the wall, he might go after Mila's parents next. "I'll contact you as soon as they're in place."

"Got it."

"Use any means possible to get the truth," I added. The Fagans would know they had my permission to compel one of the humans on site, either a thrall or someone on Andre's staff.

I signed off and sat back. "They should have an answer for us in a few hours," I told Mila.

Her face fell. "We can't leave now?"

I shifted on the chair to look at her. This time, I couldn't stifle the groan.

"Christ, I'm sorry." She wrapped her arms carefully around me from behind and laid her cheek against mine. "You're too hurt to go anywhere."

"It's not so bad," I lied. "But it's going to take a few hours for the silver to work its way out of my system. Meanwhile," I added grimly, "I need to talk to Airi." I wasn't going anywhere until I'd reestablished control over my security and what remained of my staff.

Pushing to my feet, I made my way back to the living room for another glass of blood-wine.

"But even if I wasn't hurt, I wouldn't risk Joey by rushing in without a plan. My guess is the building's a nest—smaller than a coven, but there could be as many as a dozen vampires based there. Plus, we don't know for sure Joey's still there. If he is, and we go in before we're ready, they might move him somewhere else and it could take weeks to track him down." I drained the wine and set down the glass. "So for now, there's nothing we can do. You might as well shower, have something to eat."

"Okay. Yeah." She pushed her hair from her face, looked blankly at her blood-stained hands. "I guess I could use a shower."

"Go." I took her by the shoulders and turned her toward the bathroom. "I'll get you some clean clothes."

My phone had survived undamaged in my closet. I reinstated the house security system, then arranged to meet Airi in the dining room, which like my suite, was relatively untouched.

Mila's rooms, though, had been trashed. A message, I suspected, from Redbone to her.

After leaving Mila's clothes on a chair in the bathroom, I washed up and pulled on a fresh shirt and pants. By then my head felt clearer, and the pain from my abdominal wounds had subsided. Still, until the silver passed out of my system, I'd be achy and too damn weak, and craving blood any way I could get it.

Mila reappeared, clean-smelling from her shower, her damp hair in a braid. I took a few minutes to quiz her on what, exactly, Redbone had wanted her to do.

But she couldn't tell me much more than what I already knew. Redbone had ordered her to get close to me any way she could. The mic in the earring allowed him to listen in on our private conversations, and the GPS had allowed him to track her, and thus, me when we were together.

"I know he was just using me to distract you," Mila said. "I feel so bad..." She trailed off, dark eyes troubled.

"Hey." I slid my fingers under her braid to cup her nape. "You did the right thing. They had Joey—you had no choice."

"I'm just glad I don't have to lie to you anymore." Her throat worked. "It was tearing me up inside."

"There's one thing I'd like to know. Why didn't you tell me sooner? Write me a note or something?"

Why didn't you trust me to help? my heart asked.

Fuck, I was pitiful. But she should've trusted me.

"I couldn't." The look she gave me was stark. "Andre said that if I warned you, he'd know."

What the hell? I stared back.

"We have a mole. Trust no one."

I'd been so busy trying to convince myself that Mila wasn't the mole that I hadn't thought it through. And then all hell had broken loose.

But it made sense. Someone on the inside had to be feeding Andre intel. And not O'Brien. He hadn't been part of the inner circle—not even close.

"I'm sorry." Mila eyed me anxiously. "I wanted to tell you. So bad. But I couldn't let them hurt Joey."

"It's okay, cher. I understand. But think—did he say *how* he'd know?"

A regretful shake of her head. "You have to understand, they didn't tell me much. To them, I was just another empty-headed thrall. The best way to get to you."

I drew her into my arms. "That's where they fucked up."

Fortunately, Lougenia had made it to her safe room in time, although her assistant as well as the human gardener had died in the attack. I'd already given Lougenia the all-clear, and as Mila and I took seats at the dining room table, she bustled about the kitchen in her uniform and fuzzy pink slippers, preparing a snack for us—a hamburger for Mila, a couple of rare steaks for me.

Daisy and Diesel settled under the table next to my feet. The wolfdogs were the heroes of the night. Daisy had singlehandedly held off two vampires before being knocked unconscious by a stun gun, and Diesel had made it to the helipad, drawing a trio of outside attackers who'd been dispatched by my security. Unfortunately, Redbone had realized it was a trick and headed to the beach with Stefan and Martin while Airi and her team were occupied.

Mila was barefoot. I glanced down to see her scratching Diesel behind his ears with her toes. The dog's eyes were slit in bliss. Mila had made another friend.

Lougenia set our plates on the table and went back for two more rare steaks, one for each wolfdog. A promise is a promise, after all. The dogs waited for my nod before tearing into the meat. I attacked mine only a little less ravenously, chasing it down with gulps of blood-wine.

"Get some rest," I told Lougenia. "everything else can wait until tomorrow."

The housekeeper looked shell-shocked, her round cheeks pale. Her assistant had been killed right outside the safe room.

But she firmed her chin. "No, I'll do it. I couldn't sleep a wink now, anyway. I'll be in the kitchen, cleaning up the mess those *fils-putain* left."

Airi hurried into the dining room. Her hair was in its usual sleek ponytail, but there was a knife hole in her uniform over her heart. She looked pale, but otherwise all right, and I was in no mood to pamper her. As my chief of security, the blame for this rested squarely on her shoulders.

I invited her to sit, then leveled a look at her. "Report."

Besides Airi, just two members of my security team had survived: Umar and Paco. That left four vampires and a dhampir dead, as well as Lougenia's assistant Chandra and three human soldiers. But Redbone had lost people as well: the two men on the beach, and three more vampires at the heliport.

Tomas had been informed and was on his way out to Montauk with a couple of soldiers. We also had people looking for Redbone, but I didn't hold out much hope. One of his men had probably already picked him up somewhere along the coast.

Meanwhile, no one was being allowed in or out. Umar and Paco were patrolling the grounds.

Airi straightened her already-straight spine another notch. "First, I want to apologize, sir. O'Brien was apparently working for Redbone." O'Brien was a recent vampire hire.

I made an impatient movement. "You have nothing to apologize for. O'Brien came with a recommendation from Lieutenant Mraz, and he passed my checks as well."

The enforcer nodded uncertainly.

"So I don't want your apology, I want some goddamned answers. How the fuck did Redbone get through our security? And don't tell me O'Brien let him in."

Two red spots burned on the enforcer's cheeks, but she met my gaze square on. "That's exactly what happened, sir."

"That system is airtight, with checks upon checks."

"Yes, sir."

"So how did O'Brien get access to the system in the first place? The man was a soldier. He didn't have that kind of clearance."

"I don't know how he got access," she admitted, "but he introduced some kind of bug that took down our security for thirty seconds. By the time the backup system kicked in, Redbone and six other vampires were inside the grounds. And thanks to O'Brien, they knew every one of our weak spots."

"O'Brien shouldn't have been able to take the system down for two seconds, let alone thirty. I want to know what went wrong ASAP." I didn't raise my voice, but both women heard the lethal edge.

Airi swallowed audibly, and beside me, Mila tensed.

I ignored her to keep my gaze on Airi. If Mila was going to be my mate—and I was damned if I'd let her go a second time—then she might as well see what life with me meant. I'd been attacked in my own house, my woman endangered.

If O'Brien wasn't already dust, I'd have ripped his head right off his body. And if Airi didn't explain the failure in my security to my satisfaction, she was going to follow O'Brien to her final grave by sunrise.

"Yes, sir," the enforcer replied. "I'll get on it right away."

I jerked my chin in acknowledgement. "Lieutenant Mraz will be here in a couple of hours. He'll want a full report."

Airi looked a little sick. Nobody wanted to get on Tomas's bad side.

"Of course," she murmured, and rose to return to the vampire bunker, where the op room and the bulk of our security equipment was located.

"Take Daisy and Diesel with you. They can patrol the perimeter until Tomas arrives with reinforcements." I snapped my fingers at the wolfdogs. "Go with Airi. Outside."

When we were alone, I turned to Mila. "You haven't eaten."

"I can't," she said with a listless shrug. "I keep thinking about Joey."

"Just a few bites," I coaxed, cutting her hamburger into quarters. "Here." I brought a piece to her mouth.

She took a tiny bite.

I sighed. "Mila. You have to eat. You've lost too much blood in the past couple of days. You need red meat."

When she just shook her head, I set the piece back on her plate and took her hand. "You're not doing your brother any good by starving yourself."

Her chest heaved. "I'm so scared," she confessed. "You don't know what they're like. Martin and Stefan—they kept touching me, watching me. Like they fucking *owned* me. I had to ask permission even to go to the bathroom."

My jaw tightened. I took a harsh breath. "Redbone?"

She shook her head. "Martin and Stefan. But Redbone knew what was happening. He said..." Her throat worked. "He promised me to them first."

"He's dead," I said coldly. "That's a promise."

"Good." But she stared down at her plate with a worried frown that wrenched my heart. "How soon do you think we'll know anything?"

"The Fagans are the best in the business. They should have answers for us by morning. Now eat." I tucked a strand of hair behind her ear. "For Joey—and for me. Please?"

She straightened. Her face took on that too-serene look, but she picked up one of the pieces I'd cut for her and determinedly chewed.

I finished the last of my steak. Of all the things that had come out tonight, I was most disturbed by Redbone's warning that if Mila helped me in any way, he'd know.

Could Rafe's mole be that highly placed—maybe even someone in my father's inner circle?

Or had Redbone been bluffing? Just planting doubt in Mila's mind had been enough to keep her quiet.

The uncertainty was making me edgy.

Hopefully, Tomas had discovered something that could help. He was already on his way out to Montauk. We might have our differences, but he was my father's oldest friend, his brother-in-arms.

Right now, he was the only man at headquarters I trusted completely.

❧ 19 ❧
MILA

Gabriel ordered me to get some rest while he stayed up to speak to the lieutenant who was on his way out from Manhattan. I made him promise to wake me as soon as he heard anything about Joey and returned to his suite.

His rooms were larger than mine, but as simply furnished. The bedroom had a large painting of a thunderstorm looming over the ocean and a four-poster bed made of bleached wood. The coverlet was a soft pigeon-gray.

I brushed my teeth and stripped down to a T-shirt and boyshorts. Leaving the lights on, I crawled onto the king-sized mattress and passed out. I don't know how long I slept, but Gabriel still hadn't come to bed when I jerked awake, terror for my brother pressing on my chest like a sack of rocks.

Andre would've made it back to Manhattan by now. Which meant Joey might already be a blood slave. It might be illegal, but everyone knew that some vampires kept blood slaves anyway.

And Andre was furious with me. Not only had I helped Gabriel fight him off, I'd staked Stefan myself.

I moaned and pressed my knuckles to my mouth.

You had no choice. You had to fight back.

But every time I shut my eyes, I pictured my brother locked in one of those basement cells, pale and drawn, waiting for the vampires to come for him.

When Gabriel finally came to bed, I was staring tensely up at the ceiling. He dimmed the lights and pulled me into his arms.

"Did you get any sleep at all, cher?"

"A little." I cuddled into him. "What if they—?" My breath scraped in.

"Tell me."

My fingers spread out on his bare chest. Beneath my hand, his heart beat slow and steady. I moved my fingers lower to feather over the healed-over knife wounds. Wounds that would've left a human in intensive care for weeks—or dead.

"What if they kill him?" I whispered, as if speaking it out loud would somehow make it happen.

His grip on me tightened. "They won't."

"How can you be so sure? You didn't see Andre, I did. The agreement was that if I did anything to help you, Joey was his."

"I'm sure because they're smart. As long as Joey's still useful to them, they won't hurt him."

"Useful to them? How?"

"As bait," he said succinctly. "They know I'll come after him."

I closed my eyes. "Because I agreed to the blood bond?"

He nodded against my hair. "But even without the bond, I'd go after Joey. This is personal now. They used him to threaten you, and then planted you right in my household. I can't let them get away with that."

"Oh, God." Bile filled my throat. "I didn't want this. I *never* wanted this."

"There was nothing you could do to stop it. It's been coming for a long time. Now, relax." His fingers stroked down my spine, powerful, comforting.

My breath sighed out. Gradually, my muscles released. I cuddled closer, careful not to press against his wounds. His enticing scent filled my head.

He continued to murmur to me. Telling me I was safe now, to let go, get some sleep.

My eyelids drifted down, but I forced them open and drew his head to my neck. "You're still hurting. Drink from me."

I felt his hesitation. "I shouldn't. You've already given me too much today."

"Gabriel," I said. "You need it. How are you going to stake that prick if you're too weak?"

His mouth curved against my skin. "And here I thought you were all sweetness and light."

I snorted. "Stop talking and drink already."

"Yes, ma'am," he said in a meek tone that didn't fool me for a second.

I felt the prick of his fangs, and then the suck of his mouth. Something warm curled through me. Not the high I'd gotten when he'd fed from me during sex, but something more profound. My heart turned over in my chest.

In that moment, I knew I was in deep. Way deeper than last time.

He didn't take much before licking the small wounds closed. "Thank you. You were right—I did need fresh blood."

"Mm." I stroked his nape. Was it wrong to feel so happy when my brother was still Andre's prisoner? But I sank into the good, contented feeling, enjoying it while I could.

Gabriel sighed, a low, satisfied sound. When he tried to move away, I tightened my grip, keeping his head on my shoulder. His eyelids drifted down to form thick black crescents against his cheeks. His body went lax, and his breathing slowed to almost nothing.

A short while later, my eyes closed, too. This time my sleep was dreamless.

The next thing I knew, he was gently shaking me awake. "We found him, Mila."

My eyes popped open. "Joey?"

A somber nod. "It's like you thought. He's locked in one of the basement cells."

I swung my legs out of bed. "You're sure?"

"As sure as I can be. Fagan says a thrall confirmed Joey's still there. We're sending a couple of men to check it out, but I'm leaving now."

"Yes." I looked around for my shorts, then halted, frowning. "*You're* leaving now?"

He nodded. "It's almost morning. Most of the vampires will be asleep by the time I get to Manhattan. Even if they're not, they'll be sluggish."

"But...you're taking me, right?" When he pursed his lips, I grabbed his arm. "You are *not* leaving me here. I'll go crazy, wondering what's up. And Joey's going to need me—you said so yourself."

"Fine." He blew out a breath. "You can come. But only to Manhattan. You can wait at my penthouse. It's only ten minutes away."

"Fair enough." I glanced at his body, naked except for a pair of black boxers. The wounds were barely visible red lines on his lightly tanned stomach, but I couldn't forget how much blood he'd lost, and not just from the knife wounds. Andre had ripped into his throat like an animal. "What about you? You sure you're up to this?"

He rubbed a hand over his belly. "This?" he scoffed.

"Yeah, that." I put my hand over his. "If I lost you now..." I bit my lower lip.

"Hey." He caught my hand, brought it to his mouth. "I really am better. And it has to be me. I don't trust anyone else to extract your brother."

He pressed a kiss to my palm and curled my fingers around it. My throat tightened.

"Thank you," I managed to say.

"Thank me when we get him back. Now, get dressed. We leave in ten minutes."

"I'll be ready."

At some point, my new clothes had been moved to Gabriel's walk-in closet, what was left of them, anyway—the pricks had slashed up most of them. But two dresses, a pair of sneakers and a motley collection of shirts, shorts and a pair of cropped jeans had survived. And they'd somehow missed the underwear, even the sexy stuff.

I pulled on a tank top and the cropped jeans and twisted my hair into a messy bun. Meanwhile, Gabriel dressed in slim dark pants and a green T-shirt. He tucked a switchblade into each pocket, and wordlessly handed me a third.

I looked from it to him. "Thanks," I said, closing my fingers around the silver handle.

"Hey, you earned it." He handed me a leather duffel bag. "Bring some extra clothes. We'll stay in Manhattan for at least one night, maybe two."

I nodded and added some clothes to the duffel bag. The switchblade went into my back pocket.

Lougenia met us in the foyer with an insulated lunch bag packed with food and drinks. She was neatly dressed, the fuzzy slippers nowhere in sight, but her face was drawn and she had dark smudges under her eyes.

"Here." She handed me the lunch bag. "I packed you some breakfast."

I took the bag and pulled her into a hug. "I'm so sorry about Chandra."

"It should've been me." Lougenia's voice was harsh with sorrow. "She was so young. Had her whole life ahead of her."

"I know." I hugged her tighter. "I know."

She drew a slow breath and let it out before pulling away. "Thanks, *ma p'tite*."

Gabriel squeezed her shoulder. "You okay?"

She gave a listless shrug. "I called Chandra's family a few minutes ago. Told them you'd be in touch."

"Good. I'll take care of them, don't worry. I'm sorry, Lougenia."

She nodded and shuffled down the hall, looking like she'd aged a decade since yesterday.

Outside, the sun had risen on a beautiful summer day. A cool breeze ruffled my hair, and white, cottony clouds dotted a wide blue sky.

It was...jarring. Like the weather had somehow mixed up its

signals and sent sunshine when it should've been smothering us in dark storm clouds.

Gabriel slung the duffel bag over his shoulder and took my free hand. The helicopter had been damaged in the attack, so he'd decided to drive us himself instead of taking the limo, saying, "They'll be watching for that."

When we reached the garage, the big blond vampire I knew only as Tomas waited next to a blue sedan along with a dark-skinned female vampire. My step faltered.

Tomas's mouth stretched in a smile I knew not to trust. "So this is Mila."

A chill ran over my skin. Why was he pretending we hadn't met?

Gabriel set a hand on my lower back. "This is Lieutenant Mraz. He'll be heading the team to extract your brother."

This was the lieutenant?

I gave Mraz a jerky nod, playing along until I could get Gabriel alone. "Nice to meet you."

An automatic response that I instantly wished I could unsay, because it *wasn't* nice to meet him—not this time, and not the first time, either.

The big blond vampire never lost his smile, but his gaze raked over me, taking in every detail from the sunflower on my tank top to my purple tennis shoes. Dismissing me as a weak, silly human.

I lifted my chin—and smiled right into his cold, muddy-yellow eyes. All I cared about was getting Joey back. If pretending to like this grinning bastard of a vampire was necessary, then I'd pretend with everything I had.

"Why are you bringing her?" Mraz asked Gabriel.

"Until my security here is fully back on line, she'll be safer at my penthouse."

Mraz moved a big shoulder, clearly not caring if I lived or died. In fact, I'd bet good money he was disappointed I'd survived the night.

We headed out, me and Gabriel in a silver sports car; Mraz and the other vampire following in the sedan.

As we pulled onto Route 27, I unzipped the insulated bag and stared at the sandwiches, searching for the best way to put this. Gabriel clearly trusted the blond vampire. He wouldn't be heading the team to rescue Joey otherwise.

Gabriel spoke first. "I didn't know you knew Lieutenant Mraz."

So he'd picked up on my uneasiness. "I wouldn't say I know him, but we met. Once."

"When?"

I zipped and unzipped the bag.

Three years ago, it had been Tomas Mraz who'd given me a hundred thousand in cash to leave town. He'd also advised me—strongly—to depart without telling Gabriel.

"Don't contact Prince Gabriel," Mraz had said. "Not even to tell him you are leaving. He is half-vampire, and we're possessive bastards. He will not accept that you do this thing for his own good."

God, I'd been a coward. I'd told myself that sneaking out of town was best for both of us, but that was a lie. It had been for me, because I didn't have the courage to tell Gabriel straight to his face that I was leaving.

"Three years ago, right before I left."

"Ah."

What did that mean? I darted Gabriel a look. "Who is he, anyway? A lieutenant—that's pretty high up, right?"

"He's my dad's righthand man."

"So you trust him?"

"Why do you ask?" Before I could answer, he muttered a curse. "Tomas was the one who threatened you, not my father."

"Lieutenant Mraz?" I shook my head. "No."

"The truth, Mila. No more lies. I can't help you if you won't tell me exactly what happened."

"But it is the truth."

"Is it? Mraz gave you the money you used to leave and told you never to come back. You're not going to tell me my father wasn't behind that."

I sucked in a breath. "You want the truth? Fine. Your dad did want me gone, but I could've turned down the money. Mraz didn't threaten me into leaving. Nobody did. I'm sorry, but that's the God's honest truth."

His nostrils flared, the only indication I'd hurt him. "Go on."

I fiddled with the zipper, trying to order my thoughts, as we entered a nature preserve. Short, salt-bitten pines lined either side of the highway. A sign announced we'd entered Napeague State Park.

"Your mother came to see me first."

"My mom?" His chin jerked back. "Why the hell would she do that?"

"To find out how serious things were between us. And when I said I loved you, she hugged me and said, 'Oh, honey. Bless your heart,' then invited me back to your house for coffee."

"And?"

I moved a shoulder. "I went."

Rosemarie Kral had served me coffee and sugar-dusted beignets in a gazebo draped with thick wisteria vines. Nearby, butterflies had flitted among the summer flowers, and cicadas had chirred in the trees.

Gabriel's mom had a dhampir's inhuman beauty. Her chic jade dress fit her perfect body like a glove, and her smooth golden-brown skin was unlined except for tiny smile lines like parentheses on either side of her mouth. "I like you," she'd said with a kind smile—and proceeded to break my heart.

"She said I seemed like a sweet girl. Which is why she wanted me to know what my life would be like if I—if we mated. Not that you'd asked me," I hurried to say. "But she seemed to think you were going to."

A muscle jumped in his jaw. "I see."

"Don't be mad at her. She was nice to me. She said it was for my own good, that I should know what it was like for a human in your world."

Rosemarie had seemed genuinely concerned for me. After we'd finished our coffee, she'd invited me for a walk in her gorgeous garden, where she'd linked her arm in mine and explained what her life was like.

A bodyguard everywhere she went.

A mate who never aged so that she'd been forced to become a dhampir if she didn't want to leave him broken-hearted when she died.

And meanwhile, her human friends and family kept aging at the normal rate.

"But you love him, right?" I'd said.

"With all my heart." Her smile was poignant. "But what you're really asking is was it worth it? I'd say yes, except a part of me thinks I was selfish. I only considered myself and Karoly. But there are three other people involved."

My heart sank. "Gabriel and his brothers."

Rosemarie nodded, her expression troubled. "No one told me how hard it would be for them. Karoly says it toughened them up, but I'm their mother. To a vampire, a dhampir is a lesser life form. They'll never consider Gabriel and his brothers their equals. And with you, Mila, it would be even worse. Gabriel is half vampire, but your children would be only a quarter vampire."

Gabriel downshifted. I watched the ropy muscles in his arm flex. He was so strong, so capable. How could anyone, even a vampire, believe he was somehow less than them?

"Go on," he said, tight-lipped.

"She said you and your brothers have had to fight for every inch of respect. That behind your back, the vampires say you're weak. She thinks that when your father is gone, they'll try to block you from becoming primus. That you'll be fighting off challengers left and right."

He cursed, low and vicious, his fingers white-knuckled on the steering wheel. "And you listened to her?"

Setting the insulated bag on the floor, I toed off my sneakers and hugged my knees into my chest.

After leaving Black Oak, I'd driven to the park adjoining the Krals' land and walked for hours. My heart felt like it had developed cracks. They fractured and spread outward until I thought I'd break apart.

Knowing that if I stayed with Gabriel, I would be a liability. That the syndicate vampires would sneer at me and our kids.

And that I'd always be on edge, wondering if this was the night I'd lose him to a challenge.

"The next night," I said, low-voiced, "you asked me to accept the blood bond."

A hard glare. "When—*if*—you said yes, I was going to ask you to mate with me. A human marriage ceremony, too, because I knew that would make you happy. I even bought the fucking diamond ring."

A crater-sized lump filled my throat. "I...I didn't know. I hoped, but..."

"Why didn't you just tell me? Why run? You *knew* I wouldn't have forced you to accept. Hell, I even told you to take some time to think it over. Instead you left everything behind, even your family. What the fuck was that about?"

The hurt in his voice made me hug my knees harder.

"I did know," I said lowly. "I didn't run because I was afraid of you, or what you would do. I want you to know that."

"What else was I supposed to think? A short note ending it—no explanation, just that you were leaving and I wasn't to try to find you—and then you disappear. Your own parents didn't know where you were."

I opened my mouth to say I was sorry, then shut it. Some things, you couldn't make right with an apology.

"Mraz said that you wouldn't let me go. That it was best to make a clean break."

"And you believed him over me? I promised the decision was yours. You could've trusted me that much at least."

I took a deep, pained breath. He was right, and I was wrong.

"I effed up. Big time. But I did it for you—and for our kids."

"The hell you did." His look was alive with fury. "I never said a thing about kids. I wanted *you*, Mila. Yeah, I want kids someday, but I have two brothers. When—if—I take over as primus, I'd be happy to name them or their children my heirs. Fuck, my father's probably going to live another five centuries or so anyway."

"Well, maybe *I* want kids," I shot back.

"*Then we'd have them.* And I'd protect them with every resource at my disposal. Which by the way, is a hell of a lot."

We glowered at each other. Then I sighed. "There's more."

"Go on."

"That last night, after I left you, Lieutenant Mraz was waiting.

He told me that if I didn't leave, you'd never be primus. That as a dhampir, it was going to be hard enough for you to fight off challenges once your father died. A vampire mate could protect herself, but me, I'd be a weakness. Something they could use to get to you."

It had been too much, coming after my talk with Rosemarie Kral.

I'd caved.

Shame tightened my stomach. "I couldn't do that to you, Gabriel." I was speaking to my knees. I made myself turn my head, look at him. "The syndicate is your life. I know how hard you've worked to earn the right to be the next Kral Primus. A human mate will just bring you down."

He snarled. "The hell with the syndicate. You think I didn't consider that before I asked you to accept my oath? You're mine, Mila. I'd burn the whole damn thing to the ground before I'd let anyone hurt you. And if I can't fight off a challenge, then I don't deserve to be Primus."

"Don't you see?" I cried. "Mraz was right. I *am* a weakness. It happened just like he said—Andre Redbone used me and my brother to get to you. Maybe you're right about kids; we could've figured that out. But Mraz said a challenge is to the death. How many could you fight until you lost?" My voice broke. "You almost died tonight, Gabriel. Because of me."

"It's *my right* to protect you. You think I want to live if it means I can't have you?"

"D'you think I could live knowing I was responsible for your death?" I shot back.

His answering growl was more animal than human.

I stiffened my spine. It was the truth, damn it. I was *not* going to apologize.

For a time, we drove in silence. Gabriel stared straight ahead, a muscle jumping in his cheek.

"There's one thing I don't understand," he said at last. "Why did you keep running? I let you go. I promised the decision was yours, and I meant it—the blood bond, us mating... You could've trusted me that much, at least."

He doesn't know.

I'd told myself he didn't, that if he knew he'd have stopped them, but I hadn't been sure. Maybe he'd just wash his hands of me. After all, he was a rich, powerful syndicate prince, and I'd walked out on him without even saying goodbye.

"Someone found out about us," I said. "A vampire, maybe more than one. They've tried to kill me three times."

"*What?*"

We were in one of the small, pretty beach towns that dot Long Island. Gabriel swerved to the curb and slammed on the brakes. Tomas continued past, stopping a little further up the street.

Gabriel shut off the car and turned to me, his expression pure predator. "Why the fuck didn't you let me know?" His phone was on a small shelf between us. Before I could answer, it lit up. He tapped it and barked, "I need a minute here, Tomas."

Gabriel unbuckled our seat belts, then dragged me toward him so we faced each other across the console.

Green eyes blazed into mine. "You should've got hold of me. It's because of me you were targeted. If someone was threatening you, the least you could've done is contact me so I could stake the motherfucker."

I shoved at his chest, but it was like pushing on solid rock. "I didn't know what to do, damn it. They didn't just threaten me, they threatened my family. If I returned to you, if I even tried to contact you, they'd kill them one by one, starting with my nonna first." My voice broke.

"Who?" He tightened his grip on my shoulders. "I want names."

"That's just it," I returned, fighting back tears. "I don't know. The calls are always anonymous, and the voice is disguised. It's just this weird computer voice—you know, like a robocall. And the vampires always attacked after dark, so I didn't even get a good look at them. I'm not sure how I got away, actually."

"They were toying with you." He squeezed his eyes shut. Beneath my hands, his heart beat heavily. "You could've died, damn it. And I wouldn't have known until it was too late." His Adam's apple bobbed in a noisy swallow. "You could've died."

"But I didn't."

"So you kept on the move."

"I kept thinking they'd give up." I moved a shoulder in a helpless shrug. "I mean, how long were you going to wait around for me, anyway?"

"They would've never given up. To a vampire, you're prey, and they like to stalk their prey—especially the old ones, the vampires who've forgotten they were ever human. It's a fucking game to them."

A chill ran down my spine. I *had* felt like prey.

Outgunned and outsmarted every step of the way, like a mouse being toyed with by a cat.

Except it was multiple cats with unlimited resources at their disposal, and I was just a single poor, defenseless mouse.

Gabriel buried his face in my hair. "They would've never given up," he repeated in a raw voice. "Especially since they know that killing you would gut me. Because Mila? I would have waited for you forever. That part of me is all vampire. When we mate, it's for life."

My heart stumbled. My arms came tightly around him. "I *did* miss you. Every single fucking day. I knew it was a mistake almost as soon as I left. But then the threats started... I swear, if I could've come home, I would've."

"Gods," he gritted. "I could kill Mraz right now. And my father, too. I know he was behind this. Mraz doesn't make a move without his say-so."

I stroked his nape. I didn't know what to say, because he was probably right. I'd wondered myself if it had been Karoly Kral who'd sent the vampires to kill me.

It's why I'd been reluctant to tell Gabriel the whole story. Part of me had been afraid Gabriel wouldn't believe me, and the other part hadn't wanted to hurt him. Because if the primus was that against his son mating with me, where did that leave us?

"All right. All right." Gabriel dragged in a breath and pulled back to meet my eyes. "Promise me you won't run away. That you'll give me a chance to work this out. That you'll give *us* a chance. And

I don't mean because you accepted that thrice-damned blood bond."

I nodded. The lump in my throat had grown larger, but I knew he needed to hear the words.

"I promise," I said in ragged tones.

His gaze searched mine. Then he exhaled. "I'm going to hold you to that."

"I mean it. I swear."

"Okay." He gathered me close again. We clung to each other for a few seconds, and then he set me away. "Let's go rescue that brother of yours."

We reached Manhattan a little after nine a.m. and wended our way through the heavy traffic, Tomas behind us. A short while later, the blue sedan peeled off toward Central Park while we continued north to Gabriel's penthouse on the East River.

Tomas was going to stake out the building while Gabriel waited to hear from the Fagans.

My knee started jumping. I could barely sit still. I wanted to leap out of the car and race across town to Joey.

Gabriel set a hand on my knee, stilling it. "We'll get him back."

I threaded my fingers through his. "Yes." I refused to believe anything else.

Gabriel started speaking calmly, not saying much at all. Trying to soothe me.

And I appreciated it, even though it didn't work.

Outside my window, New York was going about its business. We passed a woman in a short pink skirt walking a shih tzu with a matching pink halter and leash. A man in a dark blue suit strode by, brief case in hand, and hailed a taxi.

Around 80th Street, Gabriel nodded at a high-rise on the river. "That's my building."

He'd explained earlier that he kept the top three floors for himself. He lived in the penthouse, and the two floors below housed his offices, a gym, and living space for his staff, including his Manhattan housekeeper. The lower five floors were rented to local businesses. For security purposes, Gabriel's three floors were separated from the bottom five floors and could only be reached by private elevator.

"You'll be guarded at all times," he informed me. "There are security cameras in all the main rooms, and I've already alerted my people that you'll be in the penthouse. Two guards will be on duty in the foyer."

I'd listened to most of this with only half a brain, but when he paused, I sent him an incredulous look. "You own the whole building?"

"Yeah." He headed down the ramp into the underground garage.

I blinked. Who the hell owned an entire Manhattan apartment building? "Just how rich are you?"

He lifted his shoulders, let them drop. "Fuck if I know. I'd have to ask my accountants."

I shook my head. "Vampires."

We took the elevator up to the penthouse. The foyer ran the length of the building and was lush with tropical plants lit by a trio of colored-glass skylights. Normally, I would've been all over it, but today I only spared a quick glance around.

Two uniformed vampires stood to one side of the elevator, hands clasped behind their back. When Gabriel nodded at them, the closer man dipped his chin.

"Everything's quiet, sir."

"Good. This is Camila," he said, addressing them both. "You're to treat her like she's the most precious thing in the goddamn world, understand? Anything happens to her, and I'll have your heads."

Their expressions didn't change. "You can count on us," the first man replied.

As we headed into the living room, Gabriel's phone buzzed. He glanced at the screen. "It's George Fagan."

I grabbed his arm. "Joey?"

"Yes." His grin all teeth. "He's there."

20

GABRIEL

I left Mila in the capable hands of Jessa, my scarily efficient Manhattan housekeeper, and headed back down the elevator. As I reached the parking garage, my burner phone buzzed. A string of nonsense letters and numbers preceded the message, identifying it as from my father.

Have evidence SI is holding Z.

So he'd confirmed that Slayers, Inc. was involved.

I stared at the screen. Why hadn't my father sprung Zaq? But I'd barely absorbed that when I received a second text.

Get rid of the woman.

My fingers clamped on the plastic case. Tomas had been busy.

I was about to return the phone to my pocket when a third text flashed onto the screen.

Or the deal is off.

The hell it was. A crimson-tinged fog clouded my vision, and blood hammered in my ears.

Because of my father's interference, I'd spent three years without Mila. Not only that, she'd almost died because I hadn't been there to protect her. It might even have been Father who'd sicced the vampires on her, although that wasn't his style. No, he'd have slit her throat instead and buried the body so deep I'd never have found her.

Still, it was his fault that Mila had been hunted like a goddamn animal.

And now he had the balls to order me to get rid of her?

I dropped my head back, stared at the elevator ceiling.

Disobey Father, and I could kiss goodbye any chance of ever being primus. Obey, and I'd lose Mila.

It wasn't even a choice. As the elevator door slid open, I jabbed out a text and hit *send*.

She stays.

I shoved the phone into my pocket and strode to my car.

Tomas and a small band of some of our best men waited under the trees in Central Park across from the building. Like me, they were dressed for action in dark T-shirts and tactical pants. Tomas stood at their center, watching me approach through mirrored sunglasses, his customary smile playing on his lips. His sensitive skin was shaded by a black fedora. Even his hands were protected by leather gloves.

My molars ground together. At that moment, I could've easily staked Tomas and walked away grinning. But I needed him to get Joey out. The lieutenant was a smart, no-holds-barred fighter and the men trusted him. Hell, I did, too—at least in this. Other than my brothers, there was no one I'd rather have at my back during a fight.

With him were two vampire enforcers who, like Tomas, were old and powerful enough to resist the day sleep. He'd also called in three dhampir soldiers and a couple of human grunts who did duty as chauffeurs.

George Fagan had texted me the building plans, and I'd forwarded them to Tomas. Meanwhile, Tomas had ordered a grunt to pose as a deliveryman to distract the doorman. An enforcer had slipped into the building with him, concealed in the shadow dimension, and raced through the building at lightning speed.

The grunt was reporting back as I arrived. He hadn't been past the foyer, but he confirmed that the doorman was a dhampir. "I saw his fangs."

"How many men are on duty in the foyer?" I asked.

"All I saw was a doorman. But he does duty as security—a big dude with scary eyes. No human would mess with him."

The vampire enforcer returned at that point, and Tomas dismissed both grunts to wait with the cars, saying, "Be ready to leave on a moment's notice."

The men nodded and jogged off.

The enforcer was bulked-up for a vampire, with hard black eyes in a broad face and a head shaved smooth as a billiard ball. He'd been forced to stick to the hall and the few rooms which happened to be open. Even in the shadow dimension, we have a physical form that's something like thick smoke, and we can't walk through walls.

"As far as I can tell," he said, "the apartments on the lower level are given to thralls."

"Their favorites," said Tomas.

"Or maybe it's a brothel for blood slaves," I said.

The enforcer nodded. "I definitely scented humans—maybe more than one—imprisoned in the basement. But the basement door was solid steel and locked down tight so I couldn't verify if it was the Vittore kid."

He proceeded to run down possible security issues, including the dhampir doorman, the placing of the security cameras on each floor, and the extra level of security for both the basement and the penthouse floor.

"The basement door can only be accessed by a security pad requiring iris recognition," he added. "Or a damn good security expert."

I raised my brows, impressed. "Good work. What's your name?"

He straightened to his full height. "Isaac Bajoie."

"From New Orleans?"

"Yes, sir."

"So Redbone is your kapitán?"

"He is." Bajoie's full lips pinched together like he'd tasted something bad.

"Speak," Tomas commanded.

"Redbone is inside. I sensed him." His gaze shifted back to me. "Be careful, sir. I'm not in his inner circle—not since I came to New York to work for your father—but I hear things. This is more than an unhappy kapitán. He's working with someone."

A growl emanated from Tomas's chest. "You should have reported this to me."

"Yes, sir."

I raised a hand, halting Tomas from rebuking him further. It was clear Bajoie had been torn between loyalty to my father and his kapitán.

"This person Redbone's working with. You have a name?"

"No. And that's the honest truth," he said with a glance at Tomas. "I swear on the Dark Mother herself."

I nodded. "You'll inform us immediately if you hear anything."

"That's a direct order," said Tomas.

"Understood." Bajoie seemed relieved at the order to inform on his kapitán. Redbone had clearly made at least one enemy in New Orleans.

I turned back to Tomas, and together, we worked out a plan. Tomas would enter the building on the pretext of a meeting with Redbone while the rest of us slipped in as shadows. Tomas would take out the doormen, and then we'd split into two groups. Me, Bajoie and two dhampirs would take the basement while Tomas and the others disabled the security cameras and remained in the foyer to fight off any attackers.

Unfortunately, we'd all have to take our physical forms, leaving us vulnerable.

Tomas gave me a dubious glance. "You are sure you can handle this? You lost much blood last night, and the silver must be causing pain to you."

I scowled. "I'm fine." I turned to the men. "For now, we're just there to get Vittore. A quick, surgical strike. Stay in the shadow dimension whenever possible. But if you see Redbone, stake him. The man's a traitor. I'm officially declaring open season on him. Any questions?"

These were professionals. There was little reaction except for a few eyes widening.

I jerked my chin at the building. "Let's do this, then."

We split into three groups. As the first men headed across the street, I pulled Tomas aside. "There's something you should know. Father has confirmed that the slayers are behind Zaq's kidnapping. We have to assume they're behind this, too."

Tomas nodded, unsurprised.

"You knew?"

He moved his broad shoulders in a shrug. "Karoly said not to tell you, but me, I think you should know. They worked Zaquiel over."

My stomach lurched. "Bad?"

Another shrug. "He will heal."

"So my dad knows where he is."

"Yes."

"So why the hell hasn't he busted him out? It's been a fucking week."

"Their security is as good as ours. Better. They allow nobody to see him but a couple of trusted people. If Karoly goes in before he's ready and fails, they will move Zaquiel—or kill him. They may be waiting for your father to do exactly that. Then we will lose them both."

I made a disgusted sound. "Gods."

Logically, my father was probably right to hold off, but my gut burned at the idea of Zaq at the mercy of Slayers, Inc. The people who called us monsters and dedicated their lives to stalking us.

It should be me, damn it, not my big-hearted younger brother. The kid who brought home injured birds and motherless kittens, even when my father sneered that he was too human.

The second group left while I silently cursed my father and his methodical way of working. As the men left the cover of the trees, they faded one by one into the shadow dimension, undetectable by even another vampire, until only me and Tomas were left.

I glanced across the street at the apartment building, anxious to get going. If I couldn't rescue my own brother, at least I could save Mila's.

Tomas raised a bushy blond brow. "You understand what this means?"

"That the slayers are probably gunning for me, too? That Redbone may even be working with them? Yeah. I understand. Now, let's get Vittore the fuck away from these bastards."

I stalked forward, slipping into the shadows as I left the trees. The physical world became soft and slightly out of focus, like walking through a fog at twilight. At my side, Tomas faded into the gray mist. One second he was there, the next he was gone, invisible even to me.

I crossed Fifth Avenue. The humans I passed looked right through me. They couldn't see me, and yet they moved out of my path, some primitive instinct warning them of the predator walking among them.

Tomas came out of the shadows to enter the building. He wrapped on the heavy walnut door. When the doorman opened it, he elbowed his way inside, barking, "Tell your kapitán that Lieutenant Mraz is here."

Still in the shadows, I slipped in behind through the door before it closed.

The dhampir's dark brows shot up. "He's taking his day sleep, sir."

Tomas's smile was dangerous. "Then wake him up."

"Yes, sir." The dhampir went behind the curved wood reception desk to pick up a phone. Tomas lunged over the desktop, shoving a silver dagger into his back and up into his heart. The doorman dropped to the marble floor.

While I let the rest of our men inside, Tomas coolly retrieved his dagger, wiping the blade clean on the staked dhampir's expensive black coat before leaving with his team to search the building for Redbone and the rest of his vampire nest.

Meanwhile, I turned to the basement. The door was solid steel and locked down in three different ways, including a silver band to repel any unwary vampires. Our security expert—another dhampir —was already disabling the security pad.

A minute crawled past.

I released the catch of my switchblade.

"Come on, baby," the dhampir muttered, and then gave a muted sound of triumph as the door swung open.

I led the way downstairs, followed by Bajoie and two dhampirs. The basement was a concrete-and-steel dungeon. No windows, and only a single forty-watt bulb for illumination.

I counted six doors, three of them open. Behind two of the locked doors, I sensed vampires. My gaze locked on the third door, where the scent of human was strong.

I started toward it, then halted, nape tingling. I spun around as a man materialized on the step behind me.

Andre Redbone, gold eyes shining in the gloom.

How had he found us so quickly? He should've been fast asleep. But there was no time to think about it.

Redbone lunged, fangs out. No knife or stake, and his only clothing was a pair of tight black pants.

A part of my mind registered that we'd caught him by surprise as I flung up my left arm to block him. Bajoie leapt to my aid, but I was already bringing my switchblade up with my right hand.

"He's mine," I snapped, and sensed rather than saw Bajoie fall back.

During our fight on the beach, Redbone had had the edge, but now the sun was fully above the horizon. Even a powerful vampire like him was slower, sleepier. This time, the playing field was even—

and all things being equal, I'd put my combat skills up against a vampire's any day.

With a feral grin, I twisted my hand and aimed an underhand blow at the unprotected spot right below his ribcage, drawing first blood. He jerked back, but not before I pressed it up toward his heart. I missed, but a dark stain bloomed on his abdomen, tinging the air with the scent of iron.

He swore and touched the wound, his confidence shaken. We eyed each other grimly. I feinted right and he lunged at me.

I was waiting. I punched the knifepoint into his chest, aiming a little to the left to pierce his heart. Blood spurted. I'd hit the widow-maker, the artery that carries fresh blood into the heart. Sever the artery, and the heart stops dead almost immediately.

But Redbone was strong. His hand clamped on mine.

"Half-breed bastard." His fangs glinted, sharp and white, in the dim light.

I thought of how he'd treated Mila—and shoved the blade deeper. "This half-breed," I snarled, "will see you in Hades."

His eyes glazed over, and then he slumped forward. I jerked out my blade and let him fall to the concrete.

"That was for Camila," I said as he stared up at me, dull-eyed. "And this is for me." I punched the blade into his chest a second time and watched as his skin blackened and began to crumble to ash.

As I cleaned the blade on Redbone's pants, Isaac Bajoie clapped me on the back. "Nice job, sir."

Yep, Bajoie definitely hadn't been a fan of his kapitán.

I grunted in acknowledgment and gestured at our security expert. "Open the damn door."

He lurched into motion. "Yes, sir."

As soon as he had it unlocked, I ordered the others to stand back in case it was a trap and went to open it, but Bajoie stepped forward. "Allow me."

The enforcer's expression was respectful. I understood he was volunteering himself as a guinea pig like a good second would.

I jerked my chin in assent, and he kicked open the door.

Joey Vittore was pressed against the opposite wall, hands clenched, his youthful face haggard. Fear came off him in waves.

The cell was pitch black. The bastards had kept him in the dark.

But he bravely raised his fists, baring his teeth. "Stay back."

Bajoie took a few steps inside and gave me a thumbs-up. "It's clear."

I was already moving forward. "It's me," I told Joey. "Gabriel Kral."

"Yeah?" he said without dropping his fists.

"We're here to take you home. Your sister Camila sent me."

He did a doubletake. "Gabriel? S'that you?" He blinked rapidly, and then lowered his fists and took a wobbly step forward. He grabbed my arm. "You're not a dream?"

"It's me." I urged him out the door. "I'll explain everything. But first, let's get the hell out of here."

He stumbled into the hall, then dug in his heels. His curly black hair was matted against his head and his pupils were enlarged as if he'd been drugged. Even the feeble hall light made him wince and put up a hand to shield his eyes.

My gaze locked on the bite wounds on his throat. The bastards had already started feeding on their new blood slave.

"What about Mila?" he asked hoarsely. "We have to help Mila."

"She's fine." I squeezed his arm. "I have her safe. It's over, Joey."

He passed a shaking hand over his face. "Okay. Okay."

"Let's go." I urged him forward again. "She's at my place, waiting."

"Thank God," he whispered. His eyes closed, and he swayed on his feet.

I grabbed him before he fell, and half-carried, half-walked him to the stairs. When he looked at the first step as if he didn't know what to do with it, I slung him over my shoulders in a fireman's carry and jogged up the steps while Bajoie and the two dhampirs took another look around the basement.

In the foyer, I set Joey on his feet again. "Can you walk?"

"Yeah." He pulled himself upright. "Sure."

I slid an arm around his waist anyway. "Lean on me."

As we reached the front door, Tomas appeared. "You go ahead with the boy. I'll stay here and help clean things up. Most of the vampires are still asleep, but we found locked rooms on several of the floors."

"Blood slaves," muttered Bajoie.

I hesitated, but until we were sure whom to trust, I didn't want to let Joey out of my sight. "All right. If they're holding blood slaves, take them to a safe house."

You couldn't just release a blood slave. If they'd become addicted to the high, they had to be weaned off the blood slowly, like any addict. Otherwise, the shock to their system could make them deathly ill.

Tomas lifted a brow. "Your father?"

My father didn't allow blood slaves in the Kral Coven, but he turned a blind eye to what the other covens did.

"I'll clear it with him. There are two vampires locked in the basement, too. Find out why." I waited for his nod and then jerked my chin at Bajoie. "You. Come with me."

"Yes, sir."

Outside, I deposited Joey in the front seat and handed him an orange juice. "Drink."

He obediently brought the bottle to his lips. The poor kid was parched. He drained the bottle in a couple of gulps.

Bajoie stood guard until we were both safely in the car, then inserted his large body in the car's tiny backseat. As I pulled into traffic, Joey finished the juice and slumped in his seat, eyes half-closed.

I glanced again at the bruises on his face and arms, and flashed on my brother, bruised but defiant, the silver chaining his wrists.

At least Joey's bruises weren't recent; he'd probably been roughed up the night he was kidnapped. Still, he'd clearly been drugged, and treated more like a dog than a human being. He smelled rank, and he'd obviously been wearing his Baltimore Rat T-shirt for the past week.

My jaw tightened. I wondered what the slayers would think if they could see how their vampire allies had treated Joey.

We were almost to my building when he roused himself. "Mila's all right?" he asked again. "She's with you?"

"She's fine, don't worry."

"You're sure?" His throat worked. "Those dicks said if I didn't cooperate, they'd hurt her."

"She's safe at my apartment. You'll be able to see for yourself in five minutes."

I pulled into the garage. Joey exited the car without any help, but Bajoie and I stepped up on either side just in case.

He glanced from the big enforcer to me. His eyes narrowed. "Kral," he spat out. "You—you're one of them." He turned and hobbled away as fast as he could.

I swore under my breath. Mila had kept the fact that I was a Kral from her family, but I'd assumed they'd eventually figured it out.

"Joey. I got you out of there, didn't I? Now come with me. Mila's waiting for you."

He leaned against a concrete wall, breathing heavily. "Prove it."

"Fine." I pulled out my phone. "Mila? Joey wants to say hi."

"Joey?" Her gasp was audible. "Where are you?"

He took the phone. "In a parking garage with two fucking vampires."

"Oh, God. I'm sor—"

I'd had enough. I nipped the phone from Joey's fingers. "We'll be right there." To him, I said, "Come," putting just enough compulsion in my tone to get him to obey, and wrapped an arm around his shoulder.

But he shook me off to walk the few feet to the elevator on his own. On the way up, he leaned against the elevator wall, chest heaving like an old man with emphysema.

Mila waited in the foyer. At the sight of her brother, she clapped her hands to her mouth.

"*Joey.* Ohmigod. You're safe." She darted into the elevator and threw her arms around him. "*You're safe.*"

I guided them out of the elevator and told Bajoie to go back to

Redbone's nest to help with the cleanup. "My own security can handle things from here."

"Yes, sir."

Mila still had her arms around her brother. As the elevator door closed behind the enforcer, she sent me a look over his shoulder. "Andre?"

I drew my finger across my throat.

"You're sure?"

"I staked him myself."

Her eyelids squeezed together. "Oh, God. Oh, God." She held out a hand to me, her dark eyes bright with tears. "I don't know why I'm crying," she said, sniffing. "But thank you. Thank you so much."

My heart constricted. Didn't she know I'd do anything for her?

I wrapped my fingers around hers. "He's your brother. That makes him family. But he's hungry—I'll tell Jessa to make him something to eat."

"Oh. Right." Mila sprang into action, seating Joey on the couch, getting him water, bringing him a plate of cheese and crackers while Jessa prepared something more substantial.

I made sure they had everything they needed, then sat on the opposite side of the room checking my texts so they could have some privacy.

After downing two glasses of water and the entire plate of cheese and crackers, Joey began to revive. Mila got up to show him to a spare bedroom where he could shower. They paused in the hall to mutter about me. They kept their voices low enough that I could've tuned them out, but fuck that. I needed to know what I was up against with Mila's family.

"He hasn't let you call Mom and Dad?" Joey demanded.

"They took away my phone. Not Gabriel. Andre Redbone."

"Like Gabriel couldn't have given you a new phone."

"It's...complicated."

"The hell it is," Joey said in a furious whisper. "Sounds like you're a prisoner, same as I was. Just because the man feeds you and sets you up in his pricy penthouse doesn't mean he's going to let you go."

"It was Redbone who had me kidnapped," she hissed back. "Remember?"

"Then you can leave whenever you want?"

A pause. "Well, no. But I don't want to. I—"

He made a disgusted sound. "For Chrissake, Mila. Would you listen to yourself?"

She blew out a breath. "Go take a shower. You need to eat, rest. Then we can talk."

"Fine. But we *will* talk about this. And if Kral won't let you leave, I'll stake the motherfucker myself."

"The hell you will. The man saved your life."

"To make points with you."

"You know what? We'll talk about this later when your head's clear."

"My head's fine," Joey gritted.

"I'll get you some clean clothes."

Mila was shaking her head when she came back into the living room. I kept my eyes on my phone.

She heaved a breath. "You heard that, didn't you?"

I moved a shoulder. "If you want to keep a conversation private around me, make sure you go into the bedroom and shut the door. Better yet, go into the bathroom and shut that door, too."

She sighed. "I have to tell him about the blood bond, but right now I don't think he could handle any more." She dropped onto the couch, slid me a look. "You *are* going to let me contact my mom and dad, aren't you?"

I scowled. Because part of me didn't want her to contact her parents. If I lost her now, it would gut me.

She accepted the blood bond, my darker half growled. *That's forever. Only you can break it now.*

To save her brother, returned my other half. *Force her to honor the bond, and you really are the monster the slayers say you are.*

Mila's face fell. "Never mind." She jumped up again.

"No, wait." I pulled up the Vittore's number on my phone and handed it to her.

Because trust had to begin somewhere.

A tiny crease appeared between her eyes. She looked from the phone to me like there might be a catch.

"Go ahead." I closed her fingers around the case. "Text your mom and dad. Just basic information, though—that Joey is with you, and you're both safe. It's for their safety as much as yours. And tell them Joey will be home tomorrow afternoon. I'll send him in one of the limos."

Her mouth quirked. "He'll like that." She sat back down and snuggled into me, legs folded to the side. "I do love you, Gabriel. In case you're wondering."

My heart punched in my chest. I'd thought she'd never say those words again—or that when she did, I'd believe her.

I stared at her, arrested.

She slanted me a shy sideways smile, then bent her head and tapped out a message to her parents.

21

MILA

In the time it took Joey to shower, Jessa not only produced a pair of shorts and a couple of T-shirts in his size, she prepared a breakfast of eggs, bacon and home fries.

Gabriel had gone to his study to work, so me and Joey were alone at the dining room's rustic slate table. The T-shirt hung on my brother's too-skinny frame, and under his dark scruff, I saw fading bruises. But it was the puncture wounds that made my stomach clench.

He's okay. And Andre's dead, a heap of ashes and bones.

It was still sinking in that everything really was okay. Just yesterday, I'd been trapped in a nightmare, blood-bonded to a man who didn't trust me and sure I was going to lose either Joey or Gabriel, or both.

My brother finished his breakfast and eyed my plate. "You going to eat the rest of your bacon?"

The tears took me by surprise. How many times had Joey asked that when we were both teenagers?

"It's yours—all of it." Swiping the tears away, I handed him the plate. "I missed you, squirt."

He stopped eating long enough to reach across the table and squeeze my hand. "Back at you, Mila-Bila."

Jessa appeared at my elbow with a coffee pot. About my age, the housekeeper had a frizzy red topknot and a body that was all muscle. In her free time, she was either a runner or gym rat, or both.

"More coffee?" she asked.

I cast her a grateful look. "Please."

While Joey finished my breakfast, I sipped coffee and peppered him with questions. I was hungry for any news—him, my parents, Nonna, our cousins.

Nonna had taken a trip to Italy and enjoyed seeing all her old friends so much she'd almost stayed for good, but she was back in Baltimore now. Cousin Sara was married with a baby on the way. As for Joey, he was partway through a chemical engineering degree.

But Mom and Dad were just going through the motions, not sure if I was dead or alive. "It's like you dropped off the face of the earth," Joey said. "They reported it to the police, hired a private detective to look for you." He didn't tell me again that I should call them, but his disapproval weighed like a thundercloud in the air between us.

My throat clogged. "I'm sorry," I managed to say. "But I did it for them. They threatened you, Joey. All of you."

His jaw set. "The private eye said they should give up—that you were probably dead."

My stomach turned over. "Oh, God. I didn't think—I mean, I left a note."

"Yeah. But who knew what happened after that? You couldn't even send us a fucking Christmas card?"

I glanced at the kitchen where Jessa was polishing the stainless steel refrigerator, and lowered my voice. "I was afraid to."

"Whatever." Joey shoved back his chair and rose to his feet. "I'm going to bed. Jessa said I could sleep in that room where I took the shower."

"That's right." The housekeeper stopped working long enough to flash him a professional smile. Polite but no real warmth. "The bed's made up and I put fresh towels in the bathroom."

"Thank you." Joey turned to leave, then hesitated. "You sure you're okay?"

"Of course, I am. I'll be right here when you wake up."

"Okay." He dragged a hand down his face. "I'm too tired right now to ask what the fuck is up with you and Kral. You can tell me when I get up."

My mouth dropped open. Since when did I have to explain myself to my kid brother?

"What?"

"You heard me." He was already out of the dining room.

I was tired, too, but I couldn't sleep, so I went exploring instead.

The penthouse's main rooms were on an open plan, with high ceilings and jewel-toned skylights that let in muted sunlight. The kitchen flowed into the dining room, which flowed into the living room, where a wall of smoked-glass windows overlooked the East River. Like the foyer, the living room was filled with tropical plants and potted flowers.

This, I thought, was Gabriel's real home, not the beach house. A large, cozy cave, with slate floors and rough wood walls, some painted black, others left unpainted. Edison light bulbs hung from rustic bronze fixtures, and the furniture was a mix of more slate and bronze, with the chairs and couch covered in earthy reds and oranges. The paintings were large, slashing abstracts, and one wall held built-in shelves spilling over with books, games and primitive stone statues.

The place was spotless. I was almost afraid to touch anything in case Jessa went batshit crazy on me. Something about her made me uneasy.

I mean, who irons socks and underwear? But earlier, when I'd glanced into the utility room off the kitchen, she'd been pressing Gabriel's T-shirts, and on the counter next to her was a stack of freshly-ironed socks.

The master bedroom was on the opposite side of the apartment from the kitchen, along with the two guest bedrooms. Gabriel was still in the study next to the master bedroom, but Joey's door was ajar, so I peeked in.

He was face down on the mattress, arms and legs by his sides like a felled log. His upper body was bare, the sheet pulled up around his narrow waist.

My chest squeezed. He'd slept like that when he was a kid, too. He'd go-go-go like a maniac all day, and then when night came, drop into bed like someone had cut his strings.

My fingers tightened on the doorjamb. He was safe. That's what mattered.

I backed out of the room and glanced at the closed study door. But I could hear Gabriel on the phone, so I returned to the living room and stood at the windows, gazing down at the East River through the darkened glass.

The summer sun refracted off the water in glittering shards, and kayaks and sailboats vied for space with tourist-heavy cruise boats circling the island of Manhattan. They seemed so far away, so distant. I wondered if that was how vampires felt, observing humans...like we were creatures from another planet.

A brush on my nape was the only warning that Gabriel emerged from his study. A shiver went up my spine, a good shiver. I smiled and turned to face him.

He stared back, unsmiling. He'd showered and changed into a fresh T-shirt and pants. He smelled clean, male.

"You can't go outside," he said. "We still don't know who sent those vampires after you. But my guess is this is bigger than just Redbone and his nest."

"That's okay. I don't want to leave Joey anyway. But—" I hesitated, biting my lip, but I had to ask. "It couldn't have been your dad, could it? I mean, he's the one who sent me away."

"I've been asking myself that. But it's not his style. He may not be all warm and fuzzy, but he wouldn't have toyed with you like that. He would've just ordered the hit and been done with it."

Goose bumps prickled my skin. I rubbed my arms. "Right."

"I *will* talk to him," Gabriel promised grimly. "But he's...away right now." Something in his face warned me not to ask questions. "Here." He pressed a cell phone into my hand. "I want you to have this. I put my phone number in it. I have to go out again, but you can use the phone to call your mom and dad if you want. It's a burner phone—it can't be traced."

"Thank you." I rose on my toes to kiss him.

He touched my face. "I have to get back to the building to help with the cleanup, and then I have to head down to the syndicate's building in the Village. With my father out of town, I'm working double-duty right now."

"Okay."

I must have looked disappointed, because he tugged on a curl that had escaped my bun. "You and Joey will be fine. I'm leaving a couple of guards to watch over you two."

"It's not that. It's just I thought we could spend the afternoon together."

"Not today." He smoothed his thumb and forefinger down the curl. "You probably won't even see the guards; one's in the foyer where the elevator lets out, and the other's keeping an eye on the service staircase. It's off the utility room." He nodded at the kitchen. "They've been told that no one other than Jessa is allowed on this floor. But I thought you'd feel better if you had a phone, too. I loaded the app for my security system on it."

Taking the phone back, he showed me how the app worked, including the panic button that would call the guards and another button to alert him.

"If you need Jessa," he said as he returned it to me, "she'll be on the floor below in her apartment. There's an intercom in the kitchen." He lifted my chin with the edge of his fist and studied me with unreadable eyes. "We'll talk tonight, okay?"

My heart jittered. Something was wrong. "About what?"

"Where we go from here, for one thing."

Oh. I nodded. "All right."

He gave me a hard, open-mouthed kiss, then strode out of the room.

As the elevator doors closed behind him, I felt a surge of panic. I took a deep breath and glanced down at the phone.

Gabriel was right, I felt safer having it with me. But we both knew he hadn't just given it to me because of that.

Even more than the stiletto, it was a sign of good faith. I wasn't a prisoner anymore.

So what was the problem?

Uneasy wings fluttered in my stomach. I shook it off to consider the phone. I wanted to call my mom and dad, but after my talk with Joey, I wasn't sure I could deal with their questions.

Later, I thought. When I wasn't so tired.

I curled up on the couch and fell asleep.

※

When I woke up, Joey was rummaging in the kitchen for a soda. Whatever they'd drugged him with seemed to have worn off. His eyes were clear, and he had some of his old energy back. We ate a late lunch together, then went into the living room.

I sat on the couch while he moved restlessly around the room: fiddling with the sound system, picking things up and putting them down, staring out the window at the river.

I blew out a breath. "Joey, please—sit down. I know it's hard, but Gabriel wants us to stay put for today."

"Right." He sneered. "And he's the boss, I guess. Where the fuck is he, anyway?"

"He went back to the vampire nest to help with cleanup, and then he had to work. And it's for our own safety. You know that."

He just shook his head, then flopped onto the couch opposite me. "So. You said at breakfast that you worked on an organic farm?"

We spent the next hour catching up. When I'd left, he'd been a high school senior, and now he was three years into an engineering degree.

"I have to work my ass off," he said, "but I figure it will be worth it." His face fell. "I have an internship at a chemical company this summer. I just hope they'll take me back after all this."

"Gabriel will talk to them for you."

"No." His mouth flattened. "I'll handle it myself."

I jerked a shoulder. "Suit yourself."

An awkward silence fell until Joey jumped up again. "Let's play rummy. He must have a deck of cards around here somewhere."

We found a couple of decks in a cupboard and played a game of gin rummy to five hundred points. Joey won, as usual.

He grinned as he gathered up the cards. "I still got it."

I tossed my pencil at him. He snatched it out of the air and tucked it behind his ear.

"You got it, all right," I retorted. "A big fat ego."

He chuckled, and then sobered. "Mila." He shuffled the deck and set it on the coffee table. "Come home with me. Mom and Dad —you broke their hearts, leaving like that. You need to make it right with them. And what the fuck was that money for?"

"You didn't use it?"

"Are you kidding? The only thing Mom and Dad used it for was to pay the guy searching for you. There's something like $25K left."

"Tell them to use it, please. I won't need it now."

"No way. Mom put your name on the account. All you have to do is show some ID and it's yours."

"Joey." I passed a hand over my eyes. "Don't you understand? It's done. I'm with Gabriel now. But I *will* make it right with Mom and Dad—I just have to talk to Gabriel first."

"So you *are* a prisoner."

"No!" I drew a slow breath, made myself answer calmly. "I told you, we're together now. But I can't just up and leave."

"For Chrissake, Mila." He plowed a hand through his dark curls. "What's wrong with you? If you don't care about me, what about Mom and Dad? And Nonna—you know you're her favorite. She still says a rosary for you every night."

My stomach lurched. "I'm sorry I left that way. But I didn't have a choice—I had to get right away."

"But why?"

"Because I fell in love with a dhampir, damn it. And not just any dhampir—Gabriel Kral, heir to the Kral Syndicate. Karoly Kral was *not* happy that his son was in love with a human. And later, when I thought I might be able to come home, I was told to stay gone—or they'd come for you guys next."

"Those motherfuckers." Joey shot to his feet. "That's it. We're out of here—*now*."

He lunged around the coffee table and grabbed my arm.

"No!" I dug in my heels. "You don't understand."

"The hell I don't." He dragged me toward the hall.

"*Listen to me.*" I shoved my face into his. "I don't *want* to leave."

The guard stationed in the foyer planted himself in front of us. "Miss? Is everything all right?"

Joey growled at the guard, but the man stared back coldly.

"We're fine," I hurried to say. "My brother's just upset about..." I trailed off. "Everything's fine. Really."

The vampire narrowed his eyes at Joey. "Dial it down," he suggested in a hard voice. "I don't care if you're her brother, this is Prince Gabriel's woman and our orders are to keep her safe."

Joey's hands fisted at his side, but a look of shame crossed his face. "Sorry," he muttered to me.

With a curt nod at us both, the guard returned to the foyer.

"Jesus," Joey said. "Let's go somewhere private, all right?" Without waiting for an answer, he headed down the hall to his bedroom.

I sighed and followed. The instant the door shut, Joey took my hands.

"You see what it will be like if you stay. Come home, damn it. If Gabriel is such a good guy, he won't stop you."

"You're still not listening." I pulled my hands from his. "*I love him.* And besides, we have...an agreement."

His mouth thinned. "What kind of agreement?"

My stomach tightened. Blood bonds didn't have a good rep in the human world. But he had to know, and so did my parents.

"I accepted his blood bond." I was careful not to say when and why, because if my brother realized I'd accepted the bond to save him, he'd go ballistic.

"You're his *thrall?*" Joey sank onto the edge of the bed.

I wrapped my arms around myself. "It's not like that. A blood bond is more than just a thrall contract. And besides, I want to stay. I never wanted to leave in the first place."

Joey's lip curled. "How do you know he's not compelling you?"

"Because he swore he wouldn't—not ever—and I believe him."

"Vampires will lie through their teeth if it gets them what they want."

My chin jutted. "Not Gabriel. He loves me."

"You really drank the Kool-Aid, didn't you?" He shook his head. "A vampire or dhampir—or whatever the fuck he is—doesn't give crap about humans like you and me."

"He rescued you, remember? When he was hurt himself. Those bastards attacked us last night. He almost died, but this morning he dragged himself out of bed to save your ungrateful ass."

"Hell." My brother dropped his head into his hands. His thin shoulders heaved. "So you're not coming home with me tomorrow?"

"No. Soon, though." I hoped. I wasn't sure exactly how a blood bond worked, but Gabriel's mom didn't seem to be a prisoner.

She's Karoly's mate, not his blood-bonded thrall, countered an uneasy little voice.

Still, Gabriel had said he loved me, that three years ago, he'd intended to ask me to be his mate. Maybe that was even what he wanted to talk about tonight.

"I don't like it," Joey said, but he sounded resigned. "And Mom and Dad won't either when they hear why you left. We're a family, and families are there for each other."

"I know." I sat down and bumped him with my shoulder. "I love you, squirt."

He heaved a breath and wrapped a wiry arm around me. "Love you, too."

❧ 22 ❧

GABRIEL

After leaving Mila, I returned to Redbone's Fifth Avenue nest. Tomas had left to take his day sleep, leaving Isaac Bajoie in charge, but I wanted to make it clear to the surviving vampires that Redbone had been a traitor, possibly even working with the slayers to engineer a coup against my father.

Five of the nest had been sent to their final grave during the Montauk attack, but that left another half-dozen still in Manhattan. The two youngest had slept through the commotion, but by the time I'd arrived the four older ones were standing around in the penthouse salon, sizing each other up.

The jockeying for kapitán had already begun. The coven had the right to select their own leader, but until they did, I wanted someone I trusted in charge.

Brenda, the owner of the building, sidled up to me. "Prince Gabriel." A long-legged blond vampire, she was hot as hell and she knew it. She slicked the tip of her tongue over full red lips. "I hear you were the one who sent the kapitán to his final death."

"That's right." I eyed the wolf tattoo on the side of her neck. She'd recently made enforcer. "Congratulations on your promotion."

"Mm." Leaning closer, she traced a finger down her neck and

into her cleavage where her soft white breasts were displayed to full advantage by her skimpy purple dress.

She was either trying to seduce me, or get close enough to stab me with the dagger I was sure she had strapped to her thigh. Either way, I wasn't in the mood for games. I took her by the shoulders and set her back a few feet.

"Enough. I'm here as the primus's representative. Gather the rest of your nest and have them meet me here in ten minutes."

A slow blink of crystal-blue eyes. "Even the sleepers?"

"Yes. Unless they're too young to be awakened, I want everyone in the salon ASAP, including Isaac Bajoie." The other enforcer was on a lower floor, ensuring the safe removal of the enslaved humans.

When she still lingered, I showed my fangs. "*Now*, Enforcer."

She straightened. The pout left her lips and I saw the lethal vampire who was the real Brenda. "Yes, sir."

When the group was assembled—four men and two women—I brought them up to date in a few pithy sentences. "Kapitán Redbone was staked for attacking me. Not only that, he kidnapped my woman and her brother. This entire nest is now under the primus's control."

I sent a hard look around me, daring them to argue. The vampires stared back with expressions varying from respect to sneers, but no one spoke.

"Isaac Bajoie is now the coven's acting kapitán," I added. "The nests in Louisiana are being informed as we speak."

Per tradition, the challenges would take place at the main coven nest just outside of New Orleans, and I had a feeling that Bajoie would toss his hat into the ring.

Bajoie was standing a little to my left. He blinked, then squared his shoulders. "Thank you, sir."

"Where's the primus?" one of the older men dared to ask.

I moved forward, got right in his face. "Taking care of business. That's all you need to know."

Bajoie ranged himself at my side, backing me up. The man looked from him to me and gave a curt nod.

"And," I added, my eyes still trained on the vampire who'd

spoken, "this nest is being punished. Your blood slaves are being transferred to a rehab facility as we speak. You will drink only from paid thralls for the next decade, or I will personally see that you all join your kapitán in the final death."

They didn't like that. But no one had the balls to openly defy me.

I jerked my chin at Bajoie. "Confine them all to the basement for the thirty days. They're to be fed only once a week—and no fresh blood. Only blood-wine."

Let them see what it felt like to be locked in a cell with barely enough nourishment to survive.

That settled, I left Bajoie to finish up and headed to Syndicate headquarters. Something was niggling at me. Logic said that Andre Redbone had been the mole. He wasn't part of the inner circle, but as a kapitán, he had the kind of access that might have allowed him to circumvent our security.

And yet, it didn't quite add up...

I worked through the afternoon, tapping into our ultra-secure network to try to prove or disprove that Redbone had been the mole, but came up empty-handed. I even risked a text to my father, informing him that Redbone was a traitor and had been eliminated, but that I hadn't yet determined if he was our mole.

Father didn't reply, but then, I hadn't really expected him to.

Dinner came and went. I was avoiding my talk with Mila, and I knew it.

I got up from my desk and stretched—and stifled a groan. My body had taken a beating these past twenty-four hours. The wounds had pretty much healed, but the silver poisoning had left me stiff and aching.

And I was craving blood again. Even three glasses of blood-wine and the thick slab of rare filet mignon I'd had for dinner had barely taken the edge off. I could've called for a Syndicate thrall, but I wanted Mila.

The phone rang. I tensed, but it was only my mother.

"Mom? What's up?" I put her on speakerphone and sat on the edge of the desk.

"Not much," Mom replied. "Just that my oldest son was nearly staked last night and *he hasn't even called me.*"

I snatched up the phone and turned off the speaker. "Where'd you hear that?"

"Wrong answer," was the grim reply.

I sighed. "I didn't want to upset you, all right? You have enough to worry about right now."

I heard her teeth snap together. "Still the wrong answer."

"I'm sorry, okay? It was Andre Redbone. But I survived, and he's no longer a problem. I sent him to his final death myself."

"Andre?" She sucked in a breath. "That low-down, dirty *fils-putain*. He's been to our house, drunk my wine. Told me how much he admired my damn flowers. He even promised your father to support you if it comes to a challenge."

With each sentence, her voice got louder until I had to hold the phone away from my ear.

"He lied," I said flatly when she finally paused for breath. "Anyway, during the attack, I found out he'd kidnapped Mila's brother."

A short silence. "So that's why she came back."

"Yeah." I brought Mom up to date on everything that had happened since last night, up to and including Joey's rescue. "The pricks locked him in a dark cell for a week. Kept him drugged, too, so he wouldn't give them any trouble. A twenty-one-year-old kid."

"That poor boy. He's all right? And Mila, too?"

"They're fine, just shook up. Redbone didn't physically hurt Mila, but he fucked with her mind pretty bad." I rose to my feet, paced across my office. "I'm not going to let her go, Mom. I...can't."

"You really do love her."

I closed my eyes. "Yeah." My voice hardened. "She told me what you did, that you invited her to the house and tried to scare her off."

"Is that what she said?"

"No," I admitted. "She thought you were genuinely concerned, that you just wanted her to know what life with me would be like. But you had no right to do that. No right at all."

"She had a right to know, Gabriel. Your father had to fight his own people for years because they thought I made him weak, and then he had to break heads all over again to get them to accept you and your brothers as his heirs."

My fingers clenched on the phone. I drew a slow inhale through my teeth. "D'you know the hell you put me through these past three years?"

Her voice softened. "I'm sorry about that. I know you missed her. But if she was that easy to scare off, maybe you're better off without her."

"It wasn't only that. Father sicced Tomas on her. Told her that if she didn't leave, her family would be next. And they didn't stop there." My tone was bitter. "She's had Kral enforcers after her ever since she left. I'm pretty sure he didn't want to kill her—just keep her scared and on the run."

Because if Karoly Kral had actually wanted Mila dead, she would be.

Mom's swallow was audible. "I didn't know."

"Yeah," I said grimly. "It's one thing to chase her away. But they hounded her, told her that if she came back to Maryland, they'd target her family next. She was afraid even to contact her parents, and she lived in fucking roach-infested apartments because she couldn't keep a job long enough to make any money."

"Oh, cher."

"In fact, Father contacted me earlier. Told me to give Mila the boot, or else."

"And I suppose you told him to go to Hades."

"You bet I did."

She blew out a breath. "If you two could only see how much you're alike..."

My spine stiffened. "The hell we are."

"Mm," she said noncommittally, and changed the subject. "You want to mate with Mila, don't you?"

My brows lifted. Trust my mom to cut to the heart of the matter. I'd barely admitted that to myself. "Yes."

"Oh, Gabriel." She sounded sad. "Have you thought this through? At least your father could argue that you and your brothers were half-vampire. If you have children with Mila, they'll be three-quarters human. They might not even be able to drink blood."

I growled. "You think I don't know that?"

A long pause. "Or, you could turn her."

My heart lurched with a mix of trepidation and hope. "To dhampir?"

It had been at the back of my mind all day. But it was too risky. Only half the humans who attempted the transition to dhampir made it. The rest died a painful death.

"Unless she'd let you turn her to vampire."

I expelled a breath. "She can barely stand to be in the same room as a vampire."

"And she's young," Mom murmured. "She'll want kids. As a dhampir, she'd have an easier time getting pregnant than she would as a vampire. Plus, she'd be able to have more than one."

"I know. But I can't lose her again. Not a second time."

"Then set her free."

I scraped a hand down my face. "I can't."

"You don't know what you'd be asking, Gabriel. I went through it. You didn't."

Mom was right; I hadn't gone through it. But I remembered when she had—and I never wanted to go through anything like that again.

"And my transition came later," she added, quiet but relentless. "I was a good twenty years older than Mila is now. I'd had a chance to live, to raise you boys. Not that I was ready to die, but Mila—she's what, twenty-five? Her life is just beginning."

"You don't know her," I countered. "She changed, those three years she was gone. You should've seen her last night. She staked Stefan herself, and if not for her, Andre might've drained me until I was too weak to fight him off."

"She's strong, then. That's good. She'd have a good chance of making it through the metamorphosis."

"But what if she dies?" My voice cracked on the last word.

"Then set her free," Mom repeated. "Because if you don't, you might as well put her in a cage. You won't be able to guarantee her safety otherwise."

Mila, in a cage? I might as well clip the wings of a wild woodland bird.

"There has to be another option." I was gripping the phone too tight. I forced my fingers to loosen. "I can't lose her, Mom. Not this time."

"Oh, cher. The way things are in the syndicate right now, you may not have a choice. If you don't lose her to the transition, you'll lose her to another Andre Redbone."

"You think I don't know that?"

"I guess you do." Mom heaved a breath. "This is getting us nowhere. But whatever you decide, I want you to know you have my full support. Make sure you tell Mila that, too."

"I will. And Mom? Thanks for listening. It...helps. I love you."

"Love you, too," she said, and ended the call.

Shoving my hands into my front pockets, I stared at the floor. Turning Mila to a dhampir was the obvious solution. My father could hardly object to our mating when his own mate was a human-turned-dhampir.

But for a human, the transition to dhampir was a difficult, dangerous thing, with only a fifty/fifty chance of survival. Mila would have to drink a vampire's blood while still fully alive. The vampire couldn't bring her to near-death as happened when making another vampire.

My mother's transition had been harrowing. After she'd drunk my father's blood, he'd locked himself in a room with her while she'd undergone a painful, hours-long metamorphosis.

I dug the heels of my hands into my eyes, stomach churning.

My brothers and I hadn't witnessed the metamorphosis, but we'd had to listen to Mom's screams until Father finally emerged from the room with her unconscious in his arms. Together, we'd buried her in the dirt. No coffin, or she might not have been able to claw her way out once she came back to life.

For the next seven days, the four of us had stood vigil over my mother's grave, not knowing if she'd live or die. Like a virus, no one could predict if the metamorphosis would be fatal, or result in the birth of a dhampir.

I'd sworn I'd never ask anyone to go through that for me. I'd be smarter than my dad, choose a vampire mate. After all, as the Kral crown prince I had my pick of beautiful vampire females.

Then I'd met Mila.

Bile filled my throat. Gods, I'd been selfish.

But from the moment I'd seen Mila hovering like some faerie creature at the edge of my mother's garden, I'd known I had to have her—and I'd pursued her with a single-minded ruthlessness that few women could've resisted.

I turned back to my desk, but I'd had my fill of work for the day. I sent Mila a quick text to say I was on my way back to the penthouse, then leaned over to sign off my PC.

An encrypted message from Tomas popped up on the screen.

Need to see you ASAP. You are still in the office?

I sank into my chair, dropped my hands into my head. Gods, the last thing I wanted right now was to deal with my father's grinning lieutenant.

But I replied in the affirmative and sat back to await his arrival.

23

MILA

After dinner, Joey and I watched an old Godzilla movie. Jessa had cleaned up and left us alone in the penthouse, so we made our own popcorn and sat on the couch, laughing as the monster stomped its way through a toy-like cityscape. By the end of the movie, Joey was slumped on the couch, lids drooping. As the credits rolled, he stood up and with a bone-cracking stretch, announced he was going to bed.

"Okay." I followed him down the hall to his room, reluctant to let him out of my sight even though I knew he was safe now.

"G'night." He opened his arms and I went into them. He was bigger than when I'd left. Maybe an inch taller, but his shoulders had broadened.

My baby brother had turned into a man.

I bit my lip, trying not to get weepy. "Guess I can't call you squirt anymore."

He snorted. "Like anything could stop you." His arms tightened on me. "Pleasant dreams," he said, just like Mom had every night when we were kids.

I hugged him back. "Pleasant dreams."

Gabriel still hadn't returned. I peeked in the master bedroom, on the opposite side of the study from Joey's room, and sucked in a breath. It was the most romantic bedroom I'd ever been in.

Creamy walls reached to a ceiling that sloped inward at the top, so that it felt like I'd stepped into a billowing tent. The vintage bronze bed had four posts topped with a curved canopy draped with off-white linens. The windows were covered with soft, light-filtering cellular blinds, with more linen swags draped over rods at the top. On one wall hung an enormous antiqued-gold mirror, and the rustic wood night-stands held small gold lamps, their metal shades punched out with stars.

The bathroom was all warm terra cotta tiles in browns and golds and greens. The tub was a long cream rectangle and the glass shower stall was shaped like a circle with a rainfall showerhead. Set in the ceiling was a smoky green skylight so you could look up at the Manhattan skyline.

But before I took a shower, there was something I had to do. I sat cross-legged on the bed and took out my new phone.

I stared down at the screen. I still hadn't called my parents, but that was cowardly. Mom and Dad didn't deserve that. And it had been so long since I talked to them. I ached to hear their voices.

I pulled up the keypad and entered Mom's number.

She answered immediately. "Hello?"

I wasn't prepared for the rush of tears at the sound of her voice. I brought my hand to my eyes, dragged in a breath.

"Mom?" I whispered.

A heartbeat passed and then she gasped. "Mila?" Her voice hitched. "Is that you?"

"Yes," I managed to say. "Yes, it's me."

"Ohmigod. Chris! Chris—come here. It's Mila."

She put the phone on speaker, and then the two of us were sobbing while Dad kept saying, "You're all right? D'you need anything?"

"No, no." I sniffed and reached for a tissue. "I'm fine. Just happy. It's so good to hear your voices."

"We've been right here," was my dad's gruff reply. "It's you who left and never got in touch."

My stomach twisted. "I know. I'm so sorry. But I was afraid that if I had any contact with you, they'd hurt you."

"Damn it, Mila."

"No, listen."

We spoke for over an hour while I did my best to explain everything that had happened from the day I'd left. I glossed over the bad parts of my three years on the run, but I could tell they were hurt that I hadn't come to them for help. Like Joey, they couldn't seem to understand that I'd done it to protect them.

Still, they were my parents. Warm, loving. They forgave me.

At the end, my dad said, "Well, as long as you're happy, Camila."

"I am," I said. "I love him."

"Then we'll love him, too," Mom stated firmly.

Tears welled in my eyes again. "I know you will."

"So?" Dad asked. "When are you coming home? Your mom misses you."

"Soon," I said. "I promise."

My dad grunted.

"Can we call you at this number?" Mom asked.

"Yes. Absolutely."

A text from Gabriel popped up, saying he was on his way back to the penthouse.

"I have to go now," I told them. "But I'll call you tomorrow, okay?"

"Love you," said Mom.

Tears pricked my eyes again. "Love you, too," I said and ended the call.

24

GABRIEL

Tomas's smile was triumphant as he strode through my door. "We have found her. The slayer."

I rose from my chair. "Who?"

"Lougenia."

My stomach dropped. "No. I don't believe it."

"We have the proof."

"Then there's some mistake. There's no fucking way Lougenia is a slayer. She practically grew up with my mom. Her mother works for the Fortier family in New Orleans."

"Her family members also work for Redbone's coven. Here." Tomas shoved his phone across the desk at me. "See for yourself."

I scrolled through the evidence. A photo of Lougenia speaking to Stefan on the streets of Manhattan. An encoded message from her phone to Redbone, dated a month ago. A large payment to an offshore account that Tomas had traced to Lougenia's younger son.

"We have a mole. Trust no one."

I pinched the bridge of my nose. Alone, no one thing was conclusive, but taken together, they were definitely suspicious.

I handed the phone back to Tomas. "I agree, it doesn't look good. But any of this could've been planted. And Lougenia's never even been to headquarters—she wouldn't have the kind of access that whoever is behind this has."

"But she could be helping them. I will look into it," Tomas said with a decisive nod.

"No." I was damned if I'd let him question Lougenia. People had a way of ending up dead when Tomas was involved. "I can handle it from here."

The big man folded his arms over his chest. "Your father asked for me to take care of her."

I leveled a stare at him. "No," I repeated. "My housekeeper, my problem."

A shrug. "He contacted me. We talk of many things. He has heard about you and Redbone, and he is not happy about this thing with Mila."

"I know," I said shortly.

But Tomas wasn't finished. "He says that if you keep the woman, he will strip your title and rank, and name one of your brothers as the heir."

I scowled. "The hell you say."

Trust my father to up the stakes. Not only was he going to renege on the deal to promote me to oversee the southeastern covens, he was going to strip me of my position as crown prince. And probably demote me from enforcer back to soldier.

My stomach burned. I'd earned that promotion, and my designation as an enforcer. But if Mila was the price, then he could take his threats and choke on them.

Mila was staying. That was non-negotiable.

"Let him try," I shot back. "Zaquiel doesn't want it, and Rafe won't do the job I can. He's a tracker, not a businessman."

"As you say."

Tomas was being too agreeable. A terrible suspicion tightened my chest.

My switchblade jumped into my hand. I leapt over the desktop. Tomas took a step back, but didn't try to evade me.

I touched the silver point to his throat.

"Touch Camila Vittore," I said, low and deadly, "and you won't live to see another moonrise. I'll stake you myself. I don't care what your fucking orders are."

Tomas's hazel eyes narrowed to cat-slits. "You are the ass."

"Yeah, you already told me that. But Camila is *mine*. Stay the fuck away from her or I'll carve your heart out."

A curt nod. "But *I* will handle Lougenia—Karoly's orders."

I released him. "Agreed." I didn't like it, but Father was the primus. "But only to question her. None of this is proof that Lougenia's a slayer. It's not even proof she's working for them. Until I get to the bottom of this, you're to treat her like she's your own goddamned mother, understand?"

Disdain flickered over Tomas's broad face. I could almost hear him thinking: *Spineless half-breed.*

After all, the housekeeper was merely a human, and a servant at that.

And we both knew that at the first opportunity, he'd report my deficiencies—in detail—to my father. Well, fuck them both. I refused to condemn Lougenia without a fair hearing. If that made me weak, then so be it.

And I was damned if I'd give up Mila *or* let my father strip me of my rank. I might have been born the crown prince, but I'd more than proved myself over the years.

Tomas's mouth twitched up in an insolent curve. "We are done here?"

I jerked my chin in assent.

"I will leave for Montauk, then." He turned on his heel and left.

I stared after him, going over the conversation in my mind. But although Tomas had nodded when I told him to stay away from Mila, he hadn't actually agreed not to touch her.

Holy Dark Mother.

Fear sank icy claws into my nape. My father wouldn't dare set Tomas on Mila. Would he?

But he had three years ago. What made this time any different?

Retracting the switchblade, I shoved it into my pocket while with the other hand, I punched out a call to one of the guards stationed in my penthouse.

"Lock down the apartment—now. No one gets in, even Lieutenant Mraz. *Especially* Mraz. Is that clear?"

"Yes, sir."

Cutting the connection, I strode into the outer room and told my P.A. to order me a limo. "And I want it *now*."

Shanice was a human in her fifties with cropped gray hair and warm brown skin. Nobody and nothing rushed Shanice, and yet she got things done faster and more efficiently than any of my past three P.A.s.

One look at my face and she set down her coffee to press a button. "The boss wants a limo ASAP."

"Five minutes," was the reply.

"Make it three," she returned and reached for her coffee again.

I took the stairs to the surface at a run.

The two bodyguards charged after me. "What's up, boss?" one asked as I reached the surface and looked around for the limo.

I chose my words carefully, unwilling to accuse my father and Tomas without proof. "I've received intel that someone might target my new thrall." That was close enough to the truth, and as vampires, that was something they'd respect.

The guards nodded gravely. They might not understand love, but they understood possession. No self-respecting vampire would tolerate another man messing with his thrall, especially one who'd accepted the blood bond.

The limo arrived and we piled in, one man in the back with me and the other riding shotgun in the front seat.

As we pulled into traffic, I called Airi and gave her the news about Lougenia.

"You're sure, sir?" she asked. The enforcer didn't have much use for humans, but even she trusted Lougenia.

I massaged the bridge of my nose. It had been a long day, and it was about to get longer. "Actually, I think she's been set up. But we can't take any chances. Take her into custody. Tomas is coming out to interrogate her. See that she's treated well."

"Of course. And sir? We found the bug in the system that

allowed O'Brien to let in Redbone and his men. I have our best tech working on it right now."

My brows lifted. "Good work. But you're on probation for the next thirty days. Any further fuck-ups, and you're gone."

"I understand, sir. Not to excuse myself, but it looks like the bug was planted. A virus inserted remotely into our security system."

"Hm." It wasn't Airi's fault then, but I didn't rescind the probation. She should've instructed our tech team to watch for something like that.

"I promise it won't happen again."

"I know," I said softly. "Because if it does, I'll know who's responsible."

My next call was to Mila's burner phone.

She didn't answer.

I opened my security app, but everything was quiet. I called my security again and was informed that her brother was sleeping, and Mila was in my bedroom.

I couldn't verify that last because as at the beach house, I'd refused to put cameras in the master suite. I was damned if I was going to be spied on in my own home, and besides, cameras could be used against you.

I tried Mila two more times and then told myself she was sleeping, too. After all, she'd been up most of last night.

I stared out the tinted window, my finger tapping an impatient rhythm on my knee. Something was bothering me about Joey's rescue. At the time, I'd thought Redbone had found us in the basement way too quickly, but in the heat of the moment, I'd forgotten about it.

But how *had* Redbone gotten past Tomas? He was the man who'd taken a team to the penthouse. Could he have let Redbone escape? Even warned him somehow?

And how had Tomas known Joey was in the basement in the first place? The door had been locked—his scout couldn't have gotten through it without leaving the shadow dimension.

"Trust no one."

And my father himself had suspected someone at headquarters was involved.

But Tomas? No fucking way.

Everything in me recoiled in disbelief.

The Slovak vampire had been at my father's side every step of the way as they built the Kral Syndicate to the multibillion-dollar empire it was today. Father trusted Tomas with his life—literally. In addition, Tomas had mentored me and my brothers, teaching us how to fight, cluing us in on the nuts and bolts of how the syndicate ran. He'd spent plenty of one-on-one time with us. Hell, if he'd wanted us gone, he could've arranged an "accident" years ago.

And yet, it made an awful kind of sense. Who else could've alerted Redbone? There was no way the vampire had just happened to wake at the very moment we were breaking into the basement. Even if he had, Tomas and his team had supposedly disabled the security, including the cameras, so how had Redbone known exactly where to find us?

And it was Tomas who'd recommended I'd hire O'Brien.

The limo halted on the street in front of my building. I was out the door like a shot, the guards on my heels.

The elevator ride up seemed endless. As I stepped into the foyer, the guard on duty came to attention. "Good evening, sir."

"Any problems?" I demanded.

"No, sir. Everything's quiet."

"Camila's still in my bedroom?"

"Yes, sir," he said to my back as I strode down the hall, the bodyguards still with me.

By the time I passed the living room, I was running. I headed straight for the master bedroom, heart pounding a tattoo against my ribcage, terrified that Tomas had somehow gotten to Mila.

She wasn't there.

My chest seized. Then I saw her phone on the nightstand—and heard her humming a happy little tune in the bathroom.

The air whooshed back into my lungs.

Footsteps sounded. "Gabriel? Is that you?"

"Yes."

The bathroom door opened, and Mila stood framed in the doorway in nothing but one of my T-shirts, the switchblade clutched in her hand. She'd showered, her hair a dark tangle around her shoulders. The soft white cotton clung to her damp body, revealing the shadowed outline of her nipples and the curly hair of her mound.

She looked both sexy and badass at the same time.

My mouth dried. "Get out," I told the guards without taking my gaze from her. "And shut the door behind you."

"Yes, sir. We'll be on the seventh floor if you need us."

I waited until the door closed behind them before speaking. "I called you," I told Mila. My voice sounded harsh in my ears.

"You did?" She glanced at the phone. "I was in the shower. Is something wrong?"

"Not now." I dragged in a breath, willing myself to calm down, and held out a hand. "Come here."

✣ 25 ✣

MILA

In the glow of the metal-star lampshades, Gabriel's face appeared almost devilish, the sculpted planes in stark relief against the darkness.

Our eyes met, clung.

"Come here," he repeated, hand outstretched.

I set the switchblade on a nightstand. Even having heard his voice and knowing in advance he was on his way back to the penthouse, I'd instinctively snatched up the knife before opening the door. My heart was still pounding from the flood of adrenaline. I had a feeling it would be a long time—if ever—before my hypersensitivity to possible danger calmed.

The dozen steps I took to him seemed more like floating. He waited, lean and dark and mine.

Only when I had set my hand in his was I anchored again.

He turned me so my back was against the door. A tap on the control pad, and the lock clicked shut.

He set his hands on the door, caging me. A thrill went straight to my clit. God, that dominant stuff did it for me, and the man knew it. Coming on top of the shot of adrenaline, it made me instantly wet.

"Joey's okay?" he murmured.

I nodded, my gaze on his mouth. The lower lip was a little fuller than the upper lip, which somehow made it so sexy.

"Thank you." I lifted my eyes to his. "I don't know how I can ever repay you."

His gaze seemed to eat me up. "I'd do anything to make you happy, Mila. You must know that."

"Yeah?"

"Anything." His thumb traced my lower lip.

Pleasure shivered down my spine. My eyelids drifted down.

"Even release you from our blood bond."

"Mm." I barely heard him. His heady masculine scent filled my senses. I could practically taste it on my tongue.

"Right now, I could still break it. But I'll be honest. If you stay much longer, I don't think I could let you go." His fingers traced over my collarbone.

More pleasure slid over me. My breasts grew heavy, the tips prickling with need. But I forced my eyes to open as I replayed his words in my head.

"Let me go?" *What the what?* "But you said I was yours, now. That you *love* me."

His eyes closed as if he was in pain. "I do. I'll always love you."

"Then what is this about?" My stomach lurched. "Are you saying you *want* to break the bond?"

His hand closed around my nape. He brought his mouth to the side of my neck. Warm lips traced over the pulse point.

"I can feel your heart beat," he said thickly. "You know what that does to me?"

My breath sped up.

His mouth opened on my skin. "I want you." His voice was raw with need. "I wake up wanting you. I fall asleep wanting you. I have you and I only want you more."

Sharp fangs pressed against the point he'd been kissing. I pressed my inner thighs together as heat seared down my spine. For a few seconds, I forgot everything except how good it had felt the first time he'd drunk from me: his mouth hot against my throat. His hard body inside mine. The incredible orgasm that, like an ocean wave, had seemed to lift me up and toss me down, leaving me limp with pleasure.

But I refused to be distracted—because damn it, I'd asked a question and he hadn't answered. I pushed against his shoulders.

"Answer me. Do you want to break the blood bond?"

He stepped back, leaving a full yard between us. "It doesn't matter what I want. Say the word, and I'll release you from it."

I stayed where I was, my back against the door. The lust-induced haze had cleared, leaving me puzzled and a little afraid. "What do you mean?"

His nostrils flared. His hands fisted. But his voice was cool, controlled. Very much the crown prince.

"You would never have accepted the bond if not for Joey."

A vise clamped my lungs. "No! That's not how it was." I paused, struggling to think. "I mean, yes, it was, but I would've come back in a heartbeat if I could've. I stayed away for you, damn it. And for my family. None of it was for me. *None of it.*"

His beautiful face looked sad. "We both know Redbone forced you to come to me. He needed a spy in my house, and you were perfect. You would never have accepted the blood bond if you hadn't been desperate."

My lips felt numb. My stomach was a cold knot of fear. Everything was slipping away, and I didn't even know why.

"All right." I forced myself to mimic Gabriel's calm tones. "I guess that's true—but it's not the whole story. I told you what happened. I tried to say no. I told Andre I wouldn't do anything to hurt you. I mean, Jesus, he offered me a million bucks and I turned him down flat. But then I found out they had Joey, too."

"I know, cher. And it's okay. But that's why I'm releasing you from the bond."

I took a step forward. "What about that promise you made me make? To give you a chance to work this out—to give *us* a chance. That was just this morning for godsake!"

"That was wrong. I shouldn't have asked that of you."

We stared at each other. His face was an expressionless mask, but a muscle worked in his jaw.

Suddenly, I understood. He didn't want me to leave. He was doing it because he thought it was what *I* wanted. The icy feeling receded.

"So let me get this straight. You're doing this for me, because I only accepted the blood bond to save Joey."

A curt nod. "You can go home with him tomorrow. For tonight, you'd better sleep in another room." He reached around me to the pad that controlled the door.

I blocked his hand. "No."

His peaked black brows lifted. "What do you mean, *no?*"

"I mean no, I won't go home tomorrow." I reached for the hem of the T-shirt. "I said I loved you, and I meant it."

His Adam's apple worked. "What are you doing?"

"I'm not under pressure now, am I?" I pulled the shirt over my head, dropped it on the floor.

"No." His voice was hoarse.

"Then you know this is my choice." I set my hand on his chest. "And I'm staying right here with you."

His entire body tensed. He gripped my wrist. "Don't."

I swallowed, hurt, then noticed his eyes. The irises were rimmed with electric blue—and that muscle still jumped in his jaw.

I tugged on my wrist, and he released it. His gaze raked down my naked body, a slow, hungry sweep that made my womb clench.

He'd forgotten to bring down his hand. It hung in mid-air, and as I watched, his fingers opened and closed as if he had to force himself not to reach for me.

"Gabriel." I slid a hand around his nape and drew him down until his mouth touched my throat. "That you offered to release me? That means more than you can know. But I want this. I want *you.* Now. Forever. Whatever it takes."

🎴 26 🎴

GABRIEL

Mila's fingers were warm on the back of my neck. The faint taste of buttered popcorn clung to her breath, mixing with her own clean, sunshiny scent. The aroma of summer: boardwalks, carnivals, baseball games.

I nuzzled her throat, tempted. So tempted.

In that instant when I'd heard Mila humming in the bathroom, I'd known I had to release her from her oath. Yeah, she said she loved me, but what would happen when the reality of being with the Kral crown prince sank in?

Remain with me and Mila's whole life would change. And even if she decided to stay, she couldn't stay with me as a human. It simply wasn't safe.

Mom was right. Either I convinced Mila to transition to dhampir, or I set her free. The only other option was to cage her, and for Mila, that would be the worst choice of all.

As for asking her to transition to dhampir, I just couldn't bring myself to do it. I don't care how strong she was, 50/50 odds were too damn dicey.

I wouldn't give her up for my father.

I wouldn't give her up for the syndicate.

But I would do it for her. My beautiful, barefoot, wild-child

Mila.

I'd steeled myself to tell her she was free to go. Releasing her from the blood bond and sending her away would be like cutting out my own fucking heart, but I'd survive. Somehow.

Instead, she'd come closer, offered me her throat.

My whole being came alert, my skin prickling like a big cat readying itself to take down prey. I buried my face in the sweet underside of her jaw, my fangs alive with sensation. It didn't help that I was starving, the filet mignon and blood-wine I'd had for dinner a distant memory.

Mine, whispered the vampire that lived in my soul.

Without lifting my head, I walked her backward to the door, pinning her to the wood with my body. Spearing my fingers into her hair, I drew her head back even further and lapped at her soft, exposed skin. Preparing her for my bite.

At her aroused moan, a dark thrill vibrated down my spine. My fangs lengthened along with my dick.

"Mine," I heard someone say in guttural tones, and realized this time, I'd said it aloud.

"*Yes*." A tremor went over Mila. Her mound pressed against my aching erection. Even through my pants, I felt her wet heat. My painfully hard dick swelled even more.

I inhaled, opened my mouth, and then froze at how close I was to losing control and mindlessly sinking my teeth into her. I lifted my head and removed her hand from my nape, turning it so I could see the wrist. I stared, mesmerized, at the network of blue veins visible beneath the warm olive of her skin.

My nostrils flared. The craving was a hard, clawing drumbeat in my bloodstream.

"I want you. Now. Forever. Whatever it takes."

I pressed my lips to her wrist. The skin was petal-soft, the delicate veins pulsing gently beneath. Her breath sped up.

I traced the fragile blue lines with my tongue. Slow, exploring licks.

Her low, aroused moan hummed over my skin. I scraped my fangs down her wrist. Teasing both her and myself.

Against the door, her head moved from side to side. "Please, Gabriel."

I captured both her wrists and drew her arms behind her. The position arched her back so that her round, full breasts pressed against my chest. The beaded nipples pricked me through my shirt.

Another sexy moan. She lifted onto her toes, straining to bring her neck to me.

The blood-craving was nearly unbearable. I'd never wanted anything so bad as to drink from her right then. But I couldn't.

I forced my fangs to retract and closed my mouth.

"Go on." Her hips pressed against mine. "Do it. Drink from me. Fuck me."

My grip tightened on her wrists. The daisy blood-bond bracelet brushed against my thumb, a reminder of all I was about to give up. But it was for her own good.

"I can't." I released her and stepped back. "You. Me. It just won't work."

Confusion flickered in her eyes. She scraped her heavy hair back from her face and peered at me. "Why not?"

"Cher. You know why." I put another foot of space between us. "I'll protect you and your family—I want you to know that. I'll make sure the vampire world knows they're under Karoly Kral's protection."

"Thank you, but I don't understand. The only reason I'd leave now would be if my staying made them a target. If you can keep them safe, what's the problem?"

My fists clenched. "The problem is," I said, slowly and precisely, "is that you're not safe. I can't risk losing you again. I *won't*."

Understanding dawned. Her shoulders caved in. "Because I'm a human."

The hurt on her face nearly gutted me. "Yes. I'm sorry, but I—"

"So it's like Tomas said. I'm a liability to you."

"Mila. Don't do this. Just leave, all right?" I headed for the door, but suddenly, she was in front of me, blocking my way.

"No. Fucking. Way." She slapped a hand on my chest. "You don't just get to send me away."

I blinked. I'd never seen her so furious. She was practically vibrating.

"Sweetheart, I—"

"Shut up. It's my turn to talk now."

I gritted my back teeth. "Fine. Talk."

"All right." Her lungs heaved. Her eyes squeezed shut. Then she pulled back her shoulders and raised her chin. "If being human is the problem, then turn me. That's the only solution, and we both know it."

I studied her. Her expression was cool as marble. Yeah, I couldn't read her emotions, but everything about her tense body told me how difficult this was for her. And her fingers were knotted in front of her.

She looked about as eager to be turned as someone about to get a root canal.

"You're asking me to turn you into a vampire?"

She gave a visible shudder. "Hell, no. But you're a dhampir. That's almost as strong, right?"

Gods, I was tempted. After all, she had a fifty percent chance of making it. But I heard again my mom's screams, saw her limp body as my father emerged to carry her to a grave.

"Mila..." I spread my hands. "You don't know what it's like. My mom—it hurt so bad. Your body basically melts down and reforms itself. And after all that, you still might die."

Her throat worked.

"Yeah," I said. Reaching for her interlaced fingers, I gently pried them apart and took her left wrist so that I could press the secret catch to open the daisy blood-bond bracelet. "I, Gabriel Fortier Kral, release—"

"No!" She snatched her hand from mine. "I *do* know what it's like. Your mom told me. I've had three years to think it over. I love you, Gabriel. I'm willing to take the chance to be with you."

Gods, she was making this hard.

"Well, I'm not. You have your whole life ahead of you. I can't ask it of you. I won't lose you again."

"But if you send me away, you'll lose me anyway." She moved

closer, pressing all those sweet curves up against me. Threading her fingers through my hair. "Let's think it over, all right? We don't have to make a decision right now, do we?"

My arms came around her. Somehow my mouth was on her throat again. I inhaled deeply, as if I could take her fragrance into myself.

She nuzzled my temple. "Gabriel?"

"No," I heard myself say. "We don't have to make a decision right now."

She feathered her fingers over my nape, teasing the fine hairs there. "You're hungry, aren't you?"

I nodded against her skin. "My body's been working overtime to heal me, and that takes blood."

"Please." She angled her head to give me better access. "I want you to."

I couldn't help myself. I craved this woman, needed her body and her blood. And she wanted me.

What would it hurt to make love one last time?

Her, said my conscience. *It would hurt her—and you.*

I ruthlessly swatted the thought away. "I love you," I husked, and sank my fangs into her throat.

She gasped and arched her body against me. I supported her with one arm while I slid the other down to where she was slick and ready.

Her blood flooded into my mouth, salty and rich. Already, I recognized the special tang that was Mila.

I drew from her strongly while at the same time I played with her clit. She squirmed and pleaded, but I took my time, keeping her on the edge, waiting for the small signals that told me she was about to come: her soft groans, the erotic rocking of her hips.

When her body tensed, I took a last hard suck and plunged my fingers into her silky wetness.She moaned my name and spasmed around me, riding my hand through her orgasm. Her fingers dug into the back of my neck like she was drowning in pleasure.

I licked the puncture wounds closed but kept my fingers inside her pussy, rubbing the edge of my thumb against her sensitive little bundle of nerves until she sagged against me with a sated sigh.

"Mm." She smiled into my eyes. "Love you."

I pressed my lips to the tiny red marks I'd left on her throat. "I love you, too."

She put her hands on my shoulders and came up on her toes to give me an open-mouthed kiss. The next thing I knew, she had me backed up to the bed. She nipped my lower lip. "Sit down."

My knees immediately bent.

She inched up the hem of my T-shirt. "Raise your arms."

I did, and the shirt came over my head.

She knelt on the floor between my legs and unbuttoned my pants. She paused to press a kiss to my abdomen just below my navel, then licked her way down the happy trail of dark hair until it disappeared into my boxer briefs.

My lungs locked. She looked so damn erotic, kneeling at my feet like that, her damp hair tumbling over her bare shoulders, her rose-brown nipples brushing my shins.

"Suck me," I ordered hoarsely.

She complied—slowly. First, she eased the zipper over my hard cock. Then she set her mouth against my boxer briefs and directed a stream of warm air against my dick. My thighs hardened. It felt so damn good, that hot, fuckable mouth so close to where I wanted it, and yet still separated from my skin by the briefs.

At last, she slipped her fingers through the opening in my boxer briefs, releasing my cock. It sprang out, flushed and ready.

Wrapping her fingers around the base, she gave it a slow lick that sent an electric jolt clear to my toes. It was my turn to groan.

I grabbed a pillow and handed it to her. "Kneel on this."

She took the pillow and slipped it beneath her knees without taking her other hand—or her gaze—from my erection. Another few long, leisurely licks, and then her plump lips closed around the head.

My eyes squeezed shut in pleasure. "That's it, love." I sank my fingers into her damp hair. Not forcing her, just holding her close. "Suck me."

"Mm," she said, the vibration of her voice sending more jolts of electricity to my balls, and sucked the head into her mouth. Her hot little tongue swiped over and around it, tasting me in a way that lit up every nerve in my body.

"Take me deeper. I want to fuck that sweet mouth of yours."

She sent me a wicked look from beneath her eyelashes. Acknowledging that although she might be the one on her knees with me giving the orders, she had all the power.

Then she hummed an assent and obeyed.

A raw groan escaped my lips. My grip tightened on her hair. I guided her head back and forth, showing her what I liked.

Keeping her grip on the base of my cock, she sucked me so deep I touched the back of her throat. Then she eased up, drawing her mouth up the stalk until her lips caressed the sensitive head.

Her other hand was fondling my balls now, increasing the sensation. I pushed back into her mouth, every muscle in my body straining to go deeper.

Gods. "I'm going to come," I warned.

"Mm." She sucked harder.

It was like she'd touched a live wire to my most sensitive nerves. Light sparked behind my eyes. I was primed to explode, but suddenly, I wanted to be inside her, feeling those hot inner walls squeezing me.

I put my hand on my head, stopping her. "Come up here."

She gave a last suck and then released me. Reaching down, I pulled her onto my lap for a rough kiss. Then I pushed her against the nearest wall, face first, taking control because I knew it made her as hot as it did me.

Her fingers spread on the cream-colored surface. She cast me a look over her shoulder. Her hair was sex-tousled, her dark eyes dreamy and so damn seductive. "Do me, Gabriel. Hard."

The low, suggestive tone vibrated in my lower belly. Combined with her dreamy eyes and killer body, it almost sent me over right then and there.

I shucked the rest of my clothes and stepped closer, shaping her curves with my hands: her breasts, waist, the slope of her hips. I spent extra time playing with her ass, until she was moaning and pressing against my fingers, begging me to come inside.

I smacked her round bottom. "Open for me."

She spread her legs. I slid my fingers between her thighs, caressing and circling her sex until her soft, aroused pants told me she was climbing toward another peak. Setting a hand on the wall, I snaked the other around her waist, my body covering hers from behind.

She canted her hips to take me. I found her center and stroked slowly inside. Deep as I could...and then deeper.

A growl emanated from my throat. "You feel so good. So fucking good." I nibbled her earlobe, telling her all the sweet, nasty things I was going to do to her.

A tremor went over her. Tiny inner muscles clenched on mine. She gasped out my name, begged for more.

I set up a hard, steady rhythm. No longer thinking, just feeling. Wanting her with my whole being.

My urgency was matched by hers, the two of us feeding the heat like fire meeting fire.

Her breath sobbed in. "*Please, please, please.*"

She pushed her ass into my groin and craned her neck around, trying to kiss me.

My mouth met hers, our tongues twining around each other in a kiss that went on and on. We weren't fucking now, we were making love, the pleasure so intense it was almost painful.

My balls drew up. I slid my hand down her stomach to her clit. "Take it, cher. All of me."

Her breath jerked in. She moaned and tore her mouth from mine, lungs working. Her pussy constricted around my cock as the orgasm took her. Sensation wrapped like a fist around my balls and I followed her over the edge, free-falling in a hot, sharp burst of ecstasy.

After, I carried her to bed and pulled a sheet over us. She cuddled into me, warm and soft...and sadness ballooned in me until I could hardly breathe.

She was so young, her whole life ahead of her. Yes, she was strong, but she was still fragile in the way of any human.

If she died during the transition, I'd never forgive myself. And I didn't want her to live the kind of life where she reached for a switchblade before opening the fucking bathroom door.

I nuzzled her hair, which had dried in wild corkscrews around her face. One teased my nostril. I brushed it away and touched my lips to her temple.

She stirred. "Love you," she said without opening her eyes.

"Love you, too."

I released a breath, and abruptly, knew what to do. It had been staring me in the face the whole time.

I couldn't allow Mila to attempt the transition. And actually, as my blood-bonded thrall, she couldn't do it without my permission.

But sending her away wasn't the solution. Look what had happened the last time she'd left me. We'd both been miserable, and she'd been vulnerable to any vampire who chose to use her to strike at me.

No, the only solution was for us both to go.

It wouldn't be easy. I'd have to resign from the syndicate, step down as crown prince. It was a hell of a time to leave, with things in flux as they were. Despite Father's threats, I'd bet my favorite Jag he'd try and pressure me into staying.

And I'd be giving up everything I'd spent the past decade working to achieve.

But Mila was more important. Yeah, it wouldn't be easy, but it felt *right*.

She nuzzled my shoulder. "Something the matter?"

"No," I told her. "Everything's just fine." Tucking her close to my heart, I shut my eyes.

I t was a shadow, not a sound, that woke me. Silver flashed in the darkness.

My heart slammed into gear. I threw myself at Mila, rolling off the bed with her. We landed in a tangle of sheets on the floor between the windows and the bed.

A stake slashed into the mattress where I'd been.

I fought free of the bedclothes and looked around for a weapon. But the switchblade I'd left on the nightstand was on the opposite side of the bed along with the intruder.

Everything went silent. Then a click sounded, and the window blinds retracted. Sunlight flooded in.

Even through the specially darkened windows, the sudden change in light was too much for me. For a crucial few seconds, I was blinded, long enough for the shadow to flow over the mattress and shove me back to the floor.

A woman's powerful thighs straddled my chest. The silver stake came down again.

I knocked it away with my arm, but not before the tip tore a hole in my chest. Pain screamed through me as the silver entered my bloodstream.

I dragged in a breath as my eyes adjusted to the sunlight. "*Jessa?*"

My housekeeper glared down at me with burning eyes. She raised the stake above her head.

I grabbed her arm, but the silver raced through me like wildfire, searing my nerves, stealing my strength.

With a sneer, Jessa jerked her arm free.

Beside us, Mila rose to her knees.

Jessa flicked her a glance. "Take your brother and get the hell out of here. This isn't your fight."

"Okay. Sure." Mila lifted her hands, palms out—and lunged for Jessa.

The slayer tightened her thighs on my chest and, without taking her gaze from me, slammed a fist into Mila's throat, knocking her to the floor.

Fury rose up in me like a red-eyed wolf. I summoned everything I had and surged off the floor, clamping both hands around Jessa's throat as the stake slashed down again.

The tip caught my bicep. Another round of agony shrieked through me. My nostrils filled with the scent of my own blood.

I grimly held on to Jessa's throat. My fangs extended.

On the floor, Mila struggled to breathe. Short, ragged breaths that made my stomach knot with fear.

I had to end this. If her trachea had been badly damaged, she could suffocate right there on the floor.

I summoned my magic. "Let. Go," I said in the voice of compulsion.

Jessa's mouth twitched up. "Good try." She struck again. This time, the stake's slim point almost pierced my heart.

I gave an animal snarl, my mind awash in pain. The lucid part of me noted that Jessa was almost certainly a slayer—they were often chosen for the genetic quirk that made them immune to compulsion.

And her coolly efficient fighting technique confirmed that she must be from Slayers, Inc.

"*Gabriel.*" Mila's rasp sliced through my brain.

My head jerked up. I'd blacked out, my fingers loosening on Jessa's throat. Energy seeped out of me along with my blood.

The slayer rose up, hands locked around the stake, lips drawn back in a savage mask. I stared up at my death.

Fuck that.

I dug deep and shot upright, wrenching the stake from Jessa's hand. I turned it in the air and shoved it into her throat.

Blood spurted, drenching my chest.

Jessa's pale eyes widened. Her hand went to her throat. "*Monster.*" She had no breath to say the word, but I read it on her lips.

More blood spurted. I must've hit an artery.

Jessa's eyes rolled up in her head and she toppled sideways to the floor. I took a moment to ensure she was really dead, then crawled to Mila. She had her hands clutched to her throat.

I eased them away. "Sweetheart. Are you all right? Can you talk?"

Her throat was red, but she was already breathing more easily. Jessa must've pulled her punch; slayers try to avoid collateral damage so they don't lose human support.

"I'm—okay." Her voice was cracked and raw. She pushed herself upright. "But you——?"

She set a hand on my chest. It came away bloody. Her eyes rounded. "Gabriel?"

"Most of it's hers," I hurried to say, and tried not to wince. Even speaking hurt.

"Bitch," she croaked with a disdainful glance at Jessa, then zeroed in on my wounds. "Lie down." She guided me back to the floor. "What can I do?" She darted a worried look at the dead woman. "You think it was just her? Oh God, what if there's more out there?"

"She's alone. No one else...could've gotten past my security. Get my phone."

"Yes." She got up and grabbed it.

I pulled up the security app and pushed the panic button for the guards, then showed her the videos of the quiet apartment. "See?" When she nodded, I continued, "Why don't you go...put ice on that throat."

"What about you?"

My gaze slid to the dead slayer. The scent of her blood was almost unbearably tempting. But Jessa's last word clanged in my mind.

Monster.

Mila's gulp was loud. "Oh."

The flood of adrenaline that had allowed me to make that last, desperate lunge at Jessa had worn off. I was fading fast. The pain was so bad, I could've whimpered like a wounded animal.

Only blood would help. The craving scraped at my insides.

"Sorry." I looked away from Mila's anxious face. "But it's...fastest way to heal myself. You...go. Put ice on your throat."

"*Don't.*" Her tone was fierce. She shoved her face into mine. "Don't ever apologize for being you. Got it?"

I stared up at her. Warmth filled me, the special light that was Mila spreading to all the secret, murky corners of my soul.

"Got it."

But I waited until she'd left the bedroom before I crawled the few feet to Jessa, and fed.

🜲 27 🜲

MILA

Gabriel's people sprang into action, removing Jessa's body and cleaning his bedroom so thoroughly you'd never guess a bloody fight had taken place.

Joey had slept through everything.

I wished I'd been so lucky. As soon as I was sure Gabriel would be all right, I stumbled into the unused bedroom next to Joey's and fell onto the bed.

I was exhausted, my throat bruised. Swallowing hurt. Hell, breathing hurt.

But every time I closed my eyes, I saw the lethal flash of Jessa's stake.

I shuddered and stared at the ceiling.

Gabriel's safe, and so is Joey.

But I'd been too weak, too *human* to fight her off. One blow and I'd been tossed to the floor, where I'd lain, gasping, like a fucking fish, ten feet from the switchblade Gabriel had given me. It might as well have been on the moon for all the use it had done me.

I pressed the heels of my hands to my eyes. I *was* a liability.

I must have dozed off. When I woke again, I heard the murmur of voices—Gabriel and another man. Something made me slip from the bed. I pulled on a pair of shorts under my sleepshirt, picked up the switchblade and eased open the door. But I couldn't quite make out their words.

I crept down the dark hall, halting out of sight a few feet from the living room.

Gabriel spoke, low and mean. "What do you mean, you don't know where Zaq is? He was chained to a fucking wall."

I pressed a fist to my mouth. Gabriel's brother was being held prisoner somewhere?

"He escaped."

My brow furrowed. The other voice sounded so familiar.

"How?" Gabriel demanded.

"I don't know. But he's gone."

"Or dead, and they covered it up so well even you can't prove it." Gabriel's voice was harsh with anger. "Damn you to Hades. You should've gotten more men, gone in there—done *something*."

"Enough," the other man responded in clipped tones. "We can discuss my methods later. I have intel that the slayers themselves don't know where Zaquiel is now, which tells me he is still alive. But he's gone to ground." A pause. "It's almost as if he doesn't want to be found."

The fine hairs on my arms lifted as I finally recognized that voice.

Karoly Kral was here.

In the penthouse.

Less than twenty feet away.

My pulse spiked. I had to leave—now. Tightening my grip on the switchblade, I darted a frantic glance around me, but the only way out was past the living room.

"Hell." Gabriel's exhale was loud in the quiet. "All right. What do we do now?"

"I—" Karoly halted. "The woman is here?"

I froze. My fast-beating heart must have given me away.

"So you didn't send her away," Karoly said.

"Leave her the fuck out of this," Gabriel shot back. "You think she's weak? Out in Montauk, she saved my life. I was bleeding out, poisoned by silver. Too out of it to even think of feeding. She cut her wrist, made me drink her blood. And while I was fighting off Redbone, she staked Stefan."

I wrapped my arms around myself. God, I loved Gabriel for defending me. But his father spoke the truth. I *was* a weakness. A human who'd always be a drag on Gabriel.

But this thing between me and Gabriel was too strong. This time, I wouldn't run. This time, I'd fight.

Karoly raised his voice. "You can come out now, Mila."

I started. Then I drew a deep breath, reminding myself I was no longer alone and on the run from Karoly's hard-faced enforcers. What's more, I was blood-bonded to his son. Karoly Kral would have to learn to deal.

I straightened my spine, pulled back my shoulders and entered the living room.

"You're right." My voice came out as a hoarse rasp, but I met Karoly's gaze head on. "I *am* a liability."

"Like hell you are," said Gabriel.

But his father gave a short nod. His ebony eyes flicked to the switchblade.

The amusement I saw there made me grit my teeth. I shoved the knife into the pocket of my shorts. It's not like I'd attack him in front of Gabriel anyway.

"It's okay," I told Gabriel. "It's what everyone will say behind my back. At least your father's honest enough to say it to my face."

Gabriel glowered at Karoly. "What the fuck was up with that anyway? You convinced her to leave. Wasn't that enough? Did you have to threaten her family? Send enforcers to harass her?"

The primus raised a slim hand. "Explain," he told me. "The man wasn't any taller than Gabriel, with the same lean, catlike physique. Still, in his neat pin-striped suit, he seemed to loom over me, his eyes like flat black ice.

My nape prickled as it occurred to me that Karoly Kral had never promised not to compel me.

I nervously licked my lips. "Explain what?"

"These enforcers. I sent Tomas to pay you off, yes. In exchange, you were to stay away for two years. But you were to be left alone unless you tried to contact Gabriel."

A stunned silence fell. Gabriel and I exchanged a glance.

"But...they were Kral enforcers," I said. "I saw the wolf tattoos. They tried to *kill* me."

Gabriel narrowed his eyes at his father. "You're saying you didn't send them?"

"That's exactly what I'm saying. She'd done nothing wrong." Karoly Kral's jaw tightened. "I'm not a savage beast, to hunt a young woman for sport."

I blinked. If I didn't know better, I'd say the cold-as-ice primus was hurt his son hadn't believed in him.

"Then who did?" Gabriel demanded. There was a beat of silence. Then he swore. "Tomas. That sonuvabitch."

My mouth dropped. "Holy crap."

"What's this about Tomas?" That was Karoly.

While Gabriel launched into an explanation, I sank onto the couch. I wouldn't admit it to Karoly or even Gabriel, but I was exhausted.

I leaned my forearms on my knees, fingers tightly interlaced, and listened while Gabriel brought his father up to date on everything that had happened, starting with my years on the run and ending with the events of the past week.

Some of it was news to me, including that Jessa had almost certainly been sent by Slayers, Inc., an organization I'd never even heard of. The same organization that had kidnapped Zaquiel Kral and were apparently torturing him.

My heart hurt for both Gabriel and Zaq. I'd only met Gabriel's middle brother once, but he had the same charisma as all the Kral men, only in Zaq, it didn't have that predatory edge. It just drew you in so you couldn't help but like him.

All this time, Gabriel had been worried about his own brother. No wonder he'd been so suspicious when I'd shown up out of the blue.

Gabriel saved his biggest bombshell for last—that he believed

Lieutenant Mraz was the man behind the curtain pulling everyone's strings.

"I don't know why or how," he told Karoly. "But it fits. Tomas knows everything you know, and his security clearance lets him access any fucking thing he wants. He can act in your name, and no one would question it. Not even me."

Through it all, his father had listened closely, his expression giving nothing away. Now he shook his head. "I don't believe it."

"Then answer me this," Gabriel said. "How did Redbone know exactly where to find me this morning?"

"I don't know. But Tomas? We are like brothers." A muscle ticked in Karoly's jaw. "It's impossible."

"I know." Gabriel's hand moved, like he wanted to give his father comfort. But he checked the movement, bringing the arm back to his side. "I didn't want to believe it myself. But who else could it be?" A look of horror crossed his face. He cursed and whipped out his phone. "And I let him go out to Montauk to question Lougenia."

"No." I jumped up. "Oh, hell no."

Gabriel grimaced at me. "Afraid so."

He'd already called Airi. I crowded next to him to listen, but she was baffled. "Tomas never showed," she said. "I was about to text him to see what's up."

"If he shows," Gabriel returned, "take him into custody."

"Sir?"

"Do it. I don't care how you keep him there, but he's not to leave Montauk." He glanced at his father. "On Primus Kral's orders."

"Yes, sir," said Airi.

Gabriel ended the call. His gaze challenged his father. "Well? Where is he?"

Karoly already had his phone out. When Tomas didn't answer the call, he sent a text. The seconds ticked past as he stared at the screen, waiting for a response. Then, for the first time since I'd entered the room, his control cracked.

"He's not responding." He scrubbed a weary hand over his mouth. "I don't know what to think. The Slayers could've kidnapped him, too. Or he's in this up to his neck. Either way, I promise you, I'll find him. And when I do, I *will* get to the bottom of this."

Something about his voice made me press closer to Gabriel, who put an arm around my shoulders. "I'll give you everything I have, but I'm going to be conducting my own, independent investigation." His look dared Karoly to object.

Father and son locked gazes. Then Karoly nodded. "As you wish. As for you..." He eyed me not unkindly. "Go home to Maryland. You and your family will be compensated, and you have my promise that you will never be threatened again. I'll put the word out that you're under my personal protection."

I drew myself up to my full height. "We don't need your money, but I'd be grateful for your protection—for my family." My chin jutted. "But me? I'm not going anywhere."

Gabriel squeezed my shoulders. "We'll go together. Anywhere you want."

"No," rapped out his father. "I can't spare you right now."

"I'm sorry, sir," Gabriel said. "But it's not your decision. I'm taking Mila as my mate, and stepping down as crown prince."

His father and I regarded him with equally shocked expressions. I had to replay what he'd said in my head before it sank in.

"*No*," I said. "You can't."

At the same time, Karoly said, "You'd give up everything for her?"

"I can and I will," replied Gabriel.

"If you're worried about Camila," Karoly told him, "I give you my word she'll live out her life unharmed." To me, he said, "I assume you believe you love my son." At my nod, he continued, "Do you really think he'll be happy farming flowers with you?"

I flinched. "No," I said lowly.

Gabriel's arm tightened on me. "Stay out of this," he snarled at his father. "My mind's made up."

Karoly spread his hands. "Think about it," he said to me.

I hesitated, the weight of what I was about to do pressing on my chest and parching my throat. But looking back, I'd made up my mind to stay with Gabriel the moment I saw him again in the speakeasy. I hadn't known *how* I'd stay, but I'd known that if I somehow survived, I'd do anything necessary for a fresh chance with him.

"What if I become a dhampir?" I asked Karoly.

Gabriel stiffened. "Damn it, Mila. You don't have to do this."

The primus regarded me from beneath hooded eyes. "You'd do that?"

"Yes."

"*No*," Gabriel told me. "You're perfect just as you are. And if my father can't accept that, he can go to hell." He glared at Karoly. "Rafe can succeed you. As of now, I'm out."

I leaned into Gabriel. He'd always be there for me. That, I knew to the depths of my soul.

And I loved that he was willing to do anything for me, even resign from the syndicate.

But I didn't want to be the weak human. I wanted to stand by my mate's side, not cower behind him.

I straightened my shoulders and spoke to Karoly, not Gabriel. "I'm bonded to your son. And we're going to be married—and mated, I guess."

He arched a black brow. "Are you?"

"He hasn't asked me yet," I said with a sidelong look at Gabriel. "But he will. And if he doesn't, I'm going to ask him. So yes, I'm willing to be turned to dhampir."

"No, damn it." Gabriel's fingers dug into my shoulder. "You don't know what you're doing."

Karoly's gaze remained trained on me. "I think she does."

"Yes. Your mate explained it to me, and last night, Gabriel and I talked about it, too."

"So you understand you could die."

My already parched mouth dried further. I gave a noisy swallow and squared my shoulders. "I understand. Just tell me what I have to do."

"Mila..." Gabriel said in a broken voice. He shot his father a beseeching look. "Stop this. You know how it was when Mom went through the transition. She almost died."

Karoly's gaze went to him. "I believe your Camila will survive."

I turned into Gabriel and touched his cheek. "You said you'd free me from our blood bond. Was that a lie?"

His eyes closed. "No," he grated.

"Then either free me—or give me permission to make the transition. I need to be able to defend myself. Tonight we were attacked in your own penthouse. How do you know that won't happen again, even if you resign as crown prince?"

His nostrils flared. "You don't know what you're asking."

"The transition to vampire would be easier on you," Karoly pointed out. "You're young, strong. You'd almost certainly survive."

No fucking way. I concealed a shudder. "No. It's dhampir, or nothing."

"Are you sure?"

"Very."

"A vampire is stronger, faster. You would live longer, be more powerful."

I gave a firm shake of my head. "Gabriel's a dhampir, isn't he? If it's good enough for him, it's good enough for me."

"Mm. Of course, as a dhampir," he said to Gabriel, "she will be able to bear your sons more easily—and to give you more than one."

Gabriel's look was livid. "You think I give a fuck about that?"

Karoly moved an elegantly clad shoulder. "When you've lived as long as me, you'll find that life has a way of making you change your mind. You say that now, but later..."

"Just shut up," his son gritted.

"Please." I set a hand on Gabriel's chest. "You know this is the only solution. I don't want to live my life afraid. I've had my fill of that. I want this. If I stay human, I'll always be the weak one, the one you have to protect."

Gabriel's jaw worked. He pulled me aside. Meanwhile, Karoly crossed the room and rummaged in a sideboard for a glass of blood-wine, pretending not to listen.

"I never meant for this to happen," Gabriel said in an undertone. "Never meant for you to become a target. I—"

"Hey." I set a finger on his lips. "We can't go back now even if we wanted to. And I don't want to go back. I love you. And if this is what I have to do to have you, then I'll gladly do it."

"We can leave." He gripped my shoulders. "I have my own money. We can hole up in Montauk. Or go to some Pacific island a thousand miles from anything else."

"And do what? Work on our tans?" Actually, that didn't sound bad right now. "It might even be fun...for a year or two. But for the rest of our lives? Sooner or later we'd have to come off that island, and I'll still be a human."

"But I'd have you."

I cupped his face. "Listen to me. I'm. Not. Going. To. Die."

He scrutinized me. "You really want to do this? You're not just offering because you think it's what I want?"

"No. I've had three years to think this over. And I told you, I choose you."

"Even this so-isolated island might not be safe," Karoly murmured in his cool voice as he strolled back to us. "It seems someone wishes to ensure I leave no heirs."

"Hell." Gabriel's breath scraped from his lungs. His gaze went to the ceiling as if searching for an answer there before returning to my face. His expression was taut, the muscles of his neck corded with tension. But he gave a curt dip of his chin. "Fine. You have my permission. But if you change your mind..."

It was my turn to take a deep breath. But my mind was made up. When you're backed into a corner, sometimes the only way out is to restart the game.

"I won't," I stated and glanced at his father. "I can ask anyone I want to take me through the transition, right?"

"That's correct."

"Then I request that you, Primus Kral, turn me into a dhampir."

Karoly's smile was small but approving. "I accept. Name the date."

"A week from now. I want to go home first, spend some time with my family. Just in case—you know."

In case I didn't make it.

Karoly nodded. "You'll make the arrangements?" he asked Gabriel.

"I will." His expression was grim. "And I'll take her to Maryland myself."

"Then I will see you in one week," Karoly told me.

I gazed back calmly. Now that the decision was made, I felt strangely serene. Whether I lived or died, I believed I'd made the right choice.

"I'll be there."

❧ 28 ❧

GABRIEL

Mila had done the one thing guaranteed to win my father over. Or maybe Mom had twisted his arm; I didn't know.

But he'd come around. When we returned from Maryland, he'd even unbent enough to ask Mila how the visit had gone. For Karoly Kral, that was as friendly as it got. Apparently she was worthy of me now.

Tomas hadn't been seen since the night he'd left for Montauk. His bank accounts were untouched and his credit cards hadn't been used. At least, the ones we were aware of.

My father hadn't completely accepted that his oldest friend was a traitor. He still hoped to find something exonerating Tomas. Proof that he'd been set up, or been somehow blackmailed into aiding the slayers.

Frankly, I believed it was more likely we'd find a smoking gun aimed straight at Tomas.

"Think about it," I told Father. "How the fuck did Redbone set up a nest of blood slaves in the middle of your own city? Tomas is your lieutenant. It's his job to know about these things."

Father nodded, mouth tight, eyes shadowed. "You are correct, of course."

Pity twisted through me. It must be hard hearing that your best friend had conspired against you.

For now, we were keeping things quiet. If word got out that Father's own lieutenant had been working against him, it would shake the Kral Syndicate to its foundation.

Then there was Zaq. If he'd actually escaped from the slayers, why hadn't he come home? Either he couldn't—or he was afraid to.

At least Lougenia was in the clear. I'd hired a forensic hacker to look into my own security system, but first, I'd had him investigate the evidence against Lougenia. It had taken a couple of days, but he was convinced the evidence had been planted.

Unfortunately, he couldn't prove it. According to him, whoever had planted the evidence was very, very good. They'd set up a false identity just for this job, and routed the commands through so many servers it was impossible to tell where they'd originated.

I told him to keep looking, but if SI was behind this as well, I didn't hold out much hope he'd be able to trace it back to them. If the Tremblays or another powerful coven was working with the slayers to target me and my family, they'd have covered their tracks.

Meanwhile, Mila had spent the week with her parents. I'd had the Fortiers for dinner at Black Oak a couple of times—minus Joey—and Mila stayed each night at the mansion with me, but mostly, I left them alone. They had three years of catching up to do.

Thursday morning, Mila and I returned to New York and spent the day together—shopping; doing touristy things like taking the elevator to the top of the Empire State Building, which I'd arranged to have all to ourselves; having a late lunch at the most exclusive restaurant in Manhattan. Of course, the paparazzi found us—#DarkAngelMate was already trending on Instagram—but I'd had my P.A. prepare our way ahead of time so that we were able to shop and eat in peace.

If this was Mila's last day, I wanted to make it the best ever.

After, I took her back to the penthouse and we made love for hours. Slow, sweet love that turned me inside out and gutted me, until it took all my self-control not to beg her to change her mind.

But this was what she wanted, and I was determined to respect her decision.

Thursday evening, we flew to Long Island along with my parents. I'd called ahead. My people had already dug a grave for Mila on a cliff overlooking the ocean.

As we exited the helicopter, I placed a hand on her lower back. "I bought this house for you, you know."

"I knew it." Her eyes shone up at me.

"There's even a couple of acres for you to start your organic flower farm. You can sell them right here on the island. People in the Hamptons will snap them up."

"Oh." She drew a ragged breath, then elbowed me in the side. "Don't make me cry, damn it."

I just gathered her closer and ignored the sting in my own eyes.

Tradition calls for a transition candidate to wear red. We'd bought Mila a pretty summer dress at an exclusive Manhattan designer. While I got dressed in my suite, my mom helped Mila change in the rooms next door.

A little before sunset, I knocked on the door. "Ready?"

It was Mila who opened it. My lungs compressed. I barely noticed my mom standing behind her, smiling mistily at us both.

"You look...beautiful."

"You think?" She grinned and twirled in a circle.

"Oh, yeah," I said thickly.

The delicate coral silk clung lovingly to her upper body, baring her shoulders and cupping her breasts before widening to a flirty little skirt. A rosebud was tucked in her wavy brown hair, and on her wrist was the ruby bracelet I'd special-ordered for her from Tiffany's.

I wore a black T-shirt beneath my custom-made suit. I smoothed down the coat to hide the fear raking me like giant claws. If Mila didn't make it, I might as well plunge a stake in my own heart, because I'd be dead inside.

"I'll leave you two alone," Mom said. She gave me a quick kiss. "We'll wait on the cliff."

I nodded without taking my gaze from Mila. When we were

alone in the suite, I removed a ring from the inner pocket of my suit.

She tilted her head, curious. "What's that?"

"Your ring. The one I bought you five years ago."

Her eyes widened. "You kept it all this time?"

"Yeah." Taking her right hand, I slid the ring on her finger. It was a small yellow diamond surrounded by five petal-shaped white diamonds.

Her breath sucked in.

"It's not big," I said a little apologetically. "I figured you'd hate a big ring."

"It's a daisy." Her lower lip trembled, and then she threw her arms around me. "And it's perfect. I love it."

Her mouth sought mine. I dragged her up against me, and we kissed, long and hard and desperate. I knew she was thinking the same thing as me. That this might be the last time we ever kissed.

At last, I dragged my lips from hers—and caved. I couldn't stop myself from trying one last time.

"You don't have to do this. We can still leave for that island. Vampires hate the tropics. It's the last place they'll look."

"Gabriel. Stop trying to change my mind. I'm doing this—and I *will* survive."

"Yes." My fingers tightened on her shoulders. "*You will*. You have to."

As if speaking aloud would somehow make it true.

Her mouth quirked in a brave little smile. "Besides, I can so see myself as an ass-kicking dhampir."

I forced myself to smile back. "I'll teach you all my best moves."

"Deal." She stuck out her hand and we shook on it.

Then I enfolded her fingers in mine and together, we walked out of the beach house. That's when I saw her bare feet. Never once, in the half-dozen transition ceremonies I'd witnessed, had the candidate been barefoot.

This time my smile was genuine. By the dark gods, I loved this woman. I raised her hand to my lips and told her so.

Her eyes were luminous in the dusk. "I love you, too. So much."

My parents were waiting at the site we'd chosen, both of them wearing black like me. Mom's hair fell in a dark waterfall down her back, and like Mila, she had a red rosebud tucked into her hair. My father wore a pin-striped suit and a rose boutonniere. The setting sun painted their faces golden.

Nearby, a canopy had been erected over the open grave I'd ordered dug in the sandy soil. I'm not squeamish about death, but I shuddered as my gaze locked on the shadowed rectangular hole.

As we approached, Mom broke into a smile. "You're beautiful, *ma p'tite*. Inside and out."

Mila smiled back a little shyly. "Thank you."

My father took her hands. "You honor my son with both your beauty and your courage." For Karoly Kral, that was an open-armed welcome to the family, and Mila clearly realized it.

She blinked, then inclined her head like the future princess she was. "Thank you. I'm a lucky woman," she said with a sidelong look in my direction.

Mom beamed, her eyes bright with unshed tears. "Remember what I told you, honey."

Mila nodded. "Don't fight it. Breathe, and let the blood take me where it wants me to go."

The sun was sinking fast. It bobbed above the deep-blue ocean, a burning ball in the wash of purple and pink and orange. As night spread its dark wings across the cliff, my shoulders tightened.

"It's time," said Father. He sliced open his wrist and offered it to Mila while I watched, hands fisted at my sides.

She didn't hesitate, simply stepped forward, set her mouth to his wrist and drank.

"More," he urged. "More."

I clenched my fists.

"It's begun," Mom murmured.

I jerked my chin in assent, unable to speak.

Mila straightened away from my father. She gave me a wobbly grin, and then groaned.

A groan I felt clear to the center of my being.

Her breath scraped in and she sank to the ground, shivering.

I grated out her name. My fingers opened, closed. I ached to hold her, to soothe her. I even took a step forward, although I knew I shouldn't.

"No." Mom gripped my arm. "If you touch her, it will only hurt more."

I stilled, stomach knotted, cursing under my breath.

"Gabriel," Mila croaked.

I crouched next to her. "What, cher?"

"Nothing." Her lips lifted in a painful imitation of a smile. "Just...Gabriel." She groaned again, and then her eyes shut. She curled into a tight, shaking ball.

I dropped my head back, stared at the navy sky. The first stars pricked out, cool and bright.

Inside, an anguished howl pressed against my throat, fighting for release until I couldn't breathe. I clamped down on it. I wouldn't add to Mila's pain by letting out my own.

"Leave us," I told my parents. "I'll be all right, I promise. She asked that I be the only witness."

Mom searched my face. "If you're sure...?"

When I nodded, she opened her arms. I stood up and she gave me a hard hug.

"It won't last long," she murmured. "In a little while, she'll pass out."

I nodded, tight-lipped. "I know."

Our eyes met. Because soon after that, Mila would die.

On the sandy ground, she curled into an even tighter ball, making low, animal-like sounds that made my bowels clench.

I closed my eyes and rested my cheek against my mom's. "Gods, she's hurting so bad."

Mom squeezed me again, and then released me. "It will be okay, cher. I have a feeling."

My father gave me an awkward pat on the back. "Your woman will make it. My blood is strong."

I nodded. For once, his arrogance didn't piss me off. I just prayed he was correct.

I took a deep breath—and then my arms came around him, and

we were hugging for the first time since I was a kid.

"She *will* make it," I said.

"Yes," he said.

❧

W atching Mila die, then burying her was the hardest thing
I've ever done.

In the week that followed, I refused to leave her side for more than an hour at a time. When I did leave, I left Daisy and Diesel watching over her grave.

My father came and went. With Tomas missing and me out of commission, he had to put in facetime at headquarters. But my mother stayed for the entire seven days. At times, she would sit with me, make sure I was eating and talk about nothing much.

A tropical storm blew in from the south. The canopy was no match for it. I barely noticed the wind and rain, except to pull off my jacket and put on the dry clothes Mom brought me when she saw I was soaked to the skin.

Midway through the week, Lougenia took a turn sitting with me. I apologized for doubting her loyalty, but she said she understood.

"The evidence against me was bad," she said. "What else could you do?"

I shook my head. "I told Lieutenant Mraz it was impossible. But I couldn't take the chance."

She patted my hand. "Stop worrying yourself. It's okay. Now eat." She handed me a steak sandwich. "Your Mila's going to need you when she breaks out of that grave."

I looked at the sandwich as if it were something foreign, but I made myself eat every bite, and then downed a glass of blood-wine as well.

A short time after Lougenia returned to the house, Airi appeared on the cliff with superhuman speed. She thrust a cell phone at me. "You need to take this."

"Later." I brushed her hand away.

"It's Zaquiel," she said.

My gaze snapped up to her face.

"No," she said. "No one else knows. Zaquiel said he'd talk only to you."

"Good. Keep it that way, okay?"

"Of course."

I clicked my fingers at the wolfdogs, ordering them to stay with Mila, and strode with the phone to the edge of the cliff. "Zaq. Where are you? Are you okay?"

"I'm fine."

Relief swamped me. But—"Then where the *hell* are you? Father's been look—"

He blew out a breath. "Shut up and listen. I don't have much time—they could trace this call any second. We've been on the run for the past week."

We?

"Who's we?" I demanded.

"Listen, damn it. The short version is I was kidnapped by the slayers."

"We know. But who's we? And where are you now?"

"I can't tell you. Not over the phone." There was an odd scraping sound. "Fuck. I have to go." His voice dropped to a whisper. "Tell Father to call off the hunt. I'll be in touch. And bro?"

"What?"

"You and Rafe be careful. They're gunning for all three of us. Whoever's behind this wants to bring Father to his knees."

"Hell. You have to give me more than that. Zaq?"

But he'd already ended the connection, leaving me staring in frustration at the phone. Then I growled. "*Fuck.*"

Because I hadn't warned him about Tomas. On the other hand, if he was concerned about who might be listening in on our conversation, maybe it was for the best.

Father had returned to the beach house earlier that day. I texted him and he arrived on the cliff within minutes. Meanwhile, I tried to get in touch with Rafe with no luck. I was beginning to worry he'd been kidnapped, too.

Father took the news of Zaquiel's call with a grim nod. "Jessa was just the start. I've learned enough to know that SI is going to try again. They won't rest until I'm broken. Slay you three, and everything I've worked for will be for nothing."

I eyed him. This past week, we'd grown closer, and I heard what he was too proud—or stubborn—to admit. Not just Mom would be heartbroken if the slayers sent me, Zaq and Rafe to our final deaths.

"To Hades with that," I returned. "We're going to fight them with everything we have. I'll be damned if I let them win."

Father's face was stark. "But how do we separate our enemies from our friends? Because if Tomas—" He broke off, shook his head.

I didn't hesitate. "We stand together," I said, and held out my hand to him.

He swallowed hard and gripped it. "Yes. We stand together."

And as we stared down at Mila's grave, for the first time I understood why he'd stood back and allowed the other spawn to bully us. We'd never have survived this long otherwise.

But if Mila made it through the transition, I was going to do my damnedest to see that my own kids didn't have to go through the same thing.

And then, at last the week was over.

I'd asked to be the only person at the graveside. As the sun began to set for the seventh time, I lurched into motion, pacing back and forth on the cliff, my eyes glued to where the sandy soil covered Mila.

My love.

My life.

⚜ 29 ⚜
MILA

There are no words to describe the agony I went through.
Picture your bones, your organs, your very skin melting down, morphing to some new creature, and you might come close to understanding it. But even then, you can't really know unless you went through it yourself.

I tried to follow Rosemarie Kral's advice. "Don't fight it. Breathe into it. Let it take you where it wants you to go."

But breathing was impossible. The pain was all-consuming, like being dropped into a burning pool of lava.

I groaned—I may even have screamed—until I had no mouth or throat or tongue to make sounds with. But still it went on.

Until when at last the darkness beckoned, promising blissful, pain-free oblivion, I willingly threw myself into the abyss.

For a time I knew nothing.

I floated in the blackness, Mila and not-Mila, in a sleepy sort of peace.

From far away, I sensed Gabriel. His love was my tether, the only thing keeping me from floating up to the stars and taking my place in the endless midnight sky.

I grabbed onto it and held tight like the lifeline it was.

※

I t was the hunger that woke me.

At first, it was a low-level, easily ignored emptiness. But it ratcheted up, became all-consuming. A craving that I had to feed, or go mad.

I groaned, shifted my position.

Blood.

"Hungry," I whispered. Sand fell into my mouth. I tried to wipe it away, but my arms were trapped by my sides. More dirt encrusted my eyes.

And I needed air—now.

I clawed at the sandy soil, desperate to emerge. Twisting and kicking and shoving at the fine, smothering grains until my hand shot out of the darkness into the air.

"*Mila.*" A man's voice.

Fingers closed on my wrist, dragging me up into the daylight. After the blackness, even the fading sunlight was too bright. I blinked, trying to see from beneath my dirt-encrusted eyelids.

The man's eyes blazed into mine, the green surrounded with a brilliant blue.

Gabriel.

I tried to say his name, but my voice came out as a croak.

He set me on my feet, and then his hands were all over me, brushing away the sand and dirt, while his mouth was against my face, saying a guttural prayer.

"I need—" I wheezed.

Fangs elongated in my mouth, cool and sharp. I touched them, wonderingly, with the tip of my tongue.

Gabriel nodded against my cheek. "You're hungry. Here."

He drew my mouth to his throat. His musky forest scent was strong, familiar. I needed to taste him like I needed my next breath.

I opened my mouth and sank my fangs into him. Blood flooded my throat, rich, life-giving. I drank deeply while he stroked my nape, murmuring broken words of love.

Energy surged through me. When I lifted my head, his beloved face was incredibly clear and detailed, like someone had turned on a thousand-watt light.

I set my hand on his chest. "I can hear your heart," I said, awed. "Beating. And"—I darted a glance around—"a seagull. There."

I flung out a hand to point far offshore where the setting sun sketched a crimson slash across the twilight sky.

"Mm-hm." He smiled down at me. "You—" He broke off, shook his head.

I stepped back and flexed my fingers. Stretched.

It was my body, and yet different. Stronger, more flexible, more aware.

"I'm a dhampir?" I raised my eyes to his, equal parts stunned and thrilled. "I did it?"

"Yes." He lifted me into the air, swung me in a circle. "You did it, Mila. You. Fucking. Did. It."

I tilted my head to the sky and let loose with a loud whoop. When he set me back down, I crinkled my nose.

"I smell something. Something rank." I glanced at the wolfdogs, who sat five yards away, eyeing me with interest. "Daisy and Diesel —they rolled in something, didn't they?"

He chuckled. "Yep."

"Dead fish." I rubbed my nose. "Jesus. Is it always like this?"

"You learn to focus on what's important. The rest you ignore, like you did when you were a human."

I brushed at my filthy dress and crinkled my nose again. "I think I'm smelling myself, too." I reached behind myself to undo the zipper. "I'm going into the ocean."

"Now? But my parents are waiting to congratulate you. I think Mom has a little party planned."

"I'll tell them I had to clean up first." I dragged off my dress, held out my hand. Beneath, I wore nothing but the tiny red bikini he'd bought me that first day in Montauk. "And later?" I leaned close. "I brought that red-mesh thingy. Just in case."

His brows shot up, and then his mouth spread in a wicked smile. "Hell, they can wait another few minutes."

He took my hand, and together, we sprinted down a narrow path to the ocean. When the trail stopped on a rocky ledge thirty feet above the water, we grinned at each other—and jumped.

EPILOGUE
RAFE

I smoothed down my tux, adjusted my bowtie. A black mask dangled from my left hand. I fingered it idly, staring up at the open door of Victorine Tremblay's medieval stone chateau.

I'd spent the past week in Montreal, working my contacts, trying to find out what, if anything, the Tremblay Coven had to do with Zaq's disappearance.

A whole week I'd been close to Zoe Tremblay without being able to touch her.

Tonight, that would change. My lips curved in a smile that was pure predator.

I checked my pocket one last time. Not for a weapon; that would be asking for trouble. No, what was in my pocket was even better: an invitation to the Tremblays' annual masquerade ball.

The printer hadn't wanted to forge the invitation, even for the stupid-high sum I'd offered. The Tremblay prima ruled her city with an iron fist concealed in a sleek silk glove. But the printer was human, easily compelled. An hour later, I'd left, the invitation in hand.

Now I settled the mask on my face and strode up the chateau's marble steps—and into the heart of the Tremblay Coven.

The foyer was larger than most houses. An immense crystal

chandelier glittered overhead. Towering black vases stuffed with perfect red tulips were placed here and there on the creamy Italian marble floor.

The ballroom was visible through the double doors on the far side of the foyer. Vampires and their thralls danced on the polished wood floor. Like me, the vampires were dressed mainly in black, while the thralls wore variations on the ball's theme of red, white and black.

A Tremblay soldier asked to see my invitation. When I handed it over, he examined it closely, then patted me down for weapons before indicating the double doors. "*Entrez, M'sieur.*"

"*Merci.*" I strolled inside.

A server in a red-lace mask and short black skirt sashayed up with a tray of blood-wine. "Something to drink, sir?" she asked in a pretty Quebecois accent.

I took the wine and sipped it, scanning the crowd from behind my mask.

The Crimson Ball was traditionally held by candlelight. Candles were everywhere, hundreds of them. They flickered in the chandeliers above the dancers, and in votives on the black-clothed tables and the lush flower arrangements. The dim light softened the vampires' cold eyes, gave their skin a warm glow.

The thralls certainly seemed taken in by it. They clung to the vampires, eyes starry through their masks. Rubies and diamonds glittered on the female thralls' throats and in the male thralls' earlobes. Those who were blood-bonded wore a gold chain around their wrists.

I scented Zoe before I saw her. A spicy green scent that made my heart speed up.

There.

Unlike most of the guests, she'd made little effort to conceal her identity. Her mask was a strip of black that barely covered her eyes, and her white slip dress showed off her long golden limbs. She seemed unconscious of the bodyguard hovering nearby. No, her smile was all for the lean blond vampire looking down her dress.

The vampire fingered a lock of her straight black hair.

Zoe's smile turned chilly. She moved back a step, forcing him to release her.

A possessive fury surged through me. No man but me could stand that close to Zoe.

Touch her.

Have her.

The bodyguard's head swung around. His eyes narrowed on me.

A vampire couldn't read me like they could a human, but my muscles had tightened, my stance shifting to the balls of my feet and my hand fisting on the wine glass as I prepared to launch myself at the blond asshole.

Rein it in, you idiot. Or you'll blow your cover in the first five minutes.

I dragged my gaze away, forced my shoulders to loosen. Took another sip of wine.

But Zoe's form was seared on my eyelids. The woman had a body made for sin. High, perfect breasts. Slim waist. Taut ass. And legs that seemed to go on forever.

I couldn't resist another look.

My groin tightened. By the Dark Mother, I wanted Zoe Tremblay...almost as much as I hated her.

But for now, I had to blend in. Setting my glass on a table, I held out a hand to the nearest unattached thrall.

"Dance with me."

❧❦❧

Craved: A Vampire Syndicate Romance is now available at your favorite bookstore!

ALSO BY REBECCA RIVARD

Thanks so much for reading!

Want to be the first to hear about my vampire romances and other steamy paranormal romance books?

Sign up for my newsletter: www. rebeccarivard.com/newsletter

In return, I'll gift you with "Lir's Lady," a sexy short story from my Fada Shapeshifters world.

THE VAMPIRE SYNDICATE ROMANCES

Sexy, twisty vampire mafia romance

Pursued

Craved

Taken

VAMPIRE BLOOD COURTESANS

Steamy vampire romance set in Michelle Fox's Blood Courtesans World

Ensnared: Star

Compelled: Cerise

Learn more: www.rebeccarivard.com/vampires

THE FADA SHAPESHIFTERS

Dark shifters, seductive fae...

- *Stealing Ula: A Fada Shapeshifter Prequel*
- *Seducing the Sun Fae*
- *Claiming Valeria*
- *Tempting the Dryad*
- *Lir's Lady*
- *Shifter's Valentine*
- *Sea Dragon's Hunger*
- *Saving Jace*
- *Charming Marjani*
- *Adric's Heart*

Learn more: www.rebeccarivard.com/shapeshifters

ABOUT REBECCA RIVARD

Rebecca Rivard read way too many romances as a teenager, little realizing she was actually preparing for a career. She now spends her days with vampires, shifters and fae—which has to be the best job ever. When she's not writing, she walks, bikes and kayaks in the Chesapeake Bay area with her guitar-playing, storytelling husband.

Six of her novels have been awarded the coveted Crowned Heart Review from *InD'Tale Magazine* and the Fada Shapeshifter Series was voted Best Shifter Series in the Paranormal Romance Guild Reviewer's Choice Awards.

Her books have won the prestigious PRISM Award (*Charming Marjani*), and the Paranormal Romance Guild Reviewer's Choice Award (*Saving Jace*). Her stories have also finaled in the RONE and the HOLT Medallion.

Printed in Great Britain
by Amazon

45849052R00148